About the A

David Blake Knox has a longstanding association with the Eurovision Song Contest, and has made several TV documentaries about the event, including 2015's *Ireland and the Eurovision*. He was Head of Entertainment and Drama in RTÉ from 1990 to 1994 – during Ireland's 'golden era', when it won and staged the Eurovision contest three years in a row.

As well as working for RTÉ in Dublin, he has worked for the BBC in London and HBO in New York. He currently runs the independent production company Blueprint Pictures, which specialises in arts and entertainment series. He is the author of *Suddenly, While Abroad*, which tells the story of the thirty-two Irish merchant seamen who were held in a Nazi slave labour camp. David lives in Dublin.

Ireland
and the
EUROVISION

The Winners, the Losers
and the Turkey

David Blake Knox

NEW ISLAND

IRELAND AND THE EUROVISION

First published in 2015
by New Island Books,
16 Priory Hall Office Park,
Stillorgan,
County Dublin,
Republic of Ireland.

www.newisland.ie

PRINT ISBN: 978-1-84840-429-8
EPUB ISBN: 978-1-84840-450-2
MOBI ISBN: 978-1-84840-451-9

British Library Cataloguing Data.
A CIP catalogue record for this book is available from the British Library.

Typeset by JVR Creative India
Cover design by Mariel Deegan
Printed by ScandBook AB, Sweden 2015

For Jamie, Kirsty and Sarah

Contents

Acknowledgements

I am grateful to all those who spoke to me about their involvement in Ireland's participation in the Eurovision Song Contest over the past fifty years.

In particular, I should mention Bunny Carr, who presented Ireland's first national song contest, and who provided the commentary for the first Eurovision final in which Ireland took part. Bunny was generous with his time and memories when I interviewed him. He also showed that he had lost none of his acute sense of humour in the half century that has passed since 1965.

I would also like to acknowledge the important contribution that Liam Miller made over a number of years both to RTÉ's involvement in the song contest, and to the wider development of the Eurovision.

There are many others who have contributed directly or indirectly – to this book. They include John Keogh, Ollie Donohoe, Johnny Logan, Louis Walsh, Clíona Ní Bhuchalla, Eugene Murray, Kevin Linehan, Anita Notaro, Niamh Kavanagh, John McHugh, Pat Cowap, Michael Flatley, Jean Butler, Gerry Ryan, Cynthia Ní Mhurchú, Marty Whelan, Paul Harrington,

Caroline Downey, Darren Smith, Michael Kealy, and Glen Killane.

I want to thank RTÉ's film archive and stills department: in particular, Pearl Quinn – whose assistance was greatly valued. I would also like to thank Vinny Beirne and Angela Scanlon, who worked with me on the documentary film for RTÉ that accompanies this book.

I found an informed and insightful background to the Irish showband scene in *Send 'Em Home Sweating* by Vincent Power; in *Always Me* by Dickie Rock; and in *Goodnight, God Bless, and Safe Home* by Finbar O'Keefe. The development of the Eurovision over the years is related in John Kennedy O'Connor's *The Eurovision Song Contest: The Official History*, and in Paul Gambaccini's *The Complete Eurovision Song Contest Companion*. An entertaining and, at times, poignant approach to the contest is provided by Tim Moore in *Nul Points*. Academic analyses of the Eurovision can be found in *A Song For Europe: Popular Music and Politics in the Eurovision Song Contest* edited by Ivan Raykoff and Robert Deam Tobin, and also in *Empire of Song: Europe and Nation in the Eurovision Song Contest* edited by Dafni Tragaki.

I am especially grateful to Dr Michael Cussen, who read some early drafts of this book, and whose memories of the early years of Ireland and the Eurovision were both evocative and helpful. I also appreciate the critical insights provided by Professor Tom Inglis, whose work is essential reading for an understanding of the evolution of Irish society over the past half century.

All of my children grew up with the Eurovision as part of the soundtrack of their childhoods. Despite that, they have all managed to retain their enjoyment of the contest. I am particularly grateful to my son, Dr Jamie Blake Knox, for the analytical perspective that he brought as a historian to my understanding of the event. My two daughters, Kirsty and Sarah, also provided many shrewd, amusing and provocative insights for which I am grateful.

Their mother, Deborah Spillane, could not be described as a great Eurovision fan. In that context, I am most appreciative of the tolerance and forbearance that she displayed over many years of listening to the rest of the family discussing the contest in detail and *ad nauseam*.

I would like to thank my editor at New Island Books, Dan Bolger. The consistent popularity of the Eurovision Song Contest has often baffled and confused American observers. However, Dan has been prepared to approach the event with a fresh eye and an open mind. His close reading of my text, and his perceptive suggestions were much appreciated.

Finally, I must accept personal responsibility for any mistakes which this book contains. I accept that responsibility with some apprehension since I am aware that Eurovision fans are exceptionally well informed about the history of the contest. Many of them are undoubtedly much more knowledgeable than I am — so I ask their indulgence in advance for any errors that I may have committed.

Foreword by
Louis Walsh

When people ask me – 'Does the Eurovision matter any more?' – I ask them, 'Are you serious?' It matters to the millions of people all over the world who watch the contest every year. It matters to the artists taking part – some of them have even risked their lives just to get onto that Eurovision stage. It should also matter to the broadcasters that enter the contest on our behalf. After all, this is still the world's biggest TV entertainment show. It's often derided and ridiculed, but, over the years, it has helped to launch international stars such as ABBA, Julio Iglesias, Celine Dion, and, of course, our own Johnny Logan. Ireland has won this song contest seven times – more than any other country. Winning has been good for Ireland, and for the Irish music industry. But, in the past couple of decades, our record has been tarnished. It doesn't have to be that way. Any country – big or small – can win the Eurovision. All it takes is a really good song, a really good act – and perhaps a bit of luck. This book has been written by someone who's been connected to the Eurovision for almost as long as I have (and that's saying something). His book tells, at last, the inside story of Ireland's half-century in this extraordinary song contest – the triumphs and the tragedies. Let's hope any subsequent editions will contain news of further Irish victories.

Introduction

When I mentioned to some friends that I was writing a book about the Eurovision Song Contest, it produced a range of reactions. One of them asked me if I were writing an autobiography. Another asked why I was wasting my time with such rubbish.

This book is certainly not intended as an autobiography. However, it does concern a number of events in which I was closely involved, and it features a number of individuals who became my colleagues and friends, in part, as a result of that involvement. To begin with, I became connected with the Eurovision on a purely professional basis, but, over a period of years, I grew more engaged with the contest on a personal level, and that is reflected in this book.

For many years, both amateur and professional critics have enjoyed lamenting the banal melodies, the rare sentiments, the clichéd lyrics, and the vulgar displays of this song contest. According to Marcus Berkmann, writing in the *Spectator* magazine, the contest is an annual event that is unredeemed by 'style, flair, intelligence, wit or even the sniff of a good tune.' I don't believe that is a fair or an accurate assessment. But even if it were, it would not explain the persistent appeal of the Eurovision to many millions of viewers around the world. If it is not the songs that draw such large audiences, it must be something else. I hope this book will help to provide some explanation for its success, and its longevity.

I was fortunate to be supervised at university by the novelist and critic, Raymond Williams. He taught me that culture has a wider and more popular dimension than traditional concepts allowed. By any standard, the song contest is an extraordinary phenomenon in popular culture: it is, after all, not only the biggest, but also the most enduring live entertainment show in the world. It has been written off many times, but still manages to bounce back – bigger and bolder than ever.

In the past decade, it has begun to be taken more seriously. The contest has attracted the attention of academic analysts, and there has been a host of papers published in scholarly journals that have explored such issues as the 'Conundrum of Post-Socialist Belonging', 'The Return to Ethnicity', and 'Switzerland's Identity Struggle' – all in the context of the Eurovision contest. This book is not written from an academic perspective, but I hope that I have also taken the event seriously – though not excessively so – and have treated the performers with the respect they deserve.

The rules of the contest have changed a great deal over the years, but the fundamental elements have remained much the same. The music that introduces the event is still the Prelude to Marc-Antoine Charpentier's '*Te Deum*'. There is always a presenter, or presenters, to introduce the Grand Final. One song still represents each of the competing countries. After they have all been performed, there is some sort of entertainment – usually referred to as the 'interval act'. There is still a vote to determine the winning song, and there is still no prize for the winning act. The winner of *America's Got Talent* pockets a million bucks, but coming first in the Eurovision is deemed to be reward enough. Although it is not obligatory, the winning country is always invited to host the following year's contest.

New technology has been introduced over the years – but, sometimes, it has been viewed as counter-productive. I remember in 1992, when I was serving on the European Broadcasting Union (EBU) Entertainment Committee, we struggled with the problem of how to integrate the large number of new Eastern European entries with a contest that was not supposed to last more than three hours. The Swiss delegate pointed out that it took almost one hour of television airtime to record the votes of every national jury. He suggested that – thanks to modern technology – we could announce the result within a few minutes of the vote ending, creating space for other countries to perform. His proposal foundered when he was reminded that the viewing figures for the last hour of voting were invariably much higher than the preceding two hours of the actual performances.

The Eurovision is now open to all countries in Europe, and it does not have any formal connection with the European Union. However, the European Broadcasting Area is not simply defined by geography, but also by membership of the International Telecommunication Union. In addition, some countries outside the historic boundaries of Europe are deemed eligible to compete in the contest. The 'Eurovision family' includes countries in North Africa, the Middle East, and western Asia – as well as transcontinental states, such as Russia, which has only part of their territory in Europe. Seventy-three countries are

3

now full-members of the EBU – with a further twenty-two associate members. The applications of another six to join the EBU are currently pending. This means that more than half of the world's existing states are now connected to the EBU – and, through it, to the song contest.

In 1956, the first 'Eurovision Grand Prix' lasted just over one and a half hours. In 2014, there were two semi-finals – each of which was two hours long – and a Grand Final that lasted for more than three hours. In 1956, the contest was primarily intended for radio broadcast; although there were cameras present, the television viewership was insignificant. Since then, the TV audience for the Eurovision has grown in exponential terms: in 2014, the contest was reckoned to have been watched by almost 200 million viewers worldwide – close to twice the number who watched that year's Super Bowl in the USA. In 1956, the contest was only broadcast to Western Europe. In 2014, it was viewed widely – not only across the European continent, but also in Australia, Hong Kong, Malaysia, Canada, and many other territories.

Shelley once claimed that poets, like himself, were the 'unacknowledged legislators' of the future, and, unlikely as it may seem, the Eurovision has anticipated certain political and social developments in Europe. The contest was established before the Treaty of Rome had been signed: it pre-dates the European Union, and it may yet post-date it too. It is true that the contest has sometimes revealed the presence of simmering ethnic tensions in certain parts of the continent. It is also true that political events – including revolution, civil war and threats of terrorism – have sometimes formed a vivid backdrop to the contest. Despite all of that, the Eurovision remains one of the few festive occasions that all European countries can share together. For many, it is still a sign of hope that Europe can celebrate its musical affinities, and not be drawn back into the old seductive themes of blood and soil.

For the first half-century or so, the French language retained an equal status with English in the Eurovision – at least, in theory. French artists continue to sing in French, but English is now the undisputed *lingua franca* for almost everyone else in the contest. There have been other significant changes to the contest. In 2014, I attended the Copenhagen Eurovision. On most nights, I ended up with some of the Irish delegation in the Euroclub – enjoying a nightcap or two, and watching live performances from some of the artists in that year's final. The majority of those in the club seemed to be gay men, and the most enthusiastic reception was reserved for the Austrian performer, a drag queen called Conchita Wurst. She went on to win the contest – after receiving a large majority of televotes across the continent. No doubt, all of this would have astonished the sober and high-minded group of men who first established the contest in 1956.

They had wished to create a social and cultural occasion where the nations of Europe – which had recently spilled so much of each other's blood – might come together in both literal and figurative harmony. They wanted the Eurovision to be free of any other agenda, but, inevitably, politics have sometimes intruded. Given the turbulent history of the continent, it is, perhaps, only surprising that political controversies have not intruded more often – and with more serious consequences. In general, internal conflicts and disagreements have been expressed in fairly moderate terms. In 2014, for example, the Eurovision Grand Final took place soon after the Russian military annexation of Crimea. The Russian entry was booed loudly by the large audience at the Copenhagen show – and so were any countries that awarded high marks to the Russian act. There was more than one reason for that negative response: Russia had recently introduced legislation aimed at preventing the promotion of so-called 'non-traditional sexual relationships'. This measure was clearly directed against homosexuals, and, as a result, was deeply resented by many of the Eurovision's most devoted fans.

The Eurovision was once described to me as the 'Olympics for Gay Men', and, from an early stage, there has been much in the contest that appeals to camp tastes – the frivolity, the heightened emotion, the visual extravagance. Over the years, a considerable number of openly gay men and women have competed in the final, and it could be argued that the Eurovision has, in its own way, encouraged Europe to accept its LGBT citizens.

On the other hand, the event has been slower to reflect the multicultural nature of contemporary Europe. However, around half of the countries competing in the contest have now been represented by black or ethnic minority performers – some on multiple occasions. Indigenous minority groups have also been present on the Eurovision stage. There have been Bretons and Corsicans from France, Travellers from Ireland, Roma from Bulgaria, and members of the small Jewish community in Turkey. Songs have also been performed in Europe's minority languages, such as Romansh, Võro, Udmurt, Samogitian – and Irish.

On occasion, performers who do not correspond to what is perceived as the national ideal – or ethnic stereotype – have encountered opposition from racist groups within their own countries. Indeed, it seems from Anders Breivik's diary that his massacre of seventy-seven Norwegian civilians in 2011 was triggered in part by his rage at seeing Stella

Mwangi, an immigrant from Kenya who sang in Swahili, representing his country in that year's Eurovision. In his dairy, he described her selection as 'crap' and motivated by 'political correctness' It should, however, be remembered that Breivik was an isolated and disturbed individual, and Stella was chosen to sing for Norway in a nationwide televote in which she won an overwhelming victory.

Perhaps what appeals most to audiences across Europe is the intrinsic drama of the contest. For all its artifice, there is a sense that this event represents the prototype of Reality television. For many of those taking part, the contest offers what may seem like their one chance to break into the Big Time. Most of them will have worked extremely hard to get onto that Eurovision stage, and, behind the scenes, there is no trace of the irony that features in so much media coverage of the contest. For the performers, this is a highly competitive event, and even if there is no tangible prize to be gained, winning the Eurovision remains the stuff of dreams.

National attitudes towards the Eurovision can vary greatly. The British, for example, tend to view the contest with some disdain – often regarding the whole rigmarole *de haut en bas*. It is, perhaps, understandable that they might feel superior: the dominant language of the song contest is their own, and they are still the only European country whose popular music has a long history of global success. It may not seem so surprising that they should consider themselves as somehow better qualified to pass judgment on pop music than their continental counterparts. Despite that presumption, an analysis of the votes cast – both by juries and by public televotes – reveals a surprising outcome: the British have voted consistently in line with the rest of Europe.

7

Some western countries – such as Sweden – are proud to show their wholehearted commitment to the Eurovision. The Swedish contest to select their national entry runs over six live shows. Thirty-two semi-finalists are chosen from more than 3,000 submissions, and the final selection takes place in front of a live audience of more than 30,000 fans. In 2014, over 3 million votes were cast to select the winner, and the televised final gained an 89 per cent share of the available viewing audience – a staggering proportion of Sweden's population.

The special significance of the Eurovision can also be found in some of the Eastern European states that have emerged from half-a-century of political and social oppression. During those years, the Eurovision was one of the few TV entertainment shows from the West that Eastern Europeans were permitted to watch, and, for many, it retains much of the mystique and glamour that has now been lost in Western Europe.

Just seven countries took part in the first 'Eurovision Grand Prix' in 1956 – and Ireland was not one of them. By 2014, more than fifty countries had competed. The biggest influx of new participants came with the collapse of the Iron Curtain in 1989, and the subsequent end of the Cold War. By the turn of the present millennium, most of the countries that were once part of the old Soviet bloc had become enthusiastic participants in the contest – and sometimes their enthusiasm surfaced in unexpected ways.

In 1991, soon after the fall of the Iron Curtain, the EBU organised a conference on 'New Competition for Public Broadcasters', which was designed to give some practical advice to those eastern countries where TV stations were about to lose their State-backed monopolies. The keynote speaker at the conference was Eugene Murray, RTÉ's Head of Programme Services. He gave a detailed presentation of the complex challenges the Irish station had faced following the introduction of commercial broadcasting. After he had finished, questions were invited from the audience. The first came from a senior manager with Polish TV. He asked, 'How can we win the Eurovision Song Contest?'

This enthusiasm for the Eurovision has caused a degree of anxiety among some Western European broadcasters, and they have sometimes behaved as if the contest were their personal property – and in danger of being stolen from them. Fear of the impact of Eastern Europe's inclusion has become a familiar refrain in Western commentaries – sometimes with an unpleasantly xenophobic dimension – and, of course, such fear has not been confined to this song contest. But, for some Eastern European States, joining the Eurovision for the first time had a profound significance, and served to prove that they belonged to a modern democratic continent. It once served a somewhat similar purpose in Ireland.

The countries that helped to establish the song contest did not include Ireland; our debut was made at the tenth Eurovision in Naples in 1965. Since then, we have won the song contest more times than other nation. There were mixed results in the first twenty years, but they included two wins – in 1970 and 1980. However, the golden decade for Ireland did not really begin until 1987, when Johnny Logan won the contest for a second time. His success was quickly followed by a run of further victories, and RTÉ – Ireland's national broadcaster – went on to stage the Eurovision Final no less than five times between 1988 and 1997. It was an unprecedented achievement, and seems unlikely to be equalled – at least, not in the foreseeable future.

The Irish run of success in the Eurovision does not mean that the contest has always been revered in Ireland. Indeed, some sections of the Irish press have seemed to take a consistent delight in ridiculing the event. A few journalists appear not to have grasped that the Eurovision is designed to work as a popular entertainment show – and one that is specifically intended to appeal across the widest range of ages, cultures and nationalities. To criticise the event because it has failed to produce many songs that have become evergreen standards is a little like going to a soccer game and complaining that you had expected to see a ballet.

As it happens, the past ten or so years have witnessed a series of setbacks and disappointments for Ireland. The country has failed even to qualify to take part in the Grand Final on several occasions. When Irish acts have managed to qualify, their performances have sometimes been dismal, and they have usually finished in the lower reaches of the scoreboard.

There are a number of reasons for these failures, some of which originate outside Ireland. The advent of Eastern European countries led to a good deal of confusion within the EBU about the future identity of the Eurovision. This is reflected in the frequent rule changes that have taken place in the last twenty years – as the EBU struggled to find an equitable system of inclusion. It could be argued that Ireland, in particular, has suffered from some of the recent changes – such as the ending of the prohibition of the use of English by non-English speaking countries.

However, some of the causes of the Irish failures lie much closer to home. There has been a lack of clear direction in RTÉ's strategy for the Eurovision, and there have also been some blatant errors of editorial judgment.

The early years of Ireland's involvement in the contest were those of hope and apsiration, and subsequent years were ones of self-confident achievement. Perhaps, only a degree of hubris can explain the poor performances of the past decade. In certain respects, that development seems to parallel the progresss – or otherwise – of Irish society over the same period.

Fifty years have come and gone since an Irish singer first stepped out onto the Eurovision stage in Naples. This book is about what happened next – both on stage and behind the scenes. The stories of modern Ireland and the song contest have become intertwined over the last half-century. Both have changed greatly in recent decades – but, then, so too has the rest of Europe. Ireland was a very different country when our love affair with the Eurovision Song Contest began. Everything seemed so much simpler back in 1965.

1.
The Start of the Affair

By 1965, Ireland had established its political independence from the United Kingdom for more than forty years. In the decades that followed Independence, the new state had achieved a level of internal stability that seemed, at times, to border on stagnation. But, by the mid-1960s, there was a strong sense that social change was in the air. The generation that had won Ireland's freedom – and controlled the country for decades – finally seemed ready to step aside. In many respects, Ireland was still a deeply conservative society, but it appeared that, at last, some of the old certainties were being questioned, and new options explored.

In January 1965, the Irish Taoiseach, Seán Lemass, travelled to Belfast for an historic meeting of national conciliation with the Prime Minister of Northern Ireland, Terence O'Neill. A few weeks later, substantive reforms of the Catholic liturgy were introduced, and, in March of that year, Mass was said in English for the first time in Ireland. Later on in the year, a twenty-six-year-old medical student became the first person in the history of the Irish State to be arrested on drugs charges – though *The Irish Times* assured its readers it was 'most unlikely' that drug abuse would ever become a problem in Ireland.

The national television station, Telefís Éireann, had been launched on New Year's Eve in 1961. It operated from the spanking-new premises at Montrose in South County Dublin, and seemed to many to epitomise the emergence of Ireland as a thoroughly modern European State. As a public service broadcaster, Telefís Éireann was eligible to enter one of Europe's most popular television shows, the Eurovision Song Contest. In 1964, a formal request was made to the European Broadcasting Union – who organised the event – and it was accepted. The news that Ireland would take part in the 1965 contest led to great excitement in the country – as well as inside the young station.

The first priority was to select the Irish Eurovision entry. Ireland's first national song contest was held in March 1965, in Telefís Éireann's studios in Dublin, and was hosted by Bunny Carr. At that time, working as a presenter for Irish television was not yet perceived as a viable full-time career, and Bunny's day job was as a cashier at Bank of Ireland. When I spoke to him, fifty years after the event, he remembered the excitement that was palpable in RTÉ's studio that night. Twelve songs were performed, and the winner was chosen by voting from twelve regional juries. This has been the principal – though not the only – system used by RTÉ to select Ireland's Eurovision entry for most of the half-century that has followed. Among those taking part in 1965 were some of the biggest names in Irish show business. They included Butch Moore, Dickie Rock and Brendan Bowyer – all of whom performed with leading Irish showbands.

In 1965, showbands dominated Ireland's popular music scene, and drew large crowds to the great number of dance halls spread across the country. The showbands' basic repertoire normally included country and western songs, as well as cover versions from the current hit parade. They also sometimes played traditional Irish ballads and *céilidh* music. There were usually seven or eight members, and – unlike previous Big Bands – they always played standing up, which seemed to give a new energy and excitement to their performances. The showbands normally featured lead singers, or frontmen, who tended to attract most of the public attention and adulation. Butch Moore was the frontman with the Capitol showband, Dickie Rock with the Miami, and Brendan Bowyer with the Royal.

The types of songs these showband stars performed in the first national final were rather different to the material they usually sang while on stage with their bands. At that time, the Eurovision seemed to Irish eyes to be quite a sophisticated affair, and there was a widespread wish that whoever was chosen to represent Ireland in the Grand Final in Naples would not let the country down. For the national contest, Moore, Rock and Bowyer sang more in the fashion of American cabaret crooners, such as Frank Sinatra or Dean Martin, than in the lively and raucous style of an Irish ballroom.

One of those taking part was John Keogh. In some respects, John was an unlikely person to feature in the contest. He was the lead singer in a group called the Greenbeats, and usually played rock 'n' roll. 'I was surprised and flattered to be asked,' he told me, 'because all the other singers were well established at that time, and big stars in Ireland, and I was just starting my career.' John wasn't enthused by the song he had been given to sing. 'It wasn't bad, but it had no musical "bridge". It was just verse and chorus, verse and chorus. And it wasn't my type of music. It was an old-fashioned ballad. In fact, all the songs in the contest that year sounded as if they came from the 1950s.'

In advance of the contest, all the male singers were told that they were to dress formally. 'It was very unusual for me to wear a dinner suit,' John told me. 'One of my old teachers wrote to me after the show. He said that he was glad to see how well I had dressed, and how much he appreciated the "dignity" with which I had performed my song. I think it was the only time a Christian Brother had anything good to say about me.' According to John, those in RTÉ's audience were also untypical of his usual audience. 'The studio was stuffed with assorted dignitaries – including the Lord Mayor of Dublin, for some reason. There was hardly a young person to be seen.'

Brendan Bowyer was then considered the most popular singer in Ireland – and was often described as the 'Irish Elvis'. In 1962, The Beatles had been the support band when Brendan and the Royal played in Liverpool, and in 1965 Brendan released 'The Hucklebuck' – an infectious dance track that proved to be his biggest hit. However, despite repeated attempts, Brendan never won Ireland's national song contest. In 1965, he finished in fifth place; according to John Keogh, 'Brendan was given a weak song to perform – it wasn't his fault.'

Butch Moore won the first national final with a song called 'Walking the Streets in the Rain'. The song had been co-written by a sixteen-year-old schoolgirl, and was a fairly conventional ballad. The singer is walking away from his former lover after she has ended their relationship. He admits that he is deeply upset by what has happened, but nobody knows he is crying – because he's '*walking the streets in the rain*'. The lyrics may have owed something to the Everly Brothers' classic single, 'Crying in the Rain', which had been a worldwide hit a few years earlier.

When Butch Moore won the contest, he was already very popular on the Irish showband circuit, but his success was not greeted with universal approval. In a letter to the *Munster Express*, two 'country boys' from Waterford – Brendan Bowyer's home county – objected to what they saw as the iniquity of the vote. 'Brendan's tender feelings for his song had us enraptured,' they wrote, 'and we felt sure this was the song that would do us justice in Naples.' They still 'did not flinch' from that opinion, they continued, 'even after hearing the verdict of a "packed" jury.' The two men urged all decent Waterford people to join them in a protest against the scandalous manner in which 'the talents of Brendan Bowyer were ignored.'

The 1965 Eurovision took place in Naples, and Bunny Carr was asked to provide the commentary. Fifty years later, Bunny remembers that he had to ask permission from the manager of the bank where he worked for time off to go to Italy. He was told that he could, but that he was to keep it a secret from the rest of the bank's staff – though his manager did not explain how that might be possible.

This was Italy's first hosting of the Eurovision Song Contest. The Italian broadcaster, RAI, staged the event in studios that had been built just a few years previously. Eighteen countries participated, and the final took place in front of an invited audience of around 300. A little over forty years later, the live audience attending the Eurovision Grand Final would number more than 38,000.

Viewed from a contemporary perspective, the 1965 contest seems excessively stiff and formal. All the men in the audience wore dinner jackets and black ties, and the women were dressed in evening gowns. Although the commentators were not seen on camera, Bunny Carr told me that they were also wearing formal dinner suits. Butch wore a tuxedo, and seemed relaxed and confident. He sang well, and looked handsome and debonair on camera. Watching the grainy archive footage, I can well imagine the national pride that his professional and urbane performance must have inspired back in Ireland.

Bunny Carr was on a telephone link to his producer in Dublin, who was feeding him information about the different acts as they appeared. However, after just ten minutes, the phone connection was lost, and he had to ad-lib for the remainder of the contest. As a result, he told me, the commentary that Irish viewers received from Naples was largely a 'work of fiction'. The voting mechanism in 1965 was rather different from more recent systems, but it seems to have been equally complicated and hard to understand. Each country had ten jury members who distributed three points among their first, second and third favourite songs. These points were then added up, and the first, second and third-placed songs were awarded five, three and one votes respectively. However, if only one song were chosen by the jury, it would receive all nine points. If only two songs were chosen, they would get six and three points in order of preference. This was the shape of things to come: over the years, the EBU has displayed a marked tendency – almost a creative flair – for devising elaborate voting systems that defy simple explanation.

Butch Moore was the fifth contestant to perform that night in Naples. When the votes were cast, he finished in sixth position with eleven points. This was quite an impressive achievement – since Belgium, Finland, Germany and Spain did not manage to gain a single vote. In fact, according to Bunny Carr, this was the 'perfect' result for Ireland. 'We wanted to do our best,' he told me, 'but I think it would have been very difficult for the station at that time if we had won.' He believed that taking part in the contest brought RTÉ a new sense of authority and prestige in the eyes of the Irish public. 'Because of our troubled history, we have had low self-esteem as a nation,' he said. Engaging in the Eurovision showed that Ireland's national broadcaster could compete with larger European countries like Germany. 'More importantly,' Bunny told me, 'it showed that we could perform at the same level as the British.' Back in 1965, that seemed to matter to a lot of Irish people.

Luxembourg won the contest for a second consecutive time with 'Poupée de Cire, Poupée de Son'. This was not the last Eurovision song in which a female singer would describe herself as a living doll – and, like most of the others, its lyrics had been written by a man: in this case, the remarkable Serge Gainsbourg – who would compose his last entry for the contest twenty-five years later. In keeping with Gainsbourg's rather louche reputation, 'Poupée' was considered sexually risqué, but it went on to become a major hit in almost all European countries. For the first time, the contest was also broadcast, via the Intervision network, to Eastern Europe – where it seemed to offer those countries on the other side of the Iron Curtain a tantalising glimpse of an alternative and glamorous way of life.

There was one other significant development in the 1965 contest: the Swedish singer had unexpectedly performed his song in English. There were complaints from some of the other performers, all of whom had sung in their native languages. This led to a rule being introduced by the EBU, which stipulated that all participants had to perform their songs using one of their national languages. More than thirty years would pass before that rule was abandoned for good, and it was a regulation which some believe worked to Ireland's advantage in the years ahead.

When Butch Moore returned to Ireland, he was treated as a triumphant hero. More than 5,000 fans were waiting to mob him when he arrived at Dublin Airport, and for several months he needed a police escort when he was travelling around Ireland. His Eurovision song reached number one in the Irish charts, and he and the Capitol Showband attracted huge crowds in ballrooms all over the country. Sadly, it did not last. Butch entered Ireland's national song contest again the following year, and again in 1969. Both times he failed to qualify, and he never got the chance to sing for Ireland again.

By the end of the sixties, Irish tastes in popular music seemed to have changed, and Butch went to live in the United States. He formed a successful singing group with his wife, Maeve, and they also owned and ran a pub in Massachusetts. Butch died of a heart attack in 2001, and Maeve died in 2004.

Bunny Carr told me that commentating on the Eurovision altered the course of his life. Following the contest, he returned to his job as a cashier in the Bank of Ireland – but he soon realised how much had changed as a result of his Eurovision commentary. 'There were three of us cashiers, and I was the youngest. Normally, there was the same size queue for each of us. After the Eurovision, my queue became by far the longest. And as well as wanting cash, the customers wanted my autograph.' Not long after the Eurovision, Bunny gave up his job in the bank and became a full-time broadcaster – a career that proved highly successful in the decades ahead.

John Keogh finished in a creditable third place in Ireland's first national song contest, but he believes it made little difference to his subsequent musical career. He resumed playing rock 'n' roll with his band. In fact, he is still rocking half-a-century later, and he can still bring audiences to their feet – even if their parents had not been born back in 1965.

Butch Moore was the very first Irish entry to the Eurovision, and he acquitted himself with some distinction. He might even be credited for starting the love affair between the Irish nation and the contest – a relationship that has lasted for half a century. Like any romance, it has had its ups and downs, but, on occasion, it can still seem as intense and passionate as ever.

2.

The Boy Zone

Ireland's second national final was held in January 1966 in RTÉ – as the station was now called. Brendan O'Reilly, who later became one of RTÉ's leading sports commentators, hosted the event. There were six finalists, and they each sang two different songs. This meant that each contestant ended up with two places on the scoreboard. Dickie Rock, for example, won the competition with 'Come Back to Stay', but he also held seventh place with another song, 'Oh! Why?' The only exception to this rule was the veteran entertainer, Sonny Knowles. His two songs both finished in the same place. equal last, having failed to gain a single point between them.

Another unusual feature of this national song contest was the decision to ask the public to vote for their favourite act by postcard. There had been understandable concern about the reliability of the Irish telephone system on a live show, but the postal vote delayed the outcome of the competition for a week. It also removed much of the drama from the live broadcast of the national final.

When Dickie Rock won the national contest, he was one of the most popular singers in Ireland. By 1966, he and the Miami Showband had already enjoyed five number ones in the Irish charts – and 'Come Back to Stay' would be his sixth. Dickie had generated the sort of mass hysteria in Ireland that was normally reserved for international acts, such as the Beatles. He even became the subject of a widespread but disturbing catchphrase: 'Spit on me, Dickie.' The request originated in a Belfast club called the Boom Boom Room – where it was shouted out by a hysterical fan, and it soon spread like a rash across Ireland.

The 1966 Eurovision was in Luxembourg, and the same countries that competed the previous year had returned. In 1966, Ireland had again chosen a ballad as the national entry for the contest. The lyrics for 'Come Back to Stay' were, if anything, even simpler than the previous year. The singer's girlfriend has left him, and he wants her to come back: '*I promise I'll be true*', Dickie sang, '*and that I'll never make you blue.*' The song has a pleasant melody, but seems to lack any emotional depth. Nonetheless, Dickie gave an assured and polished performance.

Although the structure of the contest had changed very little from the 1965 final, there was one significant addition. Milly Scott represented the Netherlands with a song called 'Fernando en Filippo'. She came from Surinam, and was the first singer 'of colour' to perform on the Eurovision stage. At that time, it was still relatively unusual for black artists to appear on any European TV station. It seemed that some TV stations even preferred to use white artists pretending to be black. One of the most popular entertainment series broadcast by the BBC in 1966 was

The Black and White Minstrel Show – in which white singers appeared every week made up with black faces. The series would run for another twelve years before this obnoxious practice was finally deemed to be unacceptable.

Milly Scott was not the last black singer to take part in the contest. In fact, Portugal was represented the following year by Eduardo Nascimento, who became the first black male singer in Eurovision history. Over the coming years, it took some time before Europe's ethnic minorities began to be well represented in the contest, and the first black singer to win the Grand Final did not do so until 2001.

The winning song in 1966 came from Austria, whose singer, Udo Jürgens, had also represented his country in the two previous contests. (This would remain Austria's only win in the Eurovision until 2014 – when the 'Bearded Lady' Conchita Wurst gave Austria a second victory.) Dickie Rock finished fourth in 1966 – which was even better than Butch Moore had managed in 1965. However, Dickie later claimed to have been 'disgusted' with the result. He said he had travelled to Luxembourg 'knowing that the hopes and dreams of the Irish people were resting on my shoulders', and he believed that 'even coming second would have been a disappointment.' Dickie felt he had let down the country as well as himself. However, there were thousands of his fans at Dublin Airport when his plane landed, and he was overwhelmed by the reception.

Sadly, he was kept off the headlines of the following morning's newspapers. To mark the fiftieth anniversary of the 1916 Rising, the IRA had blown up Nelson's Pillar in the centre of Dublin – a landmark monument immortalised in the Aeolus episode of James Joyce's *Ulysses* – and Dickie later complained ruefully that the explosion had 'stolen' his Eurovision glory. Dickie entered Ireland's national contest again in 1969, and, for one last time, in 1977 – but he did not win on either occasion.

The twelfth Eurovision took place in Vienna, and the Irish artist in the 1967 contest was Sean Dunphy. Sean was the front man with the Hoedowners, a showband led by the trumpeter Earl Gill. Sean had only joined the band the previous year, but his relaxed manner and smooth baritone voice had made an immediate impact. The final was hosted once again by Brendan O'Reilly in RTÉ's Dublin studios, and the winner was again chosen following a postal vote.

'If I Could Chose' was the title of Sean's winning song. It was also a ballad, and although its sentiments were hardly original – the singer is telling his lover how special she is to him – the lyrics were unusually well written. Perhaps that was not so surprising, since they had been composed by Wesley Burrowes, who came from Northern Ireland, and was the creator of RTÉ's hugely popular rural drama series, *The Riordans*. The lyrics of this song also place the singer deep in the Irish countryside – among the *'hills of Clare'*, to be precise.

The Vienna contest took place in the splendid surroundings of the Hofburg Palace. This was – to say the least – an unusual venue for a popular music competition. It was formerly an imperial residence – the birthplace of the unfortunate Queen Marie Antoinette, and home to a succession of Habsburg kings and emperors. It had also been a centre of the Holy Roman Empire – the first attempt to unify Europe – so perhaps, in that sense, it was an appropriate setting.

The number of countries competing in 1967 was seventeen; the Danish broadcaster, DR, had withdrawn and would not return to the contest until 1978. Niels Jørgen Kaiser, the Head of DR's Entertainment Department had announced that he could think of better ways to spend the money it cost Denmark to participate. He was not alone in his reservations: from an early stage, the Eurovision had attracted a negative response from some musicians and music journalists, and that has stayed a constant feature. Herre Kaiser remained in the same role with DR for the next eleven years, but, once he had left the station, Denmark immediately re-entered the competition.

The stage that had been designed for the 1967 contest was rather different from previous years. Until then, the songs had been performed against fairly nondescript backdrops. The stage in Vienna featured three large revolving mirrors, and a staircase for the singers to make a grand – if somewhat perilous – entrance. Although the design may now seem fairly basic, it marked a turning point of sorts in the approach to the staging of the songs.

The jury system had also undergone a significant change by 1967. The EBU had determined that at least half of every national jury should be made up of jurors who were less than thirty years old. This signalled a recognition that the Eurovision still reflected the tastes of an older generation. At a time when young people across Western Europe were becoming aware of their growing influence and spending power, it was clear that their musical preferences had to be considered if the contest were to retain its popularity. Nowadays, it may all seem rather patronising, but this change was to have both short and long-term effects on the contest.

The shift in the average age of the juries may help to explain the outcome of the 1967 Grand Final, and the huge margin of its winner's victory. The British entry to the Eurovision that year was Sandie Shaw. She had enjoyed a string of hits in the preceding years – not only in the UK, but across Europe, in South America and in the United States. She had recorded versions of most of her singles in Italian, French, German and Spanish – and was well known across the Continent. She had also performed in Eastern Europe, and even in pre-revolutionary Iran.

More importantly, Sandie Shaw was a young woman who was not seen as part of the entertainment establishment. She was not only exceptionally good-looking – with her glossy bobbed hair, and Mary Quant mini-shirts, her looks were fresh and contemporary. In many ways, she seemed to embody the youthful spirit of the 'Swinging Sixties', and, more specifically, of London, which was then considered to be both the coolest and the hottest capitol in Europe. She always sang in her bare feet – which seemed to express the unfettered freedom of her spirit, and when she stepped on to the Eurovision stage, Sandie Shaw appeared to be ushering in a whole new era in the history of the contest.

Once she began to sing, it became obvious that her song was cut from a more traditional cloth. In fact, 'Puppet on a String' was not representative of Sandie Shaw's previous material. It had been chosen by a public vote in the UK – after she had performed five songs on the BBC's *Rolf Harris Show* – but it sounded as if it had been written for a German *Schlager* band to perform. In fact, its composers were Phil Coulter from Northern Ireland, and his co-writer, Bill Martin. Coulter went on to enjoy a highly successful career, and, in the years to come, he displayed an astonishing ability to compose across a wide range of musical genres. However, Sandie Shaw later criticised 'Puppet on a String' in the strongest terms: 'I hated the song from the first oompah to the final bang on the big bass drum,' she told the *Daily Telegraph* 'I was repelled by its sexist drivel and cuckoo-clock tune.'

Despite her apparent antipathy, the combination of a fashionable singer and a familiar musical idiom proved irresistible to juries across Europe, and Sandie Shaw won the contest by a landslide. Rolf Harris was commentating on the final for the BBC. This was the first British Eurovision win, and he was understandably jubilant. In the following decades, Harris would become one of Britain's 'national treasures' before he was exposed as a paedophile and rapist: he is currently serving a term in one of Her Majesty's prisons for sex offences.

'Puppet on a String' became a worldwide hit, and sold more than a million copies in Europe alone. Perhaps Sandie Shaw's feelings about the song are somewhat more ambivalent than she has claimed. I worked with her on one occasion – many years after she had won the Eurovision. Although she expressed her loathing of the song in private, she still performed it in front of an audience that night, with complete commitment and apparent enjoyment. She also re-recorded the song in a reworked version in 2007 – forty years after her Eurovision win.

Sean Dunphy had performed extremely well in the final, and, when the juries gave their votes, he finished as runner-up. This was the best result that Ireland achieved until 1970, and there was delight in RTÉ, and in Ireland as a whole. Although he had finished in second place, Sean's performance was, perhaps, somewhat overshadowed by the scale of Sandie Shaw's victory. However, Sean continued to enjoy great popularity in Ireland in the years that followed his Eurovision entry. Indeed, his last performance was given at a charity function less than twenty-four hours before his death in 2007. His son, Brian, is also a successful professional singer, and he gave his father an appropriate epitaph: 'Dad was doing what he loved right up until the end.'

In just four years, Ireland had established a commendable track record in the contest, and had been moving steadily up the scoreboard. There was a sense of anticipation that the first Irish victory was now within reach. That may explain why the national contest in 1968 was extended to include two semi-finals. Three songs were chosen from each of these, and the Irish final was held a few weeks later.

The winner of the final – by just one point – was Pat McGeegan, with a song called 'Chance of a Lifetime'. Pat's real surname was McGuigan, and he was the father of Barry McGuigan – who would become a world boxing champion, and is considered by many to be the finest fighter Ireland has ever produced. Pat's song, 'Chance of a Lifetime', was a ballad, with the singer remembering the first time he saw his lover. The lyrics are simple, but effective, and the tender, understated melody was well suited to Pat's voice.

Following Sandie Shaw's win in Vienna, the 1968 Eurovision was staged in London. It was held in the Royal Albert Hall in South Kensington, – one of the UK's best-known concert venues. This was the first time that the contest was broadcast in colour – although only five of the competing countries had the capacity for a colour transmission. In fact, even the BBC, the host broadcaster, transmitted the live show in black and white, as well as a recorded version in colour the next day, because of fears that the new technology might fail on the night.

The introduction of colour was evident in the choice of costumes made by some of the performers. Pat was the first Irish entry not to wear a black tuxedo; instead, he wore a sports coat in a vivid shade of patriotic green. The advent of new technology also affected the stage design, and the singers performed in front of a large back-projection of moving coloured shapes.

Originally, the artist chosen to perform the Spanish entry was the singer–songwriter Joan Manuel Serrat. However, he intended to sing in the Catalan language. At that time, Spain was still ruled by a Fascist government, and the Franco dictatorship ordered that the song be performed in Spanish, which was the only official language of Spain. Serrat refused to concede, and, one week before the Eurovision, he was replaced as the Spanish entry by a popular female singer called Massiel. She had been touring in Mexico when she was asked to compete, but flew back immediately, learned the song, and recorded it in five different languages before she arrived in London. Despite her late entry, she went on to win the contest.

Ironically, there was very little of any recognisable language in the Spanish song, and that gave rise to another controversy. The title of the song was 'La, La, La' – and it was aptly named, since Massiel sang 'la' 138 times in less than three minutes. The use of 'la' was a ploy that had been used before by other Eurovision songwriters to evade the prohibition of English in their lyrics, but it had not been used quite so exhaustively in previous entries.

For obvious reasons, the Spanish entry greatly annoyed those who had laboured over the lyrics of their own songs. One of these was Bill Martin, the writing partner of Phil Coulter, who dismissed Massiel's song as 'a piece of rubbish'. Once again, he and Phil Coulter had written the UK's entry. This time, it was called 'Congratulations', and was performed by the British pop star Cliff Richard. It might be argued that Martin's own lyrics do not bear much critical scrutiny: '*Congratulations and jubilations*', he had written, '*I'm happy as can be.*' Nonetheless, Cliff was only beaten to first place by one point, so it is easy to understand Martin's frustration and disappointment.

Following Massiel's victory, the EBU changed the rules of the contest to avoid any further exploitation of the 'la' loophole. In 2014, a TV documentary was screened which suggested that Spain's victory in 1967 was due to political chicanery. According to one rumour, General Franco had personally authorised bribes to ensure Massiel's victory. This has obvious appeal to conspiracy theorists, but the evidence is slender, and it seems pretty unlikely to me.

Pat McGeegan was the seventeenth act to perform in the London Grand Final, and he delivered a sensitive vocal performance of a well-written and low-key song. But it was not the night for that type of performance – or that type of song. The two front-runners, Cliff Richard and Massiel, both delivered thumping show-stoppers, and that seemed to be just what the international juries wanted to hear. Pat finished in fourth position, which was still considered a creditable performance, and his song topped the Irish charts. Pat's band, the Skyrockets, had mainly performed in Northern Ireland until his Eurovision appearance, but afterwards, they played all over the island. Pat enjoyed a few more hits in the aftermath of the contest, but then his career seemed to falter, and he dropped out of the spotlight.

Thanks to his son's victories in the boxing ring, he experienced a belated revival. Pat would accompany Barry to some of his bouts, and would sing that old favourite, 'Danny Boy', in the ring before each fight started. The choice of song had a special significance in Northern Ireland – where most of Barry's boxing career had been based. His fans included both Protestants and Catholics, and the ballad was one that was respected by both communities. Pat's most memorable ringside performance came in 1985, when he sang before Barry's world title fight with the legendary fighter from Panama, Eusebio

Pedroza. Following the Panamanian national anthem, Pat led the huge crowd in a rousing rendition of 'Danny Boy'. 'That must be some kind of first,' a bemused American commentator remarked. It was an emotional occasion, and Pat McGeegan was able to witness his son winning the world championship later that night. Pat died two years later; he was just fifty-two years old.

Pat McGeegan had performed well in the 1968 Eurovision, but Irish expectations had been running high, and there was some disappointment with the final result. For the first four years of the contest, Ireland had only sent male singers to the Eurovision; they had all sung ballads; and none of them had managed to win the contest. It all seemed to have become a little too predictable.

Perhaps it was time to try something different.

3.

Girls Allowed

The last Irish national final of the 1960s was broadcast from RTÉ in Dublin, and was hosted for the last time by Brendan O'Reilly. The winning song was decided by ten regional juries scattered across Ireland. Although this was only the fifth national song contest, four of the eight finalists had already represented Ireland in the Eurovision: Butch Moore in 1965; Dickie Rock in 1966; Sean Dunphy in 1967; and, lastly, Pat McGeegan in 1968.

However, none of these singers would represent Ireland for a second time in 1969. The winning song was 'The Wages of Love', performed by Muriel Day – a well-known figure on the Irish showband scene. Muriel was the first woman to sing for Ireland in the Eurovision. From this point on, more women than men would represent Ireland in the Grand Final.

Muriel was also the first singer from Northern Ireland to sing for Ireland in the contest. However, she was not the first Northern Irish artist to perform in the Eurovision. Ronnie Carroll from Belfast had sung for the UK in the 1962 event, and again in 1963. Since then, a sizeable number of Northern Irish singers and songwriters have represented both Ireland and the UK – on separate occasions – without any obvious crisis of identity.

'The Wages of Love' was a pop song whose bright, upbeat rhythm seemed at odds with the cautionary message contained in its lyrics. While the singer acknowledged that love can be '*very nice*', she reminded us that it also involves tears, burned fingers, and '*grey days*'. She even advised us that, if we were not careful, '*it can make you die*'. However, none of these drawbacks seemed to affect the relentless cheerfulness with which Muriel warned us of love's dangers: she bounced about the stage, smiling broadly at the cameras throughout her song.

The 1969 Eurovision Grand Final was held in Madrid, with sixteen countries taking part, and a set that featured work by Salvador Dalí. Austria had withdrawn from the contest – declining to perform in a country that was still governed by Franco's fascist regime. Muriel sang fifth on the night of the final. She wore a bright green dress with bat wings that had been made for her by a Northern Irish designer. The choice of dress not only marked a gesture towards Ireland's national colour, it also took advantage of the advent of colour broadcasting – which had become available by then in most Western European countries, though not yet in Ireland. Muriel Day had a strong and expressive voice, which was well suited to ballads, but her Eurovision pop song gave her little opportunity to display her real vocal gifts. At the close of voting, she finished in seventh place.

The 1969 contest was memorable because, for the first and last time, four countries tied at the top with the

same number of points. That possibility had never been
considered by the EBU, and so there was no tie-breaking
mechanism in place to resolve the issue. Instead, France,
the Netherlands, Spain and the UK were all declared joint
winners. The rules were subsequently changed so that such
a result might never occur again.

As it happened, Muriel Day had not been the only
Northern Irish singer to compete in the 1969 national
contest. A schoolgirl from Derry also took part in the event.
She was called Rosemary Brown – but she performed
under the stage name of Dana. Given the singer's personal
commitment to traditional Catholicism, it seems somewhat
incongruous that she shared her adopted name with a
goddess of the pagan Celts.

Dana had recorded her first single in 1967, and soon
became a familiar presence on Ireland's folk club circuit.
In 1969, she was still only seventeen years old, but she
managed to out-vote established performers such as Butch
Moore and Dickie Rock, and finished as runner-up in
Ireland's national final with a whimsical song entitled 'Look
Around'. She returned to the national contest in 1970, and,
this time, her efforts were even more successful.

Dana had been induced to enter the 1970 national
contest by Tom McGrath, the gifted RTÉ producer who
had created *The Late Late Show* – still the longest-running
chat series in the world. There were eight entries in 1970,
and three of them were in the Irish language. Most of the
finalists sang pop numbers, but Dana's entry, 'All Kinds
of Everything', was in ballad form. In its sugary lyrics,
Dana enumerates all of the things that remind her of her
sweetheart. It is a long and seemingly random inventory:
bees, postcards, snowflakes, aeroplanes – and even *'things of
the sea.'* This list was brilliantly parodied by the comedian

Kevin McAleer some years later on a show that I produced for RTÉ called *Nighthawks.*

Due to industrial action, the 1970 national final only took place a few weeks before the actual Eurovision contest. Since there were four winners in 1969, there had been some question as to which country would host the following year's event. The UK had staged the 1968 Eurovision, and Spain produced the 1969 final, so the EBU decided that only France and the Netherlands would be considered for the 1970 event. A coin was tossed, which resulted in the Netherlands hosting the contest in Amsterdam.

There were just twelve entries competing in that year's Eurovision. This was because several countries boycotted the final in protest at the inept voting system that had been used the previous year. This left its Dutch producers with an unexpected and unwelcome amount of airtime to fill. As a result, they were compelled to introduce new elements to their broadcast – and these soon came to be considered as permanent and integral features of the contest. There was, for example, an extended opening sequence that focused on some of Amsterdam's best-known landmarks. The entry for each country was also introduced by a short 'postcard', which showed each national act in their national setting. As the years passed and the staging of the Eurovision grew more ambitious, the postcards became essential if sets were to be struck between different acts. They also became a means by which the host country could showcase its national attractions to millions of potential tourists.

A number of the artists taking part in 1970 were already established stars. Mary Hopkin, representing the UK, had a successful recording career, as did several of the other performers. It was true that the Spanish entry, Julio Iglesias, had not yet achieved great international recognition as a singer – but he had been well known as the goalkeeper of the famous soccer team, Real Madrid, before a serious car accident led him to embark on a new course in his life. Since then, he has sold more than 200 million records.

In the days leading up to the contest, the UK was the firm favourite to win – so much so that they were reported to have organised a gala winner's party. Not much attention had been paid by the media to the unknown teenager from Ireland. There is an old showbiz joke that, if you can fake sincerity, your success is assured. But the sincerity of Dana's performance on the night of the Grand Final was not in question. She sat on a stool, wearing a simple *bawnin* dress with a Celtic motif – the sort that might once have been worn to an all-Ireland *féis*. There was a slide in her hair, a gap in her teeth, and she sang about butterflies and bees. She seemed to embody everyone's idea of an innocent Irish colleen.

When the voting started, it soon became clear that the contest was between Ireland and the UK. Dana did not win many high votes – and not a single top score of twelve points – but she did make gains in the middle range. When the result was announced, Ireland was ahead of the UK by six points. Mary Hopkin later described her experience in the contest as humiliating. Given that she had first come to public attention by appearing on the tacky talent show *Opportunity Knocks* – presented by the creepy Hughie Greene – her objections to the contest may seem to lack some credibility.

The impact of Dana's victory was immediate and profound. Ireland was not used to winning anything, and an international song contest still carried considerable cachet. What is more, in 1970, the Troubles in Northern Ireland were just beginning to erupt – though their full horror was yet to come. Southern Irish sympathy with the Northern Catholic population was running high, and Dana came from Derry – a city which was widely perceived, at that time, to be the cockpit of the struggle by Northern Catholics for civil rights.

In some respects, Dana seemed like the alter ego of another young woman who also featured prominently in the news coverage of that year: Bernadette Devlin. They were close in age, and they were both Northern Irish Catholics. There was even some physical similarity between the two women. However, there was also much to distinguish them. Bernadette Devlin was a political firebrand, who seemed drawn to confrontation. Dana, on the other hand, appeared unthreatening and conciliatory. For a time, they were both able to capture the popular imagination in Ireland, and, despite their very different viewpoints, they would both share a future involvement in Irish politics.

In time, a succession of IRA atrocities would cause Southern Irish feelings for the North to curdle. But in 1970, Dana's homecoming was full of political symbolism. She was flown directly to Derry by Aer Lingus – the first time that the national airline had made that connection. On her arrival, Dana reprised her winning song on the steps of the plane, and was embraced by several nuns. Later, she addressed a huge crowd from the balcony of the city's Guildhall, a former bastion of Unionist supremacy. She sang her winning song again, and dedicated her triumph to the people of Derry.

Her song became a massive hit in Ireland. It held the number one slot for nine successive weeks, selling more than 100,000 copies – an extraordinary figure, considering Ireland's population. But the success of 'All Kinds of Everything' was not confined to Ireland. Dana's single was also a major hit in the UK, Germany, Switzerland, the Netherlands and Austria – and, further afield, in Malaysia, New Zealand, South Africa, Australia and Singapore. Overseas sales for the song are reckoned to have been in excess of 2 million copies. Cover versions of the song also appeared in German, Dutch, Spanish, Romanian and Japanese.

The longevity of the song has proved remarkable. From time to time, it still crops up in TV advertisements, or for charity fundraisers. It has also acquired its own emblematic meaning: representing for many an era in Irish history that now seems naive and unsophisticated. For some, that claim to innocence can seem assumed and superficial – serving only to mask a darker reality. In his play, *A Skull in Connemara,* (1997) the playwright Martin McDonagh uses Dana's song as an ironic backdrop to a scene in which three skulls are smashed to smithereens with a hammer.

Dana enjoyed a good deal of commercial success as a singer for many years after her Eurovision win. She released over thirty singles and as many albums. But her career has proved to be much more varied than might have been predicted in 1970. In the decades that followed, Dana became increasingly identified with the more conservative wing of Irish Catholicism. She also became involved in political activism – campaigning against the introduction of divorce to Ireland, and in favour of the 'pro–life' movement.

In 1997, she ran for the Irish presidency – and, although she didn't win, she polled an impressive number of votes. Later in the year, she was elected as an MEP for the Connacht-Ulster constituency. She ran again in the 2011 presidential election, but did not fare as well on that occasion. This was due, in part, to an ugly and contentious family dispute which ended up in a British court. But, perhaps, there were other reasons for her poor result in the presidential poll. In 1970, Dana represented traditions with which many Irish people could identify. In 2011, she represented a past that many of them wanted to forget.

As far as RTÉ was concerned, 1970 marked a kind of watershed. The station had decided to accept the EBU's invitation to stage the 1971 Eurovision Contest in Dublin. This led to a sense of tremendous excitement and anticipation inside RTÉ – but also to a degree of nervousness and apprehension. RTÉ was about to join the front line of national broadcasters by staging the biggest entertainment show in the world. Would the young station be able to carry it off?

4.
The Gaiety of Nations

The first Eurovision to take place in Ireland was produced by RTÉ in 1971. This time around, Ireland was represented by another young woman. Angela Farrell had become the third consecutive female singer from Northern Ireland to win the national song contest. Although she was virtually unknown – and had never performed in Dublin before the national final – Angela had managed to outvote more established stars such as Red Hurley. This was the first time that the national contest had not been dominated by lead singers from successful showbands, and it was a further sign that things were beginning to change in the Irish entertainment scene.

Angela was only nineteen years old, and was said by the Irish press to be leading a glamorous 'double life': working in a chemist's shop in Portadown, County Armagh, during the day, and singing in cabarets in various Northern Irish clubs at night. The national final was her debut on RTÉ, although she had appeared before on Ulster Television.

Her winning entry, 'One Day Love', had been written by a Northern Irish dentist and his wife, and its lyrics are exceptionally bleak. They are addressed by the singer to her former lover – who seems to have been some sort of sociopath. Apparently, he enjoys duping women and breaking their hearts, and his response, *'when the tears start to fall'*, is simply to laugh at his victims. He has also consistently lied, cheated and deceived his ex-girlfriend. Her dearest wish is that he should get a taste of his own medicine, and she hopes that his one true love, if he ever finds her, will abuse him as badly as he has abused others. Curiously, at the close of the song, she describes her remarks merely as *'advice from a friend'*.

In the weeks leading up to the Eurovision, Angela posed for newspapers with her parents, and in the chemist's shop. It appeared that her regular backing group, the Sandmen, consisted of just two musicians. Her manager – who was also her cousin – spoke to the press about the big plans for her future. After she won the national contest, Angela had gone back to work in the chemist's, but it was reported that she intended to hand in her notice in the event of her winning the Grand Final of the Eurovision.

Until this point, only solo performers or duos had been allowed to compete in the contest. From 1970, groups of up to six people were allowed on stage, and this would become of increasing importance as the years passed. Compared to 1970, the number of participants rose again as Finland, Norway, Sweden and Portugal all re-entered after a year of absence, while Malta had its first appearance. Altogether, eighteen countries were present, and the contest was broadcast in twenty-nine countries.

The Irish entry was not the only Irish singer in the competition. Clodagh Rodgers – also from Northern Ireland – was representing the UK with 'Jack in the Box'. Her entry had obvious similarities to 'Puppet on a String': they are both robust, thigh-slapping songs. In both of them, the singer compares herself to a puppet, or doll that enjoys being (literally) manipulated by her boyfriend. The lyrics of both entries were, not surprisingly, written by men.

The previous year had been a time of political tension in Ireland, both North and South. In Northern Ireland, sectarian conflict had escalated, and a brutal campaign of terror had been launched by the Provisional IRA. In the Republic, the Taoiseach had felt compelled to ask ministers in his own government to resign. Two cabinet members – the Minister for Finance, Charles Haughey, and the Minister for Agriculture, Neil Blaney, were subsequently arrested, and charged with conspiracy to import arms illegally for the IRA.

In this context, there was some concern within the BBC over the sort of reception that the UK entrant might encounter in Dublin. This is believed to have been part of the reasoning behind the BBC's decision to choose Clodagh Rodgers as the British representative in the Dublin Contest. She had sung all six possible entries in successive weeks on the BBC's *It's Cliff Richard* show, and the winner was determined by a regional vote. Clodagh later revealed that she had received a number of death threats from the IRA because she was representing the UK.

This political background may also help to explain the BBC's choice of commentator. Terry Wogan was Irish, and had been working for RTÉ until shortly before the contest. He found it ironic that one of his first TV roles after he joined the BBC entailed his return to Ireland. He was dropped by the BBC from their Eurovision coverage the following year, but soon came back with a vengeance. For Terry, the Dublin final turned out to be the beginning of an association with the Eurovision that would last for the next thirty-seven years. Indeed, Terry Wogan and the contest became so closely linked over the decades that followed that it became commonplace for people to claim that they only watched the Eurovision in order to hear his witty and sardonic commentary.

In 1971, the Grand Final of the Eurovision took place in the ornate surroundings of the Gaiety Theatre in Dublin. The Gaiety is a traditional Victorian music hall that had originally been designed to stage light operas and burlesque shows. In some respects, the theatre seemed an appropriate location for the song contest – in others, it appeared as a rather old-fashioned venue for a modern TV event. Because of the small size of the stage, the interval act consisted of a pre-recorded film. This featured the Bunratty Castle Singers, and involved a mock medieval feast, complete with Irish songs and dancing – performed by a bevy of wholesome colleens, dressed in costumes that were vaguely suggestive of the Middle Ages. It presented an image of 'Old Ireland' that had been designed primarily to appeal to Irish-American tourists.

The contest was introduced by one of RTÉ's continuity announcers, Bernadette Ní Ghallchóir. She was a familiar face on RTÉ, and, apart from working in continuity, she had also hosted *Buntús Cainte,* an Irish-language educational programme. She sat demurely in one of the theatre boxes and welcomed Europe's viewers – first in Irish, then in French, and, finally, in English. Throughout the broadcast, she seemed utterly composed, and there was a consensus that the right choice of presenter had been made.

Although most of RTÉ's top management were ensconced inside the Gaiety watching the contest unfold, they had been compelled to run a gauntlet of their own colleagues who were picketing outside the theatre. One of those engaged in the picket was a young researcher on *The Late Late Show* called Ollie Donohoe. According to Ollie, the dispute was the indirect product of an intense and long-running *kulturkamp* within RTÉ between conservative elements and those who held more radical views on social issues such as divorce and contraception – both of which were illegal in Ireland in 1971.

The immediate reason for the picket was because the Eurovision was the first major show which RTÉ had broadcast in colour. That was related, in turn, to claims that the event was costing the station too much money – money that some believed would have been better spent on more reputable cultural projects. Some of those protesting believed that the integrity of Ireland's native musical traditions was also under threat from the dominance of bland and 'Americanised' culture. Ironically, the Eurovision contest had been designed, in part, to counteract the effects of cultural imports from the USA, such as rock 'n' roll.

It would, in any case, be a mistake to evaluate RTÉ's internal opposition to the Eurovision solely by the terms in which it liked to define itself. According to Ollie Donohoe, the intention was never to stop the contest from taking place. Another member of the picket line that night admitted to me that, once the Eurovision had begun, the protesters 'dashed off to the nearest pub to enjoy the show'. Those on the picket line were all promptly suspended by RTÉ, but, within a week or so, they were allowed to resume their usual roles. According to Ollie Donohoe, he was welcomed back warmly by his series producer – Tom McGrath – who had also directed the Eurovision Grand Final.

The only major change introduced in the 1971 Eurovision was in the voting system. The EBU had decided that this process should be more transparent, and, in order to achieve that goal, had set up a new procedure. Each country was to provide two jurors – one under twenty-five, and one over twenty-five – and each juror had to give a mark between one and five for each entry. This greatly increased the number of votes that could be cast, and, for the next few years, made it impossible for any of the competing countries to receive no votes.

For her performance in Dublin, the UK entry, Clodagh Rodgers, wore a pink top and spangled hot pants – considered to be rather daring back in 1971. Ireland's entry, Angela Farrell, also favoured pink, but her dress was a more conventional ankle-length ball gown. She sang well, and with emotional intensity, but that could not compensate for the grim and unrelenting nature of her song. Angela finished in eleventh place when all the votes had been counted. However, her song still managed to reach number four in the Irish charts. Angela released several more singles, but, within a few years, she appears to have dropped out of show business. Clodagh Rodgers finished in fourth place in the final; the first time since 1966 that the UK had not been placed first or second. Her song also charted in the UK, but it was to be her last Top 10 hit.

The winner of the contest was the French singer Séverine, representing Monaco, with 'Un Banc, Un Arbre, Une Rue'. Séverine later claimed that she had never set foot in Monaco before she was chosen to sing for the principality in the Eurovision. Her song charted highly in most European countries, and – unusually for a French-language song – it even made the Top 10 in the UK. In the next ten years, Séverine made two further attempts to reach the Eurovision Final – each time for Germany – but never progressed beyond the national contest.

Judged by subsequent Eurovisions, the 1971 contest was a relatively modest affair. In many respects, it did not differ greatly from the sort of outside broadcast coverage of concerts or sports events that RTÉ transmitted almost every week. The staging of the show could not be described as innovative, and the style of presentation now appears stilted and sedate. The biggest technical challenge faced by RTÉ was the launch of colour transmission.

Ireland was one of the last broadcasters in Western Europe to introduce colour to its screens. However, its impact was not confined to this one broadcast – or even, in a sense, solely to television. It would also affect Irish life in less obvious, but significant ways. The advent of colour seemed to signal that the country was prepared to cast off the last drab vestiges of the 1950s, and was ready and willing to catch up with the rest of modern Europe.

After the 1971 Eurovision, there was considerable pride in RTÉ that the station had passed through a major test of its professional skills with its reputation intact. There were innumerable things that could have gone wrong with the event – and none of them had. Instead, there was a real sense that the station – and, by extension, the country – had come of age, and taken its rightful place among the broadcasting nations of the world.

5.
The Love Boat

Monaco had won the Eurovision in 1971, and the EBU had written to Prince Rainier III asking if he could provide the venue and the other resources needed to stage the next year's contest. After some consideration, Rainier declined the EBU's invitation on the grounds that his tiny principality did not have the necessary resources. Instead, the UK agreed to host the final. It was the fourth time that the BBC had staged the event, but this was the first occasion it was located outside England. In 1972, the Eurovison contest took place in Scotland, and was presented by Moira Shearer, an actress and ballet dancer who had once starred in the classic British movie, *The Red Shoes*.

Ireland's national song contest was held in Cork's Opera House. There were ten songs in the final, and, in line with RTÉ's new rules, half of these were performed in Irish. '*Ceol an Ghrá*' – 'The Music of Love' – was sung by a young woman called Sandie Jones. She won the national final, and her song was – and remains – the only entry to the Eurovision Final to be written and sung in the Irish language.

'*Ceol an Ghrá*' is a ballad. The words tell how the singer hears 'the music of love' wherever she goes. '*Seo Tír na nÓg is tá sciathán in áit mo chos*', she sings ('*This is the Land of Eternal Youth, and I have wings instead of legs*'). Tír na nÓg is the mystical land in Celtic mythology whose inhabitants remain young forever. Apart from the fact that the words of the song are in Irish, and that mention is made of Tír na nÓg, there is nothing else that is specifically Irish about '*Ceol na Ghrá*' – it does not, for example, feature any traditional Irish instruments. The song has a gentle melody – rather like a lullaby – and Sandie Jones was an attractive young woman with a light and appealing voice.

Just a few weeks earlier, Sandie had joined the Dixies Showband – one of the best known in Ireland. After winning the national contest, she was catapulted into national celebrity. She received awards and invitations from all over the country. She was interviewed by the press, and she appeared on Ireland's premier entertainment series, *The Late Late Show*, with Gay Byrne. Her winning song was released, and climbed quickly to number one in the Irish charts. 'I went from relative obscurity to being a household name almost overnight,' Sandie said later. 'And that's a lot to deal with.' She must have been aware that the Eurovision had given previous winners – including Dana – an opportunity to achieve international success. Even when Irish performers had not won the contest, taking part in the Grand Final had given an enormous boost to their careers in Ireland. Either way, the Eurovision was seen as a very effective launch pad for Irish singers.

All the countries that had participated in the 1971 event were present in 1972, with no withdrawals, returns, or new arrivals. The contest was staged in Edinburgh's Usher Hall, which could hold an audience of more than 2,000. The stage design included a large screen used to introduce each national act with a still photo, and, during each performance, the artists stood before a back-projection of moving spiral shapes. That year's interval act featured the massed pipes and drums of several Scottish regiments of the British army, who paraded up and down outside Edinburgh Castle. Meanwhile, the jurors were safely sequestered inside the castle, where they were able to watch each song on TV.

The voting system that year managed to be both elaborate and rudimentary. Each country had two jury members: one aged between sixteen and twenty-five, and one aged between twenty-six and fifty-five, which was apparently considered to be the cut-off point for the right to vote. Each juror awarded one to five points for each song – other than the song of their own country. They cast their votes immediately after each song was performed, and the votes were then collected and counted. After the interval act, the jury members were shown on screen, and asked to show a card with a number from one to five for each song. The total points for each entry were then announced by Moira Shearer.

Sandie wore an elegant green dress for the final, which sparkled in the light, and she performed her inoffensive song with great conviction. During her act, there was a minor disruption in the hall when a firecracker appears to have been discharged – 1972 was a year of considerable political violence and tension in Northern Ireland, and Sandie later said that she believed this was the reason for the disruption. However, she did not allow it to affect her performance, and it was not noticeable to viewers at home, or to the jurors.

When the votes were revealed, it became clear that the Irish entry had not polled well. Indeed, the result was the poorest since Ireland first entered the contest. Sandie later admitted in a TV documentary for TG4 that she was devastated by finishing fifteenth in a field of eighteen. She believed that the political situation in Ireland had 'played a big role' in her low score. There may be a simpler explanation: '*Ceol an Ghrá*' was a likeable ballad, but – unlike the winning song from Vicky Leandros – it lacked any real emotional heft. Sandie looked beautiful, and had an appealing voice, but she lacked the vocal range and power of some of the other contestants.

After the contest was over, Sandie resumed her role with the Dixies Showband. She continued to perform and record, and to appear on television throughout the 1970s and into the 1980s. Her Eurovision song is still regarded with affection by many people, and it was the first of only two occasions on which a Celtic language has been heard in the contest (the other was a Breton song in 1996).

In 1973, a young singer called Maxi entered the national song contest with a song called 'Do I Dream?' Even though Maxi was in her early twenties, she was already something of a veteran in Irish showbiz. Her career had started when she was still a teenager as part of a trio of girl singers called Maxi, Dick and Twink. They had starred in an RTÉ series for young people with the unlikely but engaging title of *Steady as She Go-Goes*. As part of Maxi, Dick and Twink, she had also competed in the 1970 national contest that was won by Dana.

The 1973 contest involved eight finalists, and RTÉ had again stipulated that half of the songs should be sung in Irish. 'Do I Dream?' was written from the perspective of a young woman whose boyfriend has just told her that he loves her. She is confused because this news seems too good to be true. She goes on to ask herself a series of existential questions: do rivers really sparkle and quiver? Are mountains really blue and hazy? Are there many coloured flowers? Is she, perhaps, a little crazy?

In 1973, the Eurovision Final was held in Luxembourg. Advances in technology meant that this was the first time performers could be shot by moving cameras – which made the TV coverage more fluid and dynamic. The British pop star Cliff Richard, who represented the UK, was back for a second time – this time with a thumping song called 'Power To All Our Friends'. He soon emerged as the book makers' favourite to win the competition.

In the days leading up to the contest, there were reports of difficulties in the Irish camp. It seemed that Maxi was unhappy with the musical arrangement of her song, and rehearsals were interrupted repeatedly. The situation deteriorated, and Maxi was said to have threatened not to sing in the Eurovision. RTÉ took the precaution of flying out another Irish artist, Tina Reynolds, to perform in her place. Tina arrived the day before the Eurovision, but, faced with this option, Maxi agreed to go onstage and sing. However, she seemed uneasy throughout most of her performance, and never looked as if she were enjoying herself.

The complicated voting procedure that had been used in previous years was maintained in 1973. This involved each country sending two jurors to the contest. They sat in special booths – sound-proofed so that they would not be swayed by the audience reaction – and awarded points to each song. The juries were then sub-divided into six small groups, each of which was asked in turn for their votes.

This procedure was extremely slow and protracted, and lacked any sense of urgency or drama. The UK led after the first set of six votes had been cast. By the end of the third set of votes, Luxembourg had taken the lead with one of the few ballads in this final. Although the UK regained the lead for a further set of votes, Luxembourg ended up as the winner for a second successive year, with Spain as runner-up, and Cliff Richard in third place.

This was also the first time that Israel had participated in the contest. Following the murder of Israeli athletes at the Olympic Games in Munich the previous year, security was heightened at the Eurovision. It has been rumoured that the Israeli singer wore a bullet-proof vest during her performance, and the audience in Luxembourg's Nouveau Theatre was warned by the floor manager not to stand up suddenly during the show, as anyone who did so risked being shot by security agents. Despite such anxieties, Israel performed well in the voting, and ended up in fourth place, while Ireland came tenth with eighty points.

The 1973 Eurovision does not appear to have been a happy experience for Maxi. Despite that, she was not ready to give up on the contest. In fact, she entered the national contest on a further three occasions, and competed in the 1981 Eurovision Final as part of the trio, Sheeba. While Tina Reynolds' presence in 1973 proved unnecessary, in 1974, she was given her own chance to sing in the Eurovision contest.

For the first time, all of the songs that had been shortlisted by RTÉ for entry to the Eurovision were performed by the same artist. There was speculation that this represented a form of reward for Tina, having helped out RTÉ the previous year. She sang eight songs on *The*

Likes of Mike – a popular Saturday evening entertainment series on RTÉ that starred Mike Murphy. RTÉ still insisted that half of the songs should be in Irish, and, for the first time since 1967, the Eurovision was decided by a postal vote – which deferred the result until the following week. When the votes were counted, the winning song was 'Cross Your Heart'.

The song is based on a simple, but original notion. The singer is testing a possible lover, and uses adaptations of nursery rhymes – such as *'sticks and stones wouldn't break my bones'* – to show how serious she is about their potential relationship. The contrast between her serious intention and the playfulness of the childhood doggerel that she uses provides an unusual dynamic. It seems that the singer's heart has been broken in the past, but this rather sad back story is offset by the upbeat tempo of the song, and by Tina's cheerful delivery of the lyrics.

Since Luxembourg declined to host the 1974 Eurovision, it was held in Brighton, England, and is memorable for a number of reasons – some of which have little to do with music. In 1974, the fascistic Estado Novo regime was still in power in Portugal, and heavily committed to prosecuting colonial wars in Africa. A group of young army officers planned a military coup to end the dictatorship. When the opening bars of 'E Depois do Adeus' – Portugal's entry in the 1974 contest – were played on a radio station on the evening of 24 April, it served as the signal for those officers to seize control of the state. The Portuguese singer in the 1974 Contest, Paulo da Carvalho, has since been credited with performing the only Eurovision song that managed to start a revolution.

Although Italy participated in the contest, the national broadcaster, RAI, decided not to broadcast the event. This was because the final coincided with a national referendum in Italy on the introduction of divorce – which was strenuously opposed by the Catholic Church. Since the title of the Italian entry was 'Sì' – 'Yes' – and since that word was repeated on numerous occasions throughout the song, RAI concluded that the station could be accused of attempting to influence the result of the poll. As a result, the Italian entry was not played on radio or TV stations in Italy in the weeks leading up to the divorce referendum – which was passed in any case.

Tina was the last act to sing in the final. In keeping with the title of her song, she wore a dress with crossed straps. She seemed confident in her performance, and, when the results were in, she had finished seventh. That was a better outcome than it might seem because the contestants in that year's Eurovision included some exceptionally tough opposition.

Gigliola Cinquetti, who sang for Italy and was runner-up, had not only racked up a number of worldwide hits, but had already won the song contest in 1966. Mouth and MacNeil, who represented the Netherlands and finished third, had also enjoyed major chart success – not only in Europe, but in the United States. The UK was represented by Olivia Newton-John, who had performed all the UK's entries on a show hosted by the late Jimmy Saville – another BBC presenter and British 'national treasure' who was later exposed as a paedophile and serial rapist. Olivia Newton-John had also enjoyed prior international recording success. She finished fourth in this contest, but has gone on to sell more than 100 million records, picking up four Grammy awards along the way.

However, all of this pales in comparison with the subsequent career of the winners of the 1974 contest. ABBA had entered the Swedish national song contest the previous year, but failed to qualify for the Eurovision. In 1974 they were back, and that year proved rather more successful for them. Their winning song, 'Waterloo', broke with a number of Eurovision conventions, and, in several ways, changed the future development of the contest.

Until then, Eurovision acts had tended to dress rather conservatively. ABBA wore satin costumes in vivid colours that brought a glam-rock flavour to the final. They also took advantage of a temporary lifting of the language restrictions to sing in English. Their act even involved some basic choreography. Above all, the energy and flair of their performance seemed contemporary, and made all the other acts appear dated and staid.

ABBA not only brought Sweden its first victory in the Eurovision, the band also became one of the most commercially successful acts in the history of pop music. Their popular appeal, however, was not to the liking of a number of serious-minded musicians and music critics. One satirical piece, performed by another Swedish group, described ABBA as being 'dead as tinned herring'. But the band has had the last laugh. ABBA have not only sold more than 400 million records worldwide, they have also established their credibility in the music industry, and it is no longer considered strange or lame to admire their work as outstanding examples of popular music. The success of the stage show and subsequent movie, *Mamma Mia,* is ample evidence of their continuing appeal. Four decades after their Eurovision win, 'Waterloo' still sounds fresh.

Ireland was not the only county to be influenced by ABBA's stunning victory. For a decade, all of the Irish acts sent to compete in the Grand Final had been solo singers. In 1975, Ireland broke for the first time with that tradition.

6.
The Boys Are Back In Town

In 1975, it was once again the men's turn to represent Ireland in the Eurovision, and, once again, RTÉ had decided to choose the Irish act without a public vote. Tommy and Jimmy Swarbrigg were brothers with a long history in Ireland's showband scene. As well as singing and playing, the brothers also wrote their own songs. By 1973, they had launched themselves as a singing duo, and had landed their own TV series on RTÉ. Two years later, they were asked to write and sing the Irish Eurovision entry. They performed eight songs – with two of these in Irish – and the winner was chosen by ten regional juries.

The winning song was called 'That's What Friends Are For'. It was a mid-tempo number, with the singers calling on their listeners to help each other in times of need – because *that's what friends are for*. In the final verse, the call is made to everyone in the world, rather than just to those who have exceptionally needy friends.

At that time, all the stations taking part in the Eurovision were obliged to broadcast a preview programme, which featured all of that year's entries. National broadcasters were asked to supply suitable material for the show. This could be either the act's winning performance in their national contest, or a new video designed to showcase their song. In 1975, RTÉ decided to make a video of the Swarbriggs' number. Twenty years later, that video became the inspiration for an episode of the ground-breaking TV comedy series, *Father Ted*.

The video that RTÉ made to promote the Swarbriggs' Eurovision entry defies easy description. It included a number of extremely stilted scenes that seem entirely unconnected to the lyrics of the brothers' song. The Swarbriggs are seen relaxing: riding horses, playing golf, sailing, playing snooker – and, most ludicrously, tossing a beach ball with two women in a deserted swimming pool. Through all of these scenes, they laugh and smile constantly – to show how much they are enjoying themselves – in an entirely unconvincing way. There are also several unrelated shots: an unidentified woman hitching in the Wicklow hills, and an unknown man skydiving, and then gathering his parachute. The video ends with some highly contrived shots of the brothers singing in front of a wildly enthusiastic audience.

This film was parodied in the 'My Lovely Horse' episode of Graham Linehan and Arthur Mathews' wonderful sitcom. However, it could be argued that the original video was almost beyond parody, and all that the writers, and the director, Declan Lowney, needed to do was to reproduce its ridiculous and cheesy nature. Of course, it is not only RTÉ's video that is satirised in the *Father Ted* parody: the banal lyrics of the song, and its insipid melody are also part of Neil Hannon's pitch-perfect pastiche.

In fairness, there were other Eurovision performers that year who also offered inviting targets for satirists. The Dutch entry – and winner of the final – was called 'Ding-a-Dong', and was described as 'an ode to positive thinking'. It followed in the worn footsteps of other infantile ditties such as 'Boom Bang-a-Bang': *'Even when your lover is gone'*, the Dutch lyrics ran, *'Sing ding-ding-dong'*. For many, these childish and nonsensical words seemed to epitomise what they saw as the risible standards of the whole contest.

ABBA's victory in Brighton the previous year had given Sweden the right to host the contest for the first time. The venue for the event was the new International Fairs arena in Stockholm, and, once again, politics entered the Eurovision equation. In July of 1974, Turkish armed forces had invaded the island of Cyprus. In 1975, Greece withdrew from the contest in protest at Turkey's occupation of part of the island. By contrast, the Portuguese entry, 'Madrugada', was an explicit celebration of that country's Carnation Revolution – in which their previous Eurovision entry had played an unintended, but critical role. It has been reported that the Portuguese performer in 1975 had to be dissuaded from wearing his military uniform and carrying a gun onto the stage.

In fact, there were fears of other weapons being used during the 1975 contest. Intelligence reports from Germany indicated that the Stockholm Eurovision was being considered as a target by the German terrorist group, the Red Army Faction. This led the Swedish authorities to impose strict security regulations, and, happily, the event passed without any sort of violent incident. However, the concerns of German intelligence were vindicated a few weeks later when the West German embassy in Stockholm was attacked by the RAF group. Two attachés were murdered before the terrorists accidentally detonated their own explosives, and brought the siege of the embassy to a bloody end.

A record number of nineteen countries took part in the 1975 final. Apart from Turkey making its début, France and Malta both returned to the contest. Belgium and Germany followed the example set by ABBA the previous year, and sang their songs in a mixture of their national languages and English. The Swarbriggs were the second act to appear, and they also seemed to have been influenced by ABBA's choice of vibrant costumes: they wore identical electric blue suits with sparkling silver lapels.

A new scoring system was introduced in 1975, and, with some modifications, it has been used ever since. Each jury would give twelve points to the best song, ten to the second best, then eight to the third, and so forth, until their last choice of song would receive a single point. However, the points were not announced in order of rank, but in order of performance. It would take another five years before the inherent weakness of that procedure would be addressed and adjusted.

The Swarbriggs finished ninth in the competition, but, curiously, they were outvoted by another Irish act. The Irish singer, Geraldine Brannigan, had sung Luxembourg's entry, 'Toi', and the song had been written by Bill Martin and Phil Coulter. Phil also conducted the orchestra for Luxembourg, and would later marry Geraldine. Luxembourg's strong performance may have taken the edge off the official Irish entry. However, it did not deter the Swarbrigg brothers, and the following year, they were back in the national contest.

The 1975 Eurovision had received considerable criticism from within Sweden. From an early stage, there were protests against the cost of the contest, and its commercial aspects. At first, the criticism was directed towards SR, the Swedish broadcaster, but it soon developed into a more general movement against commercial music – which was dismissed as worthless, and even immoral. An alternative music festival was organised in another part of Stockholm to run on the second Swedish TV channel at the same time as the official contest. It featured an open mic, where anyone who wanted to could perform their own composition: not surprisingly, the songs were of an abysmal quality.

Perhaps as a result of the protests, SR later announced that it would not be competing in the following year's Eurovision, and would not even broadcast the contest. Their withdrawal encouraged the EBU to change the basis on which the contest was funded. From now on, each competing country would contribute to the cost, and this seemed to be excuse enough for the Swedes not only to make a rapid return to the Eurovision stage, but to become some of its most committed supporters.

Ireland's 1976 national final reverted to the format in which different acts performed the shortlisted songs. Eight finalists took part, and the winner was chosen by eight regional juries. Apart from the Swarbriggs, two other performers had also appeared in previous national contests – Cathal Dunne and Linda Martin – and both of them would eventually reach a Eurovision Final. However, 1976 was not their year. Instead, the national final was won by Red Hurley, with a song called 'When'. The song had been written by Brendan Graham, and was the first of four songs by him that would win the national contest – two of which also went on to win the Eurovision Final.

Red Hurley had begun his career as lead singer with a number of Irish showbands, and he had enjoyed a great deal of success before becoming a solo performer. Although he was considered a major star in Ireland, international success had eluded him. There was a feeling that the marketing of an Irish singer would be difficult in the UK, so long as the terror campaign of the IRA was in full spate. The Eurovision stage seemed to offer just the sort of platform on which an Irish artist could make a breakthrough into the bigger markets. This was, after all, what Dana had achieved in 1970.

Before he departed for The Hague, RTÉ made another video for the Eurovision preview show. Red Hurley's promotional film proved to be almost as strange and inept as the Swarbriggs' the previous year. Red is first seen wandering about the Irish countryside in a black evening suit and white shirt. Then, he pops up in a nightclub, wearing a white suit and black shirt. In this scene, he is standing beside a woman in a bikini, who is swinging back and forth on a trapeze over a circular plunge pool. None of this seems to have anything to do with the lyrics of Red's song – in which he pleads for his former lover to return – except for the expression on his face, which is consistently dejected.

Red arrived in The Hague as one of the favourites to win the contest. He is a fine singer, and his song was a well-crafted ballad. However, when he sang in the Nederlands Congres Centrum, his performance seemed to be out of kilter with the mood of the contest, which favoured more modern and upbeat pop songs. There were some obvious attempts to replicate the success of 'Ding-a-Dong', the previous winner: the Finns' entry was called 'Pump-Pump', and the Germans' 'Sing-Sang-Song'. The title of the Spanish entry, 'Sobran las Palabras', may even have revealed some wishful thinking: it translates as 'Words Are Unnecessary'. Red received more votes than any of these. However, he still finished in a disappointing tenth place.

The winning act was the British group, Brotherhood of Man, with a catchy song called 'Save Your Kisses for Me'. The name of the group was originally just a label given to a sequence of studio session musicians. However, when the 'Brotherhood' started to chalk up some hits, it assumed a regular identity. By the time the group appeared in the Eurovision, Brotherhood of Man was well known throughout Europe. In the Dutch contest, the two men and two women who made up the group were dressed in fetching red, white and black outfits, and performed some simple but amusing dance steps.

The lyrics of their song suggest that the singer is addressing a lover, but the final lines reveal they are actually meant for his three-year-old daughter. Eurovision viewers seem to have been enchanted by this twist-in-the-tail, and the song won by an overwhelming margin. 'Save Your Kisses For Me' became a major hit around the world – including the USA. It eventually sold more than six million copies worldwide, and is still the biggest-selling Eurovision winner of all time.

Although Red Hurley's song was a chart hit in Ireland, the Irish music scene was going through a period of significant change. Established artists, like Red, whose careers had started in the showband era, had begun to seem out-of-touch, and were being pushed aside by younger bands and newer forms of music. By the 1990s, Red's career seemed in terminal decline. He moved to the USA, but returned to Ireland at the start of the new millennium. He even auditioned for the UK reality talent show, *The X-Factor,* in front of his former manager, Louis Walsh, and was immediately rejected.

However, it would have been a mistake to write Red off. His record sales eventually began to pick up again, and so did attendances at his live performances. He has managed to re-establish himself as a credible performer as he heads towards his fiftieth year in show business, and I would not be too surprised if he decided to give the Eurovision another shot.

7.

The Bland Leading the Bland

The final of Ireland's 1977 national song contest was held at the RTÉ studios in Dublin, and was hosted by Mike Murphy. Eight acts took part, and the winner was chosen by votes from ten regional juries. Among those taking part were Dickie Rock, who had represented Ireland in the 1966 Eurovision, and Colm C. T. Wilkinson, who would do so in 1978. Linda Martin also participated – not as a soloist, but as a member of the pop group, Chips.

The winners, however, included faces that were more familiar to continental Eurovision fans. The Swarbriggs were back in the picture, with a song entitled 'It's Nice to be in Love Again'. This time, they were joined by Alma Carroll and Nicole Kerr, who were not named, but were merely, and ungallantly, credited as 'Plus Two'. Although the act included these two women, the lyrics of the song were written entirely from a male perspective. Apart from that, its sentiments were quite innocuous: according to the Swarbriggs, being in love was '*nice*'.

The Eurovision Final was staged in London, with the former newscaster Angela Rippon presenting the show with antiseptic efficiency – despite a chaotic voting procedure. The Swarbriggs both wore white suits in the final, while, by way of contrast, Nicole and Alma wore dark blue, off-the-shoulder dresses. The performance of the song now seems almost as twee and cutesy as the lyrics: the foursome paired into two couples, held hands, and gazed dreamily into each others' eyes – as if they were still teenagers.

Both the song and the performance seemed highly derivative of the Brotherhood of Man – the previous year's Eurovision winner. Nonetheless, when the voting ended, Ireland had picked up 119 points, finishing third out of eighteen entries. It was the country's best result since Dana won in 1970. Ireland may also have been helped by the reintroduction of language restrictions in 1977, which stipulated that each country must sing in one of its national languages.

The following year, the national contest was again held in the RTÉ studios in Dublin, and was again hosted by Mike Murphy, with eight finalists and ten regional juries. There were some familiar faces among the performers, including Maxi, singing as part of the group Sheeba, who would represent Ireland in 1981, and Linda Martin, a future Eurovision winner, who performed as a member of Chips. The winner of the national final was Colm C.T.Wilkinson, who had also been a finalist the previous year, and who had written his own composition, 'Born to Sing'.

Colm possessed a very powerful and expressive voice. Indeed, he was later voted one of the five greatest singers ever in a *Rolling Stone* magazine readers' poll. He was also an intensely dramatic performer, and went on to establish a very successful career in musical theatre. He is probably best known for originating the role of Jean Valjean in the West End and Broadway productions of *Les Misérables*.

'Born to Sing' is a mid-tempo ballad, and appears to have a strong autobiographical element. The singer presents himself in romantic terms as a kind of wandering minstrel – *'a travelling man'* – who understands and accepts the price that both he and his partner have paid, and will continue to pay, for his itinerant lifestyle. He claims that he has had no choice but to lead that sort of life. It does not even involve a conscious decision on his part: it is his destiny, and beyond his control, simply because he was *'born to sing'*. The love of music has inspired other Eurovision songs, but it has seldom been presented in such uncompromising and self-centred terms.

On the night of the Eurovision Final, Colm performed first in the running order. He wore an extremely tight-fitting, dark-green velvet suit that looked as if it had been moulded out of chocolate. A white scarf was tied rakishly around his neck. There can be no doubt that he invested his performance with a sense of total commitment – or demented passion, depending on your viewpoint. He stood wide-eyed, with his legs splayed, as he clawed the air and tore the raw emotion out of every syllable of each word he sang. When he reached the song's climax, he looked as if he were about to erupt out of his chocolate suit.

Colm's fierce performance was, by any standards, remarkable, and it led to acutely divergent reactions. For some, this was a dramatic *tour-de-force;* for others, it was merely a display of self-indulgent histrionics. This polarity was also reflected in the voting: half of the competing countries gave Colm very high marks, while the same number of countries gave him no marks at all. When the result was announced, 'Born to Sing' had picked up eighty-six points, and finished fifth in a field of twenty.

It was a creditable result, but many of his fans thought that Colm deserved better. However, it did not damage his long-term career, and, since the 1978 Eurovision, Colm has collected a number of prestigious awards for his work in the theatre – including the Helen Hayes Award, the Outer Critics Circle Award, and the Theatre World Award.

Ireland's 1979 national contest was held in Dublin, and was once again hosted by Mike Murphy. The winning song was chosen by ten regional juries. The finalists included Red Hurley – and Tina Reynolds, who had sung for Ireland in the 1974 contest. They entered as a duo, but this was not their night, and they ended up in last position, without gaining a single point from any of the juries.

The Miami Showband was the runner-up. The Miami occupy a special, but unenviable place in the history of popular music in Ireland. In 1975, five members of the band were travelling back to Dublin from a gig in Northern Ireland, when their minibus was stopped at a fake military checkpoint. Gunmen from the loyalist paramilitary group, the UVF, planted a bomb on their bus, but it exploded prematurely, killing two of the paramilitaries. The remaining UVF gunmen opened fire on the band, killing three of them, and leaving the other two for dead. The survivors reformed the band, and they performed in the 1979 national contest. The Miami massacre is generally accepted as marking the end of the showband era in Ireland.

Also appearing in the contest that night was a young singer who had just begun to make an impact on the music scene in Ireland. He had been born in Australia, and was the son of a well-known Irish tenor who performed under the name of Patrick O'Hagan. That night, Johnny Logan sang a number called 'Angie', and finished third. It was a promising start to his Eurovision career – and, of course, there was much more to come.

The winner in Ireland's 1979 national contest was Cathal Dunne. In 1976, he had competed in the national contest that was won by Red Hurley. This time, the outcome was reversed, and Cathal won by a large margin. His song was called 'Happy Man', and its lyrics were, to say the least, very simple: the singer has fallen in love, and, as the title would suggest, this has made him happy. In fact, the sentiments of Cathal's love song were so familiar that he even described them in his own lyrics as being '*like a love song*'.

The twenty-fourth Eurovision was held in Jerusalem, following Israel's win in the 1978 Eurovision. Nineteen countries participated, but Yugoslavia had declined to take part because they objected to the inclusion of Israel. Turkey had originally indicated that they would participate, but later withdrew under pressure from Arab states who objected to a predominantly Muslim country taking part in the Israeli contest. Yugoslavia did not broadcast the contest, but Turkey did – despite its abstention – and so did Hong Kong and Romania, for the first time.

When it came to the final, Cathal appeared nervous at the start, but he seemed to gain confidence as the song progressed, and, when the voting was over, he was placed fifth, with eighty points. The rest of the voting was extremely close. The Israeli group, Milk and Honey, led in the early stages with their song 'Hallelujah', but, around half way through, Spain overtook them. When it came to the final vote, Israel were one point behind Spain – but the last jury to announce a result was in Spain. The Spanish jury gave Milk and Honey ten points, which meant Israel had won the Eurovision contest for a second consecutive year.

The win should have meant that the following year's event would take place in Israel. However, the Israeli government turned down an appeal from the Israel Broadcasting Authority for the extra funds needed to stage the Eurovision in 1980. As a result, the IBA declined the EBU's request to hold the contest. The EBU then asked Spain, who had been the runners-up, if they were prepared to stage the event. They also declined – and so, apparently, did the UK when they were asked. Eventually, the Netherlands agreed to host the show on the understanding that it would only be a small-scale production. That was why the 1980 Eurovision took place in The Hague – where Johnny Logan would get his first chance to sing in a Grand Final.

8.
Another Year

In 1980, I was a very young and inexperienced producer in RTÉ. I had recently finished a training course, and had expected that I would be joining the station's Drama Department. That was, after all, why I had been recruited by RTÉ. I had directed and produced dramas at university; I had written a doctoral thesis on Irish drama; and I had worked with a drama company in Dublin. I was greatly surprised, therefore, when I was assigned to work in RTÉ's TV Variety Department. Later, I was shown an internal document which revealed that the purpose of the assignment had been to 'soften my cough'. Looking back, I think that was a good call: nowadays, we might term it 'counterintuitive'. Almost ten years would pass before I got to work on my first TV drama project.

Instead, one of the first programmes to which I was assigned as a producer was the station's premier entertainment series, *The Late Late Show*. At the time, the series was both presented and produced by Gay Byrne – a broadcaster of the very first rank. Gay liked to establish traditions that would run across successive seasons of his show, and one of these was the appearance of Ireland's Eurovision entry on the *Late Late* the week before the contest to perform the Irish song. I was in the green room that night when a young man wearing a white suit came in, and introduced himself as Johnny Logan.

I hadn't watched that year's national song contest, and I hadn't heard Johnny's song, but I knew that it had been written by Shay Healy. Shay had enjoyed a varied career, including stints as a cameraman, a TV presenter and a music journalist. However, I knew him best as the writer and performer of novelty songs and parodies. In fact, he had once performed one of these on TV with my future wife – to her acute and continuing embarrassment. His Eurovision song has been arranged by Bill Whelan, an extremely gifted composer and musician who would later play a central role in two Eurovision finals. Bill had introduced a soaring saxophone break to the arrangement, which gave Shay's song a more sophisticated and soulful dimension.

As I watched Johnny sing 'What's Another Year?' on the *Late Late Show*, I thought that he had a very good chance of winning the Eurovision. Although he was handsome, tall and well built, there was something open and vulnerable in his performance that seemed to match the theme of the lyrics. He seemed a little shy, but had definite sex appeal. He voice was clear and could carry a sense of underlying emotion. He was also able to hit the last high note of his song.

After Johnny returned to the green room, I told him that I was convinced he would win the Eurovision. He was polite, and diffident, and his character reminded me a little of what I imagined the young Elvis was like. I believed that, if he won that year's Eurovision, his life would change dramatically, and I thought that, if I followed him for the subsequent year, it would make an excellent subject for a documentary film. It even tied in with the title of his song.

Over the next few days, I discussed the proposal with some senior colleagues, and it was agreed that I could proceed with the film, with Mike Murphy as its presenter – provided that Johnny won the Eurovision. I watched the final on Saturday night with an unusual degree of interest, but it was not the most impressive Eurovision I had ever seen. The Dutch broadcaster, NOS, had kept to its word, and the contest was a relatively small-scale production. The Eurovision had been staged in The Hague in 1976, and in 1980 it was broadcast from the same venue. Some of the 1976 opening film was reused in the 1980 contest, and so were parts of the 1976 set. There were no filmed postcards between the songs. Instead, a guest presenter from each of the competing countries introduced their national song directly to camera. In some cases, the same person also provided a TV commentary.

Johnny was the seventeenth act to perform in the final. The lyrics of Shay Healy's song are somewhat ambiguous, and open to interpretation. On one hand, the song can seem to come from the viewpoint of someone who is waiting patiently for the girl he loves to feel the same way about him; on the other hand, according to Shay Healy, the song was inspired by watching his father trying to come to terms with the death of Shay's mother. Either way, the mood of the song is bittersweet, and suggestive of sadness and loss.

For the first time, the Eurovision votes were given in ascending order – starting with one and ending with twelve. This greatly increased the drama of the final, since it meant the last vote from each country had the maximum impact – and it is the voting system which has, more or less, been followed ever since. Halfway through, it looked as if Johnny were going to win, and he ended up doing so by a comfortable margin. When he came back onstage after the result, he was so overcome that he could not reach the high note at the end of his song. Instead, he simply said 'I love you Ireland'. Seven years later, similar emotions would prevent Johnny from hitting another top note, and once again, he declared his love for Ireland.

Both times, the declaration seemed completely sincere to me. Indeed, I sometimes felt that Johnny's connection with Ireland had the sort of intensity that can be found in those who were dislocated in some way from the country. Johnny had been born in Australia. He had lived there for the early years of his life until his family returned to Ireland and moved between various parts of the country. When he first entered Ireland's national song contest, his father and mother had already returned to live in Australia, and there was a sense that Johnny did not quite know where to call home.

Perhaps this confusion was even evident in what he called himself: his birth name was Sean Sherrard, and he had performed as Sean O'Hagan before settling on Johnny Logan. He told me that he was given his stage name by one of his managers, but he has also been quoted as claiming that he chose it himself from the main character in the movie *Johnny Guitar.*

I was at Dublin Airport when Johnny and Shay Healy arrived back. Johnny was mobbed by hundreds of fans, and seemed ecstatic about his win. This was a time when the winning Eurovision song could still enjoy immediate international success. 'What's Another Year?' soon topped the charts in almost every European country, and it seemed that a bright and lucrative future lay ahead for Johnny Logan.

But, from the beginning, problems began to arise. When he won the Eurovision, Johnny had existing contracts with two different managers, and, within weeks of winning the contest, he was in Dublin's High Court being sued by one of them. The case dragged out over several weeks. When it was eventually settled, it meant that Johnny would pay a percentage of his earnings to two managers for the next two years.

That wasn't the only drain on his resources. Johnny began an intensive tour of Europe's TV studios performing 'What's Another Year?' I travelled with him for some of that time, and so did his tour manager, a young man from the west of Ireland called Louis Walsh – later to become a celebrity in his own right on *The X-Factor*. It was hard for me not to like Louis: he was a professional working in the entertainment industry, but he was also a fan, and his interest in pop music was genuine, extensive and unpretentious. Although Louis was very entertaining company, he could be very astute in his judgments. He also had a sort of inner compulsion to tell the truth – or, at least, the truth as he saw it – which was very useful for my documentary.

Johnny spent much of the next five months crisscrossing Europe with Louis, with Colin Tully, the Scottish saxophone player, and, sometimes, with me. He would be picked up at some foreign airport by a stretch limousine, and whisked off to a luxury hotel. He would spend the afternoon or evening taping a TV show. At night, he would often dine with the local PR agent of his record company. The next day, he would be taken by limo back to the airport and flown to another city, another hotel, and another TV station. It was rather monotonous, but it was the sort of lifestyle seemed to prove he had become a real international star. Johnny didn't fully grasp that the flights, the limos, the luxury hotel rooms, and the meals would all came out of his earnings.

A few years later, and Johnny's management could simply have couriered a video of his song to every TV station in Europe, but that was not seen as an option in 1980. There was another downside to Johnny's non-stop touring: it meant that he did not release the follow-up to his Eurovision hit until five months after his win. By then, the heat of his success had cooled, and he was not helped by the choice of follow-up. There had been talk of keeping the team responsible for 'What's Another Year?' – Johnny, Shay Healy and Bill Whelan – together, but it was not to be. Instead, he recorded a ponderous ballad, written by one of his record company's favoured composers. The only thing about the song that seemed to connect directly with Johnny was its title – 'Save Me' – and its ominous refrain, *'I'm not a winner anymore'*.

Johnny confided that this was a very frightening time for him – since he had to prove he was not a 'one hit wonder'. He also told me that he had never believed that 'Save Me' was the right choice of follow-up, but he had been assured by his record company that it was a sure-fire hit. Soon after the single was released, Johnny embarked on a lengthy tour of Ireland. This involved a very large entourage of roadies, musicians and backing singers travelling around the country in what passed for a luxury coach. Johnny said that he felt he owed this size and scale of show to his loyal Irish fans.

It was not a glamorous tour – changing in the dingy back rooms of pubs, driving through the night, sleeping through the day – and it proved to be a punishing experience for Johnny, not only in terms of the distances travelled, but because the tour ended up losing a lot of money. It had not been properly promoted, and the show itself was uneven, with an uncertain mix of material: traditional Irish ballads, pop songs, rock music and a tribute to Elvis – all seemed to have been thrown together. It was as if Johnny had still to define his own act to himself.

As the tour progressed, it became increasingly clear that 'Save Me' had flopped. Johnny tried to put on a brave face, and so did Louis, who assured me on several occasions that the record was 'going great in Japan'. But it was clearly a depressing time for both of them, and as the year wore on, Johnny seemed to have lost direction in both his personal and professional life. He released another single in 1980. Its title was also sadly appropriate: 'Give a Little Bit More (Too Much Too Soon)'. Like its predecessor, it failed to chart. By the time the 1981 Eurovision came along, Johnny's career seemed to lie in ashes.

A few days before the contest, we asked Johnny how he would describe the past twelve months. He said it was both the best and the worst year of his life. He said his immediate priority was to salvage his career – 'or what's left of it'. It was a deeply disappointing conclusion to a year that had begun so well. When Louis Walsh was asked if Johnny had been ready for what had followed the Eurovision, he was characteristically direct: 'No, he wasn't. And neither were we, I should add.' He acknowledged that Johnny's Irish management simply had not been capable of dealing with the international dimension of his career. In the course of 1980, Louis learned many lessons, and, in the years to come, they would prove to be of great benefit to him.

I had spent a year following Johnny Logan around the TV studios of Europe, and the dance halls of rural Ireland, and felt pessimistic about his future. He had been given a terrific opportunity, and it seemed to have been wasted. In the years ahead, I came to realise that I had underestimated Johnny: he was not only more talented that I had thought – he also had enough grit and determination to raise his career up from the ashes.

9.
The End of the Beginning

Nineteen eighty-one was the twenty-sixth Eurovision, and the second final to be mounted in Ireland by RTÉ. Ten years previously, the event had been staged in the Gaiety Theatre in Dublin in the form of what was almost a traditional variety show. By 1981, RTÉ's ambitions had grown. The final was held in the more extensive space offered by the Simmonscourt Pavilion of the Royal Dublin Society, which was normally used for agricultural, horse, and trade shows. The Gaiety had been able to hold an audience of a few hundred; the Pavilion had the capacity to seat thousands.

There were other significant differences between the 1971 and the 1981 contests. In 1971, the main concern for RTÉ management was that the Eurovision might be disrupted by disgruntled members of the station's own staff. Ten years later, the threats were much more serious.

At the beginning of the previous month, Bobby Sands, the IRA commander in the Maze Prison in Northern Ireland, had begun a hunger strike. On the night of the Eurovision Final, Sands had been refusing food for more than thirty days.

The IRA, and its political wing, Sinn Féin, had found it difficult at first to generate public support for the strike, and there were real fears that they might try to use the Eurovision as an opportunity to gain international publicity. For that reason, the contest took place under heavy guard, with more than 250 armed soldiers and police on hand to protect the event from any possible political demonstrations from the IRA or its sympathisers. Fortunately, there were none.

The costs of the 1981 contest had also increased significantly from 1971. It was reckoned that it had cost RTÉ around £300,000 to stage the 1981 contest – a substantial figure at that time. On the other hand, it was also estimated that the Irish economy as a whole benefited by at least £2 million. The presenter of the 1981 final was Doireann Ní Bhriain, who was a well-known and accomplished broadcaster. She was fluent in Irish and at ease in French – which was still an obligatory language in every Eurovision Final. The show was directed by Ian McGarry – a professional musician as well as an experienced TV director.

The theme of the contest's opening montage was one that connected images of ancient and contemporary Ireland. It intercut shots of ruined castles and Celtic monuments with those of modern Irish art, architecture, sport and entertainment. The interval act developed that theme. It was called *Timedance,* and explored the evolving story of Irish music through the medium of dance. It contained three principal elements: the megalithic, the medieval, and the modern. The music was provided by the traditional Irish band Planxty, who performed a piece written by Donal Lunny and Bill Whelan.

Bill had arranged Johnny Logan's winning song the previous year, and he would write a companion piece called *Riverdance* for another Eurovision interval act thirteen years later. Although *Timedance* was a sophisticated and admirable piece of work, I think it lacked the type of visceral energy and sense of drama that would later be delivered by Bill in *Riverdance*. Perhaps the staging was all a little too genteel and polite to ignite an audience. Nonetheless, when the track was released as a single, it became a hit in the Irish charts.

Sheeba had won the national contest the previous month with 'Horoscopes', out-voting seven other acts. The favourite to win the national final had been a comedy song called 'My Pet Parrot', which featured a man dressed as a parrot playing a trombone. Although it didn't win, that song finished as runner-up, and received a good deal of radio airplay. If it had won the national contest, it would have been Ireland's first novelty act to appear in the final. We had to wait another twenty-seven years before Ireland would send another bird to the Eurovision to fill that role.

'Horoscopes' was an up-tempo number, with the female group singing about the '*crazy*' fascination that some people have with star signs. It was a curious subject for a pop song, and it seemed a little unclear to whom its message was addressed. The three singers did not want '*the planets*' to '*take control of our lives*', and they reminded us that '*we are terrestrial*'. This robust critique of popular astrology was, no doubt, warranted, but it seemed to me to be a trifle unnecessary.

81

For the national contest, the three singers in Sheeba looked as if they had employed the same costume designer as Ming the Merciless. For the Eurovision Final, the sci-fi motifs in their outfits had been reduced somewhat: the dresses they wore were now green and diaphanous – slightly more contemporary, and certainly more revealing of their figures. The group's routine had also become more polished than it had been in the national final. Sheeba were likeable and attractive young women, and they were well received that night. At the close of voting, they had received 105 points, placing their song fifth in a field of twenty.

Soon after the contest, Sheeba signed a recording contract in the UK, and released some singles – sadly, without much success. The following year, they entered the national contest again, but were unsuccessful. Later in 1982, they were involved in a serious road accident in the west of Ireland that effectively ended their career, although the three women competed once more in the national final of 1984.

The voting in the 1981 Eurovision was close and tense, and there were some technical problems that caused the presenter, Doireann Ní Bhriain, a little difficulty. 'I am not renowned as a mathematical brain,' she told me many years later, 'and I was a bit afraid that I was going to make some terrible mistake.' In fact, she did not make any mistakes, but there was a fault with the telephone line to Yugoslavia. Doireann waited for what seemed like an age before her call was answered. When she asked for the Yugoslav vote, she was told abruptly, 'I don't have it.' Doireann didn't panic, and, a few moments later, the correct points were added to the scoreboard.

Five countries ran neck and neck throughout the final, and, until the penultimate vote, three of the contestants were tied in the lead position with the same score. It was only the last vote that sealed victory for the UK. The winners were a group that had been manufactured for the contest called Bucks Fizz. Their entry was called 'Making Your Mind Up'. In some respects, the song felt almost as retro as the rah-rah skirts, or the display of hand-jiving that it featured – but it was catchy bubble-gum pop, and was performed with manic enthusiasm by the group.

Bucks Fizz had a squeaky-clean image, but the lyrics of the song carried a discreet sexual undercurrent, including references to being 'taken from behind'. Their performance is best remembered for the moment when the two male members of the group appeared to rip the skirts off the two female members – only to reveal that they were wearing miniskirts underneath. The move was unexpected, mildly risqué and quite dramatic – and it probably secured the UK's success. But it wasn't popular with all the other contestants. The Swedish singer, Björn Skifs, was reported as complaining afterwards that, 'This was not a song contest, it was a show – all these dancing girls, they take away from the songs.'

The Swedish singer was not alone. France withdrew from competing in the following year's contest, claiming – with some Gallic exaggeration – that the songs in 1981 were 'a monument to insanity'. There appeared to be a consensus among contestants that Bucks Fizz's victory represented a triumph of style over substance. However, that seems to be a perennial complaint about the Eurovision, and it has surfaced repeatedly in the history of the contest – most recently in the early years of the present millennium. Dickie Rock emerged from semi-retirement in 2007 to lambast the contest as a 'freak show', with its 'trapeze artists, half-naked women and all the gimmickry'. He may have been speaking in 2007, but similar sentiments were expressed by others back in 1981. In this context, it might be worth pointing out that 'Making Your Mind Up' was a major hit in most of the competing countries, and ended up selling more than four million copies worldwide.

The 1981 Eurovision was counted as another major success for RTÉ. It represented – in both creative and technical terms – a considerable advance on the 1971 production. It would be seven years before the contest would be brought back to the Pavilion of the Royal Dublin Society. It had been staged in 1981 because Johnny Logan had won the Eurovision. When it returned there in 1988, it would be for the same reason.

There were eight finalists in the 1982 national contest, and Ireland's entry was determined by eleven regional juries. The winners of the national final were the Duskeys – a family act, as their name suggests – with a song called 'Here Today, Gone Tomorrow'. The Duskeys' song was written from a female perspective. The singer's boyfriend has been unfaithful with *another girlfriend on the far side of town*. It seems that she had hoped he would change his *'rovin' ways'*, but is now close to giving up on their relationship. However, the door is not quite closed on her wayward lover, since she still implores him to love her *'all the time'* in future. It would appear from the lyrics that the singer is in a deeply unhappy situation, but any sense of emotional upset was undermined by the upbeat tempo of the song, and the remorseless energy with which it was performed.

Following Bucks Fizz's win in Dublin, the Eurovision Final was held in Harrogate in the north of England. Eighteen countries took part, and the twenty-seventh contest opened with a map of Europe. Then, the question 'Where is Harrowgate?' was asked in the main spoken language of all the competing entries – apart from Ireland. The Irish entry was in English, but the question was posed in Irish. Eventually, the camera zoomed in on a map of northern England to reveal to European viewers the exact location of Harrowgate.

No doubt, this Yorkshire town has much to commend it, but there was little evidence of its charms in the BBC broadcast. In the interval between the performances and the voting, viewers were invited to 'look at the beautiful countryside surrounding Harrogate'. What followed were several minutes of desolate vistas. We were shown ruined churches, deserted villages, bare trees and empty parkland. It all looked as if it had been filmed very early on a bitterly cold winter morning. When some human beings were eventually seen, they were dressed – unconvincingly, and for no apparent reason – as Victorians, boarding a steam train. Behind them, a man dressed in contemporary clothes could be seen walking his dog. The final sequence of the film showed a random collection of performers from the contest attending what looked like some sort of ghastly reception. Meanwhile, a chamber orchestra, dressed in periwigs and frock coats, could be observed playing in the background.

The whole film consisted of what might kindly be described as 'wallpaper' footage: visual material that is specifically designed to be ignored, or talked over. It was accompanied by a piece of equally bland music provided by Ronnie Hazlehurst and His Orchestra. As an example of popular entertainment, it made the choice of massed pipes and drums – used as the interval act in Edinburgh some ten years earlier – appear like a stroke of imaginative genius.

Even before the voting started, it seemed obvious that there was only going to be one winner. Nicole had sung for Germany. She was still a teenager, but her performance had stood out from all the others. She sat on a stool – as Dana had done in 1970 – and played an acoustic guitar that had been painted in a chaste shade of white. Her gentle ballad expressed her earnest desire for world peace. This was hardly the stuff of controversy, but it was nicely delivered by the young singer.

Ireland's entry, the Duskeys, gave a performance that was synchronised with military precision, but, when it came to the voting, they were never in contention. Nicole led from the outset, and became the runaway winner of the contest. She finished more than sixty points ahead of her nearest rival – a record at that time. Nicole went on to sing the reprise of her song in English, French and Dutch, as well as German, to the delight of the audience in Harrogate's Conference Centre. The English version of her Eurovision winner subsequently reached the number one slot in the UK Singles Chart.

Her song, 'Ein Bisschen Frieden' had been written by Ralph Siegel and Bernd Meinunger. Between them, these two have now composed more than twenty songs that have reached the Eurovision final. The majority of these have been written for Germany, but Siegel and Meinunger have also entered the national contests of other countries – including Ireland. So far, Nicole's song is the only winner they have produced, but they are still writing. Nineteen eighty-two was also the first year that Germany won the Grand Final – although they have competed in almost every Eurovision since the inception of the contest. More than 13 million Germans watched Nicole's victory on TV, but they had to wait another twenty-eight years – until 2010 – before Germany won again.

The Duskeys finished in eleventh place out of a field of eighteen. They did not enter Ireland's national contest the following year. But, then, neither did anyone else. In 1983, for the first time in its history, RTÉ had decided to withdraw from the Eurovision.

10.
Waiting for Lift-Off

RTÉ's decision to withdraw from the 1983 Eurovision had been taken as part of a series of financial cutbacks in the station's Programmes Division. RTÉ management knew just how popular the event was with Irish audiences, and that was precisely the reason why the contest was earmarked to be culled from the schedule. At that time, RTÉ management was negotiating for an increase in the TV license fee – which the Irish government of the day was resisting. The idea seems to have been that the Irish public would resent the loss of one of their favourite shows, and would express their displeasure forcibly to the government. The government would respond, in turn, by increasing the license fee to ensure that the same sorry situation would never arise in future.

What actually happened, of course, was that the Irish public was annoyed – not with the government, but with RTÉ. They tended to believe that the station had chosen – for its own reasons – to deprive Ireland of participation in this prestigious event. As it turned out, the Irish public was not denied the possibility of watching the Eurovision Final that year, since RTÉ decided to relay the BBC broadcast. The only real impact was that – without an Irish entry – the viewing figures for the Eurovision fell sharply.

RTÉ returned to the contest in March of 1984, but the sense of austerity lingered. That year's national song contest was held in RTÉ's studios, and was presented by Gay Byrne as if it were a minor part of *The Late Late Show*. Somewhat incongruously, the bulk of that night's show was spent discussing the issue of divorce, which was still illegal in Ireland. On one side of the debate were a number of forbidding priests, and, on the other, some of those who felt trapped in unhappy marriages. Periodically, Gay would interrupt their passionate dispute to introduce one of the contest's finalists. 'It's time', he would say, 'for another musical item' – and, once it was over, he would pick up where he had left off: 'You wanted to say something, Father Noonan.' The debate would grind on for another twelve years before Ireland's constitutional ban on divorce was overturned in a public referendum.

There were eight songs, and eight regional juries in 1984. The contestants included Sheeba, Ireland's entry in the 1981 Eurovision, and Charlie McGettigan, who would go on to win the Eurovision ten years later. On this occasion, however, the standard of entry was considered to be exceptionally low – so much so, indeed, that almost half of the singers received no points from any of the regional juries.

The winner of the final was Linda Martin – who, Gay informed us, had to leave immediately after the show to perform in Birr, County Offaly; not the most glamorous of locations. Linda was dressed for the national final in what was believed to be the height of fashion in the early 1980s: a white jump suit, with huge shoulder pads, accompanied by big hair, big heels and big nails. She could almost have been auditioning for a part in *Miami Vice* – the archetypal eighties' crime series that RTÉ would screen later that year. In fact, the high-energy song that Johnny Logan had written could well have served as the theme tune for that series.

There was little doubt that Johnny's song, 'Terminal 3', was by far the best of those heard that night, and so was Linda's performance. The song is an up-tempo number, with Linda singing about her feelings while waiting for a former lover to disembark from a flight from the USA. Unusually for a Eurovision song, there is quite a complex narrative related in the verses of the song.

It appears from the lyrics that the singer's lover had left her at some point in the past, when '*he turned his back, and walked away*'. Now, he is coming home: he wonders if she still loves him, and wants to renew their relationship. She has come to the airport to meet him, because he is '*all alone*', but is aware that her lover '*must have changed*' while they were separated. The song finishes without a dramatic resolution – and the future of the couple is left open-ended.

Logan claimed that he had found inspiration to write the song while waiting in Terminal 3 of Heathrow Airport for a flight home to Ireland. But perhaps the connection between himself and the song runs even deeper. At one level, the narrative of 'Terminal 3' concerns the difficulties of maintaining a long-distance relationship. At that time, Johnny was travelling a great deal in Europe – struggling to get his career back on track – while his wife and young family continued to live in Ireland. It cannot have been easy for any of them. However, the painful emotion of the song is offset by its fast tempo, and is unlikely to have been obvious to most Eurovision viewers.

On the night of the Grand Final in Luxembourg, Linda performed ninth in the running order. Because her song had been written by Johnny Logan, the Irish entry had attracted considerable media attention, and 'Terminal 3' was rated as one of the favourites to win. Linda gave a strong and committed performance, which was well received by the audience in Luxembourg's Grand Theatre.

The early voting was very close, with the lead position changing regularly. The Irish entry received maximum points from Belgium, Italy, Sweden and Switzerland, and was in contention to win for most of the contest. However, in the second half of the voting, the Swedish entry began to gather momentum – and a lot of points. By the end of the contest, Sweden had won with 145 points, and Linda came second, just eight points behind. Yugoslavia was the only country that had failed to award her any votes.

It was a very creditable result, but was agonisingly close to winning for Linda. To add insult to injury, she had been beaten to the Grand Prix by 'Diggi-Loo Diggi-Ley', a song whose repetitive melody and infantile lyrics about a pair of magic shoes seemed to many to epitomise all that was worst about the Eurovision. After many unsuccessful attempts to reach the final, Linda might have thought that her moment had come – and gone. But she later claimed that the result had only spurred her to try again. For Linda, the Eurovision story was far from over – and the same was true of her song's composer, Johnny Logan.

In fact, Johnny returned to Ireland's national song contest the following year. In 1985, a sense of change was again in the air. In March of that year, it had even become legal for adults to buy condoms in Ireland without consulting a doctor and obtaining a medical prescription. But there was little variation in the staging of the Irish national contest a few days later. The final was held once again in RTÉ's studios, and was presented once again by Gay Byrne. There were eight songs in the national contest, and the singers included Marion Fossett, who had been part of Sheeba when they represented Ireland in 1981, and Johnny Logan's brother, Mike Sherrard, who performed a song that had been written by Johnny.

The eleven regional juries voted to send Maria Christian to Gothenburg in Sweden to represent Ireland in the 1985 Eurovision. Maria was a young woman from Dundalk, County Louth, and her song had been composed by Brendan Graham. It was the second time he had written Ireland's Eurovision entry, and he would go on to write two more – both of which would win the Grand Final of the contest. This time, Brendan's song was called 'Wait Until the Weekend Comes', and it was a rather gloomy ballad.

The singer implores her lover not to leave immediately, but rather to '*wait until the weekend comes*', and see how he feels then. She reminds him that, for unexplained reasons, Sundays '*always change your mind*', and she hopes that this will be the case again. In the second verse, she begs him to wait longer – '*until the summer comes*'. In the final verse, she asks him to wait '*until the rainbow ends*' – when they will enjoy growing old together. In the chorus of the song, she repeatedly informs her lover that she is '*so afraid*' to live without him. The song was described by one critic as 'sickly' – and, for me, the passive–aggressive nature of the lyrics was accentuated by its melancholic melody. Nonetheless, it was a well-structured song, and Maria Christian delivered an appealing – although rather nervous – performance as the first act on stage in the Gothenburg final.

When it came to the voting, it was not immediately evident which country would win the contest. At first, the German entry took a commanding lead, but, in the second half of the voting, the gap between Germany, Sweden and Norway narrowed, until just a few points separated the three of them. Sweden managed to edge ahead, but, with just three votes to go, Norway's entry – 'La Det Swinge' – took the lead, and held it until the end. It was the first time that Norway had won the Eurovision; in fact, the country had received no points at all in more than one contest.

When the voting ended, 'Wait Until the Weekend Comes' had picked up ninety-one points – which included a maximum of twelve points from Italy – and had finished sixth out of nineteen entries. Only Greece and Luxembourg had failed to award Maria Christian any points. That was a solid result, since the 1985 contest is generally regarded as one of the best of the 1980s. The Scandinavium – where the final was held – was the biggest venue to date, and the set was considered to be one of the most impressive ever designed for a Eurovision.

The following year's national contest was held once again in the RTÉ studios, but it was no longer part of *The Late Late Show*, and marked the return of Mike Murphy as its presenter. There were nine finalists, and the winner was again decided by votes from eleven regional juries. Linda Martin was back – and, once again, she was singing a song written by Johnny Logan. Her hair was even bigger – and so were her shoulder pads – but this time she didn't win the national final. Instead, the winning act was a family-based group from Northern Ireland, who performed with the (for me) irritating name of Luv Bug. Prior to their Eurovision entry, the band had released a number of singles in Ireland with some success.

Their mid-tempo song was called 'You Can Count On Me', and its lyrics described another broken relationship. Once again, it appeared that the singer had been dumped without warning by her boyfriend. What seems to have made matters worse was that he had previously assured her that she could count on him until '*the end of time – plus eternity*' – the sort of promise that would surely arouse most people's suspicions. Despite being let down, the singer still wants to revive the relationship, and suggests to her boyfriend that they should '*try again*': she must have been a sucker for punishment.

Until 1985, Norway had the reputation of being the least successful country in the history of the Eurovision – finishing last on six occasions, and receiving no points at all on three of those. The Norwegian national broadcaster, NRK, had decided to stage the contest in the city of Bergen, and the obvious pride that most Norwegians seemed to take in their first hosting of the Eurovision was reflected in the presence in the Grieg Hall of Crown Prince Harald, and other leading members of the Norwegian royal family.

Luv Bug performed twelfth on the night of the contest, and the band was well received in the hall. However, when the voting began, it soon became clear that there was only one frontrunner. The Belgian entry, Sandra Kim, went on to win with '*J'Aime la Vie*' by a substantial margin. However, her age caused some controversy. In the lyrics of the song, Sandra Kim had described herself as '*fifteen*', but, in reality, she was just thirteen. When this was revealed after the contest, Switzerland, who had finished second, was reported to have appealed the result. However, the EBU decided to let it stand. Sandra Kim is the youngest winner of the contest, and likely to remain so, since the age of admission to perform in the event was raised in 1989.

At the close of the voting, Luv Bug had received ninety-six points, which meant that they finished in a creditable fourth place out of twenty entrants. The band continued to perform and record over the following years. In 1988, they moved to the UK, and changed their name to Heart of Ice. But they returned to Ireland and entered the 1992 national song contest again as Luv Bug. In 1986, they had beaten Linda Martin for a place in the Eurovision Final. In 1992, the situation was reversed, and Linda emerged as Ireland's entry. She went to Malmo in Sweden to perform another song written by Johnny Logan.

Johnny had entered songs for Ireland's national contests in 1984, 1985 and 1986 – but they had all been written for someone else to sing. In 1987, he returned to the national contest with another of his own compositions. And this time he had decided to sing it himself.

11.
The Second Coming

In 1987, I was working in RTÉ as a producer on a doomed magazine series called *Evening Extra*, when I heard that Johnny Logan was planning to enter the Eurovision Song Contest for a second time. I realised at once that he was taking a considerable gamble, and the odds of him succeeding were very long. The simple truth was that no winner of the Eurovision had ever come back to win again, and I assumed that Johnny must be pretty desperate to take that sort of risk with his career. The Irish press had given him a hard time in the years since he won the contest. There were regular articles that focused on his record flops, his personal disappointments and his financial setbacks. There was little doubt that there would be a lot more of the same if his attempts to win the Eurovision for a second time proved unsuccessful: in fact, the headlines could practically write themselves.

I hadn't spoken to Johnny for a while, but, a few days later, I went to see him play at a gig in Dublin. He was performing in the basement of a pub, and people were knocking back pints, wandering about and chatting to each other, as Johnny and his small band provided some background noise. It looked like hard and demoralising graft, but, when I spoke to Johnny later, I was struck by his new sense of purpose – and realism. He told me that he felt he had been rejected by Ireland in the aftermath of his Eurovision win. 'I took it very personally,' he said. 'It was very hard to handle. At the end of 1980, I just felt broken.'

In the words of Shay Healy, who had written the winning song in 1980, Johnny had spent 'seven years in the wilderness. And it was ignominious for him. He had fallen from grace in the eyes of the Irish public, and yet he continued to plug away. He did bad gigs, for small money.' Since 1980, Johnny told me, 'the hole had just got deeper and deeper, and darker and darker.' Eventually, he decided that the only way he could lose the label of 'one hit wonder' was to do the Eurovision again – 'and not just do it, but win it.'

This time, he had written his own song. He was clearly apprehensive about entering the contest again, but had steeled himself for whatever lay ahead. He told me that he had been discussing his plans with Shay Healy: 'I said to Shay – "I really want to do this song. It's a very personal song, and I feel very strongly about it." He said, "Then, do it!" And I said, "But if I don't win, people will laugh at me." And he said, "Sean, people have already laughed at you. You've got nothing left to lose."'

By the end of the evening, it was agreed that I would make another film about Johnny's second attempt to win the Eurovision. Soon after that, I recorded a meeting between Johnny and Bill Whelan, who had provided the soulful arrangement for 'What's Another Year?' – and who was back on Johnny's team this time around. Afterwards, I asked Johnny if I could film him playing his new song. He agreed, and he sang 'Hold Me Now' while accompanying himself on the piano. It was a slightly slower and more reflective version than the one that he would later deliver, but I was very impressed. The song was clearly close to his heart, and I thought it was even stronger – and carried more emotional weight – than his previous winner.

Ireland's national song contest was held in March of 1987 in Dublin's Gaiety Theatre, and was presented by Marty Whelan and Maxi. When Johnny sang that night, there were few watching who could have realised how desperate his personal situation was: he was heavily in debt, and had been compelled to borrow from his bank simply in order to record his winning song. In 1980, he had too many managers, and too many people giving him advice. In 1987, he had no manager, no agent, and no recording contract. In more ways than one, Johnny was on his own.

There were eight finalists in the national contest, and the winner was decided by a jury of twelve 'experts' that had been chosen by RTÉ. The jury included some friends and close associates of Johnny's – such as Linda Martin. The composition of the jury may have been questionable, but there was little argument that Johnny's song was the strongest entry that night, and he won deservedly by a handsome margin.

'Hold Me Now' is a power ballad sung from the point of view of a man whose lover is leaving him for someone else. The singer does not plead for her to stay, but accepts that their relationship is over. All he seeks is one last moment of intimacy with her. He suggests that such a moment will stay with both of them, and will provide emotional sustenance throughout the years ahead. In comparison with most Eurovision lyrics, this is quite mature material, and it touches upon themes of loss and separation that feature in a number of other songs that Johnny Logan has written. The structure of the song involves a critical key change, which occurs just before the final chorus has been reprised by the backing singers. The momentary anticipation by Johnny's voice heightens the drama of the change of key – and this was further accentuated by Johnny bending low, as if he were struggling physically in order to reach an elusive high note.

I travelled with Johnny to the Eurovision in Brussels. The 1987 final was the largest and most ambitious held to that date, with twenty-two countries taking part. There was considerable media interest in Johnny because stories of his 'wilderness years' had been widely circulated in the European press. Once again, Johnny appeared in a white suit – though this time the jacket was cut in a bolero style. In the days that led up to the final, I was further impressed by his utter determination to win, and how he seemed able to motivate the other members of his act. Later, he told me that, 'I tried to inspire not just myself, but the backing singers as well. I wanted to make the whole team work as one.'

Offstage, Johnny seemed to be under constant and intense pressure, but, when he sang in rehearsal and in the Grand Final, he gave a commanding vocal performance. As the presenter of the contest – the improbably named Viktor Lazlo – remarked in her introduction to his song, 'Johnny Logan is back, and he's looking and singing better than ever.'

For the competing artists, the most stressful part of any Eurovision usually comes during the voting. I sat beside Johnny in the green room when it began, and, for most of the time, he looked as if he were about to be physically sick. I asked him some time later how he had felt when it became clear that he had won: 'Like I was on top of the world!' he told me. 'On top of the world!'

In the reprise of his winning song, Johnny became overcome with the emotion of the moment, and was unable to reach the final top note – just as he had failed to do in 1980. Instead, he ended his performance, once again, by saying how much he loved Ireland. Johnny's father, in Australia, had asked him to give thanks to God – or Yahweh – if he won the contest, and Johnny had promised to do so. He kept his word, and began his first press conference after the contest by mentioning Yahweh – to the utter confusion of the international press. One Dutch journalist even asked me if Yahweh were Johnny's wife. The first question Johnny was asked by one of the other journalists was what he would have done if he had lost the final. 'Kill myself,' Johnny replied. He may not have meant this literally, but it gave some indication of how much he believed was at stake for him.

Winning the 1987 Eurovision marked a decisive turning point in Johnny's career. No other artist has won the contest twice, and, in the years that followed his second win, Johnny did not repeat the mistakes of 1980. He has been able to establish a very successful career in continental Europe over the last four decades, and he continues to release new albums, and to appear in award-winning stage musicals. 'Hold Me Now' was a major hit in many European countries, and there have been a large number of cover versions. The song has also retained its popularity with Eurovision fans: when I was in Copenhagen for the 2014 contest, it was voted the most popular Eurovision winner of all time.

In 1987, Johnny told me that he was finished with the Eurovision for good because he had 'nothing left to prove'. But, as it turned out, he was far from finished with the contest, and was about to set new records in its history.

12.

Beauty and the Brains

Following Johnny Logan's win in Brussels, RTÉ accepted the EBU's invitation to stage the thirty-third Eurovision in 1988. The presenters chosen to present the event were Pat Kenny and Michelle Rocca. To many, it seemed that RTÉ was aiming to match Pat's brains with her beauty, but the reality was by no means as crude, or as simple, as that.

Pat was – and is – a highly intelligent individual, who had worked most recently as a skilful and well-informed presenter in the station's Current Affairs TV Department. Pat may have come from an academic background, but he also had a keen interest in mainstream culture, and had presented a successful popular music series on RTÉ radio. Hosting the Eurovision marked a turning point in his career: for many of the years that followed, Pat would work in the station's TV Entertainment Department, and his association with the Eurovision would also continue over the next decade.

Michelle Rocca was a former Miss Ireland who had also appeared in the final of the Miss International pageant. She had worked as a model, and had been married to the Irish international soccer star, John Devine. But she was also a graduate of University College Dublin, and was fluent in several European languages. Following her presentation of the Eurovision, she went on to gain several postgraduate degrees. They may never have seemed entirely at ease in each other's company, but, on screen, Pat and Michelle proved to be a surprisingly effective combination.

The executive producer of the 1988 Eurovision was Liam Miller. Liam was also Head of Programme Services in RTÉ. He was extremely familiar with the latest developments in broadcasting technology, and had a great deal of experience in the staging of major events. But Liam was not a bloodless technocrat: he was also a creative manager, with a deep understanding of the Irish audience, and of RTÉ's relationship with its viewers. Liam was determined that the 1988 Eurovision would be an innovative and challenging production. In particular, he wanted it to attract a younger and more sophisticated audience.

Liam chose Declan Lowney to direct the 1988 final. Declan was a very talented young director with a lot of experience in editing and directing music videos, who had previously worked in RTÉ's Young People's Department. He generated some controversy before the contest when he claimed – some might say with good reason – that Eurovision was 'just an excuse for a load of TV executives to go on the piss on expenses'. Later, Declan would direct the first two series of the brilliant sitcom, *Father Ted*.

Together, Declan and Liam changed many of the traditional features of the Eurovision, and, in the process, they initiated a new phase in its development. Indeed, many of the elements they introduced have become integral parts of current contests. To begin with, the traditional scoreboard was replaced by two giant Vidiwalls located on either side of the stage. When the voting stage was reached, the screens projected images, for the first time, of the contestants backstage in the green room area. A new computer-generated scoreboard was also used for the first time.

One of the most dramatic changes was the design of the Eurovision set. The stage had been conceived by Paula Farrell, working with the chief production designer, Michael Grogan, and it was the largest and most ambitious ever built for a Eurovision contest. The final was taking place in an Exhibition Hall of the Royal Dublin Society, and the stage took up so much room that the space for a live audience was severely limited. In order to conceal the small number of people in the hall, Declan kept the audience in virtual darkness for most of the competition. When the cameras cut away to shots of spectators, they were seen in tight frames and close-ups – designed to give the impression that the hall was crowded. Meanwhile, the creative use of lighting gave great depth to the performance area. The overall impression was that Ireland's Eurovision contest was taking place in a vast and packed arena.

The interval act of the 1988 contest also broke with Eurovision convention. Liam and Declan had chosen to feature a young Irish band called the Hothouse Flowers. The band was not the usual type of musical act that appeared on a Eurovision stage: they had a contemporary edge, and the bluesy song they performed was clearly not a middle-of-the-road ballad, or pop song. The Hothouse Flowers had

104

been formed in 1985, when Liam Ó Maonlaí and Fiachna Ó Braonáin began performing as street musicians on the streets of Dublin. Within a year, *Rolling Stone* magazine had hailed them as 'the best unsigned band in Europe'.

Pat gave a lengthy introduction to the Flowers – perhaps because RTÉ realised that their inclusion would surprise some of the contest's older viewers. Pat explained that music was attractive to young people because it reflected 'their energy, their talent, and their integrity'. He said that RTÉ had decided to 'give the stage' that night to a young act, and asked them 'to show us their Europe'. With the plans for European Integration scheduled for 1992, Pat claimed that the purpose was to reveal the Europe of the future: 'A Europe post-1992, when most of the frontiers now dividing us will vanish'. Over the next few minutes, Pat promised, RTÉ's cameras would take the audience 'from the tip to the toe of Europe'.

Although Pat had claimed that the stage had been given over to the Hothouse Flowers, their lead singer, Liam Ó Maonlaí, was the only member of the band to appear there that night. He introduced the band's song – first in Irish, then in English – saying that it was intended as 'a celebration of unity, and how people can be united by pure simple music.' It was, perhaps, a somewhat naive introduction – but Liam's youth and palpable idealism ensured that it fell on the right side of piety.

After he had spoken, a video of the band – performing an extended version of their song 'Don't Go' – was played on the giant video screens in the Exhibition Hall and on TV screens in viewers' homes. The video cut rapidly and effectively between different performances of the song in eleven different European countries. It had been paid for by the European Commission – on the basis that it would advance the goal of European integration – and, at times, it seemed to me to edge a little too close to being a promotional film.

However, there was also a genuine and engaging sense of romance about the Flowers' video. We saw an Irish rock band tooling around the continent in a beat-up Citroen van – playing in city streets, on beaches and roof tops – confident in themselves, at ease with other young Europeans, and clearly having the time of their lives. The video somehow managed to make the prospect of European integration seem cool and exciting – and that was no mean feat.

The national song contest had been held in the Olympia Theatre, and had been co-hosted by Marty Whelan and Maxi, who had represented Ireland in the 1973 Eurovision as a soloist, and again in 1981 as part of Sheeba. Eight songs competed in the event, and the selection was made by a jury of twelve 'experts' chosen by RTÉ. The winning act was called Jump the Gun, and their winning song was 'Take Him Home'. In the song, the singer informs his listeners that, if they meet someone in need of help, '*it might be someone I know*' – in which case, they are requested to '*take him home*'. The lyrics fall somewhere between a plea for world peace, and a fundraiser for the homeless.

Despite the rather pious sentiments, the Irish entry was a well-written song, and it was performed with great conviction by the band. However, it was overshadowed by the preceding act, and the remarkable vocal performance of the Swiss entry. Celine Dion was a French-Canadian singer who was, at that time, almost unknown in the English-speaking world. She was much better known by the end of the contest. The voting turned into a close race between Celine and the British entry – who went by the unlikely (and adopted) name of Scott Fitzgerald. When it came to the last vote, the UK was leading by five points, but Yugoslavia gave six points to Switzerland, and none to the British song – so Celine won by a single point. This was the first step in her international career, and the last time that the Eurovision was won by a song in French. Meanwhile, the Irish entry placed eighth in a field of twenty-one, which was regarded as a reasonable result.

Ireland's national song contest was held the following year in the Olympia Theatre in Dublin, and was hosted by Ronan Collins. Eight songs competed in the final, and the winner was, once again, decided by a jury of twelve 'experts'. They had been selected by RTÉ to represent both the music industry and the Irish public, but their representative status – as well as their judgment – was clearly open to question.

The jury chose a song called 'The Real Me' – written, composed and sung by Kiev Connolly – to travel to Lausanne, Switzerland for that year's Eurovision. Kiev, and his group, the Missing Passengers, finished ahead of two former Eurovision finalists: Linda Martin, who sang as a soloist for the third time, and Nicola Kerr, a former member of 'The Swarbriggs Plus Two', whose song had the curious title of 'This Isn't War (It's Revolution)'.

The Lausanne Eurovision was opened by Celine Dion – winner of the previous year's contest in Dublin. She reprised her winning song, and then performed her first English-language single, 'Where Does My Heart Beat Now?' It was unusual for a previous winner to perform two songs in the following year's contest, but it proved to be very much to Celine's advantage. Her new song went on to become a major hit in the USA, and elsewhere, and effectively launched her international career.

The French entry to the contest caused some controversy – since the singer was only eleven years old. Some of the other countries felt it was unfair to them to have to compete against such a young child; some of them felt it was unfair to the child. As a result of the bad publicity which this generated, the EBU changed the rules of the contest: from 1989, no performer was allowed to take part in the Eurovision before the year of their sixteenth birthday. In the era of *The X-Factor* and *America's Got Talent* – where children as young as four years of age have competed – the EBU's discretion now seems like a relic from another age.

Kiev's song tells the story of someone who is addressing his former lover, and claims to be devastated after the breakup of their relationship. However, the lyrics seem suffused with self-pity, and the words 'I', 'me' or 'my' are used by the singer forty-eight times in less than three minutes. Nothing is said about his former girlfriend – except that she was thoughtless enough to have left him *'standin' in the rain'*. Any sense of the singer's heartache was further diminished by the shots of Kiev grinning into the camera throughout his performance.

The singer admits that he cannot understand why his girlfriend might want to end their relationship, and the song ends with her being informed that she must choose to accept the singer as he is, or leave him for good. Kiev was joined in the performance by a female singer: although she was not credited, she stood beside him for all of the song, and joined in each chorus. It was not clear if she were intended to represent the singer's former girlfriend, or what her precise role was supposed to be – but she and Kiev linked up during the song, and gazed into each other's eyes with apparent affection, before kissing at the end.

Kiev performed his song third on the night of the final. At the close of voting, he had received just twenty-one points, leaving him eighteenth in a field of twenty-two. This was – at the time, and for the next decade – Ireland's worst result in a Eurovision Final. Since then, Kiev has set up his own recording studio. He has worked closely with the über-nationalist folk group, the Wolfe Tones, and is said still to perform at various venues around Ireland.

Riva, representing Yugoslavia, won the contest in 1989 with a bright and bouncy pop song. She sang in Croatian, but the title of her song, 'Rock Me', was in English, and so was the chorus. As it turned out, this was the only victory recorded for Yugoslavia as a unified state. The runner-up was the UK entry, Ray Caruana – the lead singer with a band called Live Report – whose song had what proved to be the all-too-appropriate title of 'Why Do I Always Get It Wrong?' After the contest, Ray complained bitterly about the winning entry; claiming that he should have won the final, instead of finishing second, because he had the better song. He argued that the UK had 'shot themselves in the foot' by giving high points to his chief rival – seeming to forget that none of the countries in the Eurovision are allowed to vote for their own song. Ray is currently employed in the manufacture of bespoke handbags in Billericay.

I cannot claim to have taken much interest in that year's Eurovision. Ireland's entry did not appeal to me, and, in any case, for the previous few years I had been fully engaged devising and producing a late-night series for RTÉ called *Nighthawks*. It was a live show that was broadcast three times a week. It featured studio interviews, bands, solo performers, comedians – and whatever else caught our interest. For me, it entailed close to a 24/7 level of commitment. However, before the 1990 contest, I was given a new editorial position inside RTÉ, and it was one that involved direct responsibility for Ireland's participation in the Eurovision.

13.
Anywhere in Europe

I had only been appointed RTÉ's Head of Entertainment and Drama for a few months – and most of that time had been devoted to working on the station's new soap opera, *Fair City* – when I travelled to Zagreb, the capital of Croatia, for the first and last Eurovision to be held in the federal state that was still called Yugoslavia. Under Marshall Tito, Yugoslavia had been the only communist country in Europe to take part in the contest. In fact, it had been participating for several years before Ireland first entered the Eurovision.

By the time I began my new job, Ireland's entry for the 1990 Eurovision in Zagreb had already been decided. Liam Reilly had won the national final at the Gaiety Theatre in Dublin, with a song he had written himself. He had pipped 'Linda Martin and Friends' for the top spot – but Linda's turn would come around a few years later. The 1990 national final had been hosted by Jimmy Greeley and Clíona Ní Buachalla – and they would both later provide the TV commentary in Zagreb. Eight songs competed in the national event, and the winner was decided by twelve regional juries.

The winner, Liam Reilly, had competed in the national song contest in 1988 with a song called 'Lifeline', and had finished as the runner-up. He was a former lead singer of a band called Bagatelle. His band had enjoyed considerable success in Ireland in the early 1980s. Indeed, one of their songs – 'Summer in Dublin', which Liam had written – had been so popular that it seemed to be the anthem of a whole generation.

In musical terms, Liam Reilly had certain similarities to the style of Elton John – there was even a slight physical resemblance between the two men. That may help to explain why Liam was said to have received an offer from Gus Dudgeon – at that time, Elton John's producer – to begin a solo career. Liam turned down the offer, and insisted on remaining with the rest of the band. That may have showed admirable loyalty on his part, but, perhaps, it was an unwise decision. As it turned out, Liam left Bagatelle in the mid-eighties and moved to the States. He returned to Ireland a few years later.

For the 1990 national contest, Liam performed 'Somewhere in Europe'. In its themes and musical structure, the song reminded me of 'Summer in Dublin'. In both songs, the singer names a series of locations which he associates with a former lover. In the Dublin song, he refers to the River Liffey, Grafton Street, Dun Laoghaire and the 46A bus. In the Eurovision song, he covers considerably more ground. Indeed, the singer and his girlfriend seem to have wandered across most of Western Europe – including Holland, Italy, France, Germany, England, Spain and Greece. However, the couple do not seem to have strayed far from the mainstream tourist trail in any of these countries. In Rome, he tells us, they viewed the Trevi Fountain; in Paris, the Champs-Élysées; in Germany, the Black Forest; Trafalgar Square in London, and the canals in Amsterdam. He does not mention what they went to see in 'old Seville'.

The lyrics may have seemed rather naive and obvious, but Liam was not the only composer that year who had chosen Europe as the subject of their song. The collapse of Eastern European communism and the reunification of Germany formed the political backdrop to the 1990 contest, and several of the entries focused on those seismic events. The songs entered by Norway and Austria welcomed the emergence of a new Germany, while Italy celebrated the growing unity of the European continent. Eventually, Ireland would also enter a song in the Eurovision that sought to address the fall of the Iron Curtain and the Berlin Wall. However, it came seventeen years after those events – which might seem a little late in the day.

The 1990 final took place on 'Europe Day'. But, in retrospect, Zagreb may not have been the best venue to celebrate the birth of a new era in European harmony. Yugoslavia had managed for many years to exploit some of the political contradictions between Eastern and Western Europe. By 1990, the end of the old Soviet bloc meant that many of those contradictions had been dissolved – and, in effect, this also undermined the basis of the Yugoslav state. Conflicts were already beginning to open up between the different federal republics in Yugoslavia, and I witnessed some of that tension surface in heated rows over the seating arrangements for the different ethnic blocs in the 1990 final.

Later in 1990, the first democratic elections since World War II were held in Croatia. They resulted in a comprehensive victory for Franjo Tuđman's nationalist party. The following year, the seething Yugoslav disputes were to find a focus in the selection of the Eurovision entry. The winner of the national song contest was a group from Serbia. However, the favourite to win that competition had been a singer from Croatia, and there was a strong suspicion that the voting had been rigged in Belgrade. This was to result in two separate Yugoslavian commentaries being broadcast: one for Croatia, Bosnia-Herzegovina, Macedonia and Slovenia, and the other for Serbia, Montenegro, Kosovo and Vojodina. Later in 1991, open civil war erupted in the Balkans along the same ethnic divisions.

But in Zagreb, in May of 1990, there were more immediate concerns. Some Western Europeans had doubts about the capacity of TV Croatia to stage an event on the scale of this contest. Soon after the show started, it seemed that their anxieties were well founded. The first act to perform was a duo of sisters from Spain. But when Azúcar Moreno came on stage, their backing track at first failed to play, and then started ahead of the orchestra. The Spanish conductor appeared helpless, and the sisters disappeared back into the wings.

They re-emerged a few minutes later, when the fault had been corrected, and performed their song without any further hitches. Azúcar Moreno did not go on to win the Eurovision, but their song was a hit in Spain and South America. The Spanish act was the only one that encountered technical problems that night. However, there was one further glitch when it came to the voting. The telephone lines to the international juries worked well – with one exception: there were problems reaching Zadar just a few miles away, where the Yugoslav jury was based.

Some have regarded it as an omen that the Yugoslav phone lines could connect with every country in Europe except their own – and interpret this as a portent for the impending disintegration of the Yugoslav state. Nonetheless, when the result had finally been announced, it was generally accepted that the contest had been a fairly successful production.

Liam was the seventeenth act to perform in the Vatroslav Lisinski Concert Hall. His voice had lost none of its appeal since his days with Bagatelle, and I thought that his song was the strongest in the competition. If I had any criticism of his performance, it was that he seemed too understated in his delivery. Liam came across as a likeable and modest character, but he did not generate much sense of personal charisma on camera. Despite that, I was confident that he would be a serious contender in the final.

Liam's underplaying could hardly have been offered a greater contrast than the performance of Toto Cutugno, who sang for Italy. Toto was not only a well-known singer in his native country, but he had enjoyed international success in the previous decade with his song, 'L'Italiano'. Dressed entirely in white, and with jet-black shoulder-length hair, Toto delivered a dramatic and passionate plea for European unity. He assured his audience that they all shared *'the same dream'* – which was to live in a continent that was founded on *'love without borders'*.

Toto's song had not been rated as a likely winner before the final, but it was soon evident that his fiery and emotional delivery had made an impact on juries all over Europe. When the voting commenced, the three countries that quickly emerged as the frontrunners were Ireland, Italy and France. The French entry had been written once again by Serge Gainsbourg. He was not only a remarkable showman in his own right, but was something of a

Eurovision veteran, who had written the winning song for France Gall back in 1963 – as well as other entries for other countries. Gainbourg's entry this time round, 'White and Black Blues', celebrated Europe's growing sense of multiculturalism, and involved a great deal of African drumming. This would be Gainsbourg's last Eurovision song – he died the following year.

Toto took the lead for the first seven rounds of the voting. Then, Liam held top position for the next nine rounds, with France snapping at the heels of both Italy and Ireland. Ironically, it was the Irish jury that handed the lead back to Italy by giving Toto the maximum of twelve points. The Italian jury, on the other hand, did not give Liam a single point. At the close of the voting, Toto's song, 'Insieme: 1992', had won the contest – Ireland and France were tied in second place. When Toto returned to the stage for a reprise of his winning song, he had been obliged to change into a dark jacket. In the excitement of his victory, he had been doused with champagne – and that had led the dye to run from his black locks onto his white tuxedo.

Toto was back the following year – co-presenting the Eurovision from Rome – and so was Liam Reilly, though this time as the composer of Ireland's entry. Kim Jackson had been one of Liam's backing singers in Zagreb, and she had won Ireland's national contest – by a single point – with Liam's song, 'Could It Be That I'm In Love?' The national final had been held in RTÉ's studios in Dublin. There had been seven entries – one of whom was Johnny Logan's brother, Mike – and the winner was selected by ten regional juries.

The winning song was a ballad, with Kim confessing her uncertainty about the feelings she holds for her lover, and wondering if they might mean she is in love with him. Once again, Liam had produced a well-crafted song, but I felt that it lacked some of the emotional heft of the previous year's entry. Kim was a likeable and attractive young woman with a good voice, but she seemed very nervous on stage, and was, perhaps, a little overwhelmed by the whole experience of competing in the Eurovision. Her performance in the Rome final seemed tentative and unsure.

At the close of voting, Ireland's song was placed tenth – tied with the UK in a field of twenty-two. It was by no means a disastrous result – indeed, it would have been hailed as something of a triumph ten years later – but Kim appeared distraught. She felt that she had let down Ireland, and it was hard to persuade her otherwise.

The 1991 contest had originally been intended to take place in Sam Remo – where the roots of the Eurovision had first been planted. However, due to the Gulf War and mounting ethnic tensions in Yugoslavia, RAI – the Italian broadcaster – had decided to move the contest to Rome, which was perceived to be more secure. This was the last Eurovision in which Yugoslavia participated under that title. The new Federal Republic of Yugoslavia competed the following year – and it only represented Serbia and Montenegro.

Toto was helped in his presentation of the Rome contest by Gigliola Cinquetti – who had won the Eurovision back in 1964, when it was still sometimes known as the San Remo Music Festival. Toto's approach to his presenting role seemed rather off-hand. At times, he appeared profoundly bored with the whole proceedings, and he had clearly made little effort to learn how to pronounce the song titles, or the names of the artists and conductors. He also spoke in Italian for most of the time – even though it was not recognised as an official language by the EBU. The voting segment of the show was something of a fiasco – with Toto repeatedly awarding the wrong marks, and he addressed the EBU's adjudicator, Frank Neff, in the impatient terms that a soccer player might use with a short-sighted referee. Despite – or because of – Toto's eccentric presentation, a record number of seven million Italians watched RAI's broadcast.

There was only one serious technical hitch in the broadcast. This was during the performance of Carola – the Swedish entry – when the sound system broke down, and the audience in the Concert Hall could not hear her sing. However, this did not affect the television transmission, and Carola went on to win that year's Eurovision. Perhaps the most notable feature of the 1991 contest was the fact that it ran well over its intended duration. This caused acute problems for the TV schedules of a number of countries that were taking part, and it became a preoccupation of the EBU that it would not happen again.

Of all the Eurovisions that I have attended, the 1991 contest was by far the most chaotic and disorganised. I had arrived earlier in Rome than I had in Zagreb, and had more time in the lead-up to the final to observe the contest close-up. By the end of the week I spent in Rome, I thought I had identified some of the weaknesses in RTÉ's Eurovision strategy, and had begun to plan some of the changes that I wanted to introduce. I discussed these with Liam Miller, and he was in agreement with me about what needed to be done.

On the morning after the final, I came down to breakfast in our hotel, expecting to find the Irish delegation debating the previous night. However, there was another topic on everyone's lips. It had just been revealed that Eamon Casey, the Bishop of Galway, had admitted to fathering a child with an American woman some years previously. In the light of subsequent scandals that broke over the Catholic Church in Ireland, this no longer seems quite as shocking as it did in 1991. However, it was the first time that this sort of behaviour had received extensive coverage in the Irish media, and there was a strong sense that a frontier had been crossed, and things would never be quite the same again.

The news about Bishop Casey came at a time when Ireland seemed to be emerging at last from the dismal economic circumstances of the 1980s. The tide of emigration seemed to have been turned back. After years in which we had grown used to national disappointment, we were starting to have some things to celebrate. Our soccer team had not disgraced us in the World Cup. Our rugby team had begun to win more games than it lost. Our filmmakers had won Oscars, and our writers were receiving international acclaim. In U2, we had even produced the best rock band in the world. In that context, why shouldn't we also want to win the Eurovision once again?

14.
Why Not?

Ireland's 1992 national song contest differed in some important respects from all previous ones. By that stage, I had drawn the (fairly obvious) conclusion that the key to winning the contest could be found in the pre-selection procedure. It is a little like a conjuror's trick: the real work has to be done before the audience starts paying attention.

As things stood, there was no limit to the number of entries that any individual could submit to RTÉ for our consideration – and some composers sent in more than twenty songs. The sheer volume of entries meant that some members of RTÉ staff had to spend several months of every year listening to and assessing hundreds of tapes in order to reduce the number of songs to around twenty before an internal jury could select the finalists. It was not – to put it mildly – the most efficient system, or one well suited to selecting the best songs, and it cried out to be reformed.

We involved the professional bodies of Ireland's music industry in our discussions on how this wasteful procedure could be changed. It was a laborious process, but we succeeded in a radical overhaul of the existing rules. In the new dispensation, any individual was only permitted to submit one song for the national contest, and each songwriter had to provide proof of a formal relationship with an established Irish music publisher.

RTÉ was accused by some critics of acting in an undemocratic and elitist manner – and it was true that these changes reduced the chances of amateur songwriters reaching the national final. However, the new rules also reduced the number of entries by more than 90 percent – and made the whole pre-selection procedure more focused and manageable. I believed it would also increase our chances of winning the Eurovision, which was, after all, its primary purpose – at least, as far as I was concerned.

My heart sank when I saw that one of the songs that had reached the pre-selection jury in 1992 had been written by Sean Sherrard – otherwise known as Johnny Logan. Johnny had created Eurovision history by winning the Eurovision contest twice, but I thought that going to the well for the third time might be a step too far – even for him. However, while Johnny sang on the demo tape that he had submitted, he also indicated that he did not intend to perform the song himself, which I found reassuring.

Johnny's new song was called 'Why Me?' and its musical structure was very similar to that of his previous winner, 'Hold Me Now'. Like that song, it built in intensity, and involved a dramatic key change. For me, it lacked some of the emotional weight of his 1987 entry: perhaps that was because the song did not involve the heartache of 'Hold Me Now'. Instead, 'Why Me?' sought to celebrate a romantic relationship – although, as its title suggests, the lyrics also conveyed an undercurrent of personal insecurity. Initially, I was also a little doubtful when I learned that Johnny wanted Linda Martin to perform his song in the national contest.

Linda had teamed up with Johnny almost ten years previously, when she had finished in second place in the 1984 Eurovision Final with his song 'Terminal 3'. With the notable exception of Johnny, there were very few Eurovision finalists who had returned to the contest with any degree of success. In fact, only two other artists in the previous thirty-eight years had managed to win the contest after having competed on a prior occasion.

Linda had an even longer association with the Eurovision than Johnny. She was from Northern Ireland, and had begun her musical career with Chips in 1969. Chips became one of Ireland's most popular live bands in the 1970s. They competed in four separate national song contests, but failed to win any of them. Eventually, Linda left Chips, but she continued to compete in the Irish contest – three times as a soloist, and once as part of 'Linda Martin and Friends'. The 1992 contest marked her ninth attempt to win the Eurovision: if nothing else, she had displayed remarkable persistence in the pursuit of her ambition.

The 1992 national contest was held in March at the Opera House in Cork, and was hosted by Pat Kenny. Eight songs competed in the contest, and the winner was decided through the votes of ten regional juries. Linda was not the only veteran performer to appear in the 1992 contest. The band Luv Bug, who had represented Ireland in 1986, also took part – and so did Patricia Roe. Patricia had first appeared in Ireland's national final in 1980 – the year that Johnny Logan sang 'What's Another Year?' – and she took part most recently in 2014, when she was mentored by her sister: a time span of thirty-four years that surpasses even Linda's Eurovision history.

Whatever reservations I had about Linda were dispelled by her performance in the final in Cork. She looked great, and I thought that her vocals did full justice to the underlying emotion of Johnny's song. She was the clear winner at the end of the voting, and I was convinced that she was going to Malmo with an excellent chance of winning. By now, winning the Eurovision had become something of a preoccupation with me – and I knew that the head of the Irish delegation that was travelling to Sweden with Linda shared my goal.

It had become the custom – since Pat Kenny began to present the national song contest – that the producer of his TV show, *Kenny Live,* would also act as head of Ireland's delegation to the Eurovision. The producer in the 1991–1992 season was Adrian Cronin, who had a long association with the contest. However, Adrian had become ill a few weeks before the national final, and had been replaced by Kevin Linehan. I had worked with Kevin some years before on a TV series called *The Live Mike,* and I knew that he would want to win the Eurovision just as much as I did. In the weeks that led up to the contest we discussed every aspect of Linda's performance – but Kevin's attention became focused, in particular, on the dress that she would wear in the Grand Final.

Linda had already made an arrangement with a well-known designer in Dublin about her Eurovision dress. But Kevin was convinced that it was not suitable for the contest, and he was insistent that it had to be changed. 'When Linda won the national song contest,' he told me, 'she wore a dress that was too tight-fitting, and, on a number of camera angles, it was unflattering to her.' For understandable reasons, Linda was reluctant to concede to Kevin on this point. It became a test of his authority as her producer – and he was determined to have his way. He succeeded, and remained convinced ever afterwards that she would not have won the contest in her original dress.

When Linda arrived in Malmo, her song had already received a great deal of media attention. That was largely because it had been written by Johnny Logan. Johnny was something of a legend in Eurovision circles, and the press eagerly awaited his arrival in Sweden. He flew in just a few days before the final, at the end of a long and gruelling tour of Germany. I met him at the airport, and he looked utterly exhausted. Nonetheless, I ended up that night in a Karaoke club with Johnny, nursing a beer, and listening to him sing until the early hours of the morning.

Although the Eurovision is supposed to be a song competition, songwriters rarely get much notice in the lead-up to the final – and not much afterwards, for that matter. Johnny was an exception to that rule. In fact, he got more attention both from fans and the press than Linda. Perhaps that was of benefit to her – since it may have eased some of the pressure.

According to Liam Miller, RTÉ's Director of TV Programmes, when the Irish delegation arrived in Sweden, we brought with us 'an extraordinary amount of confidence that we were going to win'. In fact, he thought it was the only time he could remember that we were actively planning what we were going to do after we had won. Liam believed that 'things that in the past had not even been considered – the dress, the publicity, the presentation – were given a huge amount of attention.' For the first time, he thought that there was 'an absolute belief and a determination on our part to win.'

Twenty-three countries were due to take part in the Malmo contest – at that time, a record number of entries – but, in several respects, this was the last of the traditional Eurovisions. The collapse of the Iron Curtain – along with the disintegration of the Soviet Union and Yugoslavia – was already leading to major changes in the nature of the competition.

For the previous two years, I had attended regular meetings of the EBU's Eurovision Committee, in which we had discussed how to deal with countries from the former Soviet bloc that wanted to take part in the contest. On one hand, there was an anxiety that allowing too many new countries to participate might be like taking too many passengers on board a lifeboat, and could capsize the whole Eurovision. On the other hand, there was recognition that these were our fellow Europeans who had as much right as ourselves to be part of the song contest. In fact, several of these former communist states were geographically closer to the heart of Europe than countries such as Iceland – or, indeed, Ireland – who had been competing in the Eurovision for several decades. Until then, Yugoslavia had been the only Eastern European state to participate in the Eurovision, but 1992 was the last year in which it would appear. In reality, the so-called Federal Republic of Yugoslavia was just a shadow of the former state – and effectively only represented Serbia. As a result of the war then raging in Bosnia, Serbia was subsequently banned from the Eurovision until 2004 – in line with the sanctions that were imposed by the UN Security Council.

The 1992 show began with a computer-generated sequence, which transported viewers from the Coliseum in Rome, across the Alps, past the Eiffel Tower before coming to rest on the Ice Stadium in Malmo – the home of Sweden's leading ice hockey team. Nowadays, the computer graphics would seem laughably primitive, but back in 1992 they were regarded as state-of-the-art. The stage in Malmo had been designed around the theme of a Viking longship – with a dragon as its figurehead. Behind the ship was a representation of the Øresund Bridge – which, within a few years, would link Sweden with Denmark in both practical and symbolic ways.

Harald Treutiger – the co-presenter of the contest – welcomed viewers by reminding them of the historic context in which that year's Eurovision was taking place. 'The map of Europe is rapidly changing,' he said. 'Old countries disappear. New ones are being formed.' But Harald was optimistic about the future: 'When east is no longer East, and west is no longer West, Europe has become greater.'

In the days leading up to the final, the British entry, 'One Step Out of Time', had been considered the hot favourite to win. 'This year, it's our turn,' Terry Wogan had confidently assured his UK audience, 'or there ain't no justice.' Michael Ball, the British singer, was an attractive and experienced performer, who had starred in musicals in the West End and on Broadway. He had an excellent voice and a catchy song, but, in my eyes, he oversold himself in his performance. There was a sense that, when he tossed his hair, wrinkled his nose, or punched the air – all of which he did frequently – he was a little too conscious of his own roguish charm: as if he were singing, not to an audience, but to some imaginary mirror.

Linda sang immediately after Michael Ball in the final. I thought her performance was well judged: catching some of the darker emotions that underpinned Johnny's song without exaggeration or indulging in histrionics. I also thought that Kevin Linehan's instinct had been right about the choice of dress. Linda wore a long dove-grey evening gown that fell off one shoulder. According to Kevin, it was 'very simple, but very strong – something that gave her a classic shape, and something that she was able to carry off because she has a great figure.'

Malta established a lead in the early stages of the voting. But by the time the halfway point was reached, the UK and Ireland were also in contention. When it was Malta's turn to vote, Ireland was in first place, and we held that position to the end of the contest – with Linda finishing sixteen points ahead of Michael Ball. In fact, the UK received more top scores than Ireland – and so did Malta – but Ireland still managed to garner enough points to scoop the Grand Prix. Michael Ball later told the BBC that he would rather stick pins in his eyes than take part in another Eurovision.

At a press conference the following morning, Liam Miller declined to confirm that RTÉ would produce the 1993 contest. But the truth was we had already begun to discuss where and how we might stage the Eurovision – in fact, we'd begun that discussion even before Linda won the competition. It was the first win for Ireland since 1987, and it completed a remarkable hat trick for Johnny Logan. He is still the only person to have won the Eurovision performing a song composed for him; to have won while performing his own song; and to have won with someone else performing a song he had written.

On this occasion, the composer of the winning song attracted as much attention from the media as the winning singer. However, when we returned to Ireland, RTÉ organised a celebratory party for Linda, which went on till very late, and which involved a protracted session of discordant karaoke singing – in which I must admit I was one of the worst offenders.

It seemed like the perfect end to that Eurovision journey as far as the Irish production team was concerned. We had no idea that, in many ways, it was really just the beginning.

15.
The Cowshed in Cork

When Linda Martin won the Eurovision in Malmo, one of those watching the TV show back in Ireland was a dynamic entrepreneur called Noel C. Duggan. That same night, he wrote the first draft of a letter to RTÉ offering the free use of an equestrian centre which he owned for the staging of the 1993 contest. The centre was located in the small village of Millstreet in the northwest of County Cork. The population of the village was less than 1,500. There was no train station in Millstreet, and there were no main roads leading to Cork or Dublin. There were also no hotels in the village. And the equestrian centre was still unfinished.

It took two months for the national broadcaster to reply to Duggan's letter. But this did not mean that his offer was not being taken seriously. Duggan's proposal was better timed than he might have expected, and was helped by a number of factors that happened to coincide. The

Director-General of RTÉ at that time was Joe Barry, who came from Dunmanway, another small Cork town that was less than thirty miles from Millstreet. From the start, Barry made it clear that he was sympathetic to the idea of staging the contest outside Dublin.

So was Liam Miller – who was then a senior manager in RTÉ, and had acted as executive producer when the 1988 Eurovision was staged in Dublin. Liam would also act as executive producer of the 1993 Eurovision. He was not only a brilliant organiser, but one who relished the range of technical and creative challenges that bringing the contest to Millstreet would inevitably involve. Both Joe Barry and Liam Miller had a great deal of hands-on experience in staging major outside broadcasts – so they were not daunted by some of the logistical problems that might have alarmed less seasoned veterans. In fact, Liam told me that he believed one of the things that RTÉ did particularly well was 'special events under difficult circumstances'.

The question Liam asked himself in the days after Linda Martin's win in Malmo was: 'How can Ireland present a different type of Eurovision to the rest of Europe, and to the music industry?' Although Dublin had not been ruled out, a number of possible locations in rural Ireland were visited by RTÉ production staff in the following months. I remember RTÉ receiving an attractive proposal from Galway, but, as the weeks passed, Millstreet began to emerge as the frontrunner. According to Liam, it had two principal advantages over the other contenders: it had the space to stage the Eurovision, and a hugely willing local community to support it.

When RTÉ announced that the 1993 Eurovision would take place in Millstreet, the initial press reaction – both in Ireland and abroad – was one of scepticism and ironic amusement. The BBC even claimed that Ireland had decided to stage the contest in a 'cowshed' – for which they later apologised. In reality, it was naive and unfair to dismiss RTÉ's plans for Millstreet as a harebrained scheme that was doomed to failure. Several previous Eurovisions had been produced from less promising venues, and empty warehouses in bleak industrial estates had been transformed into modern TV studios. However, that did not mean the 1993 contest would not cause more acute problems than had been encountered before – or that it would not call for more imaginative and bolder solutions.

In fact, the Millstreet operation was by far the biggest outside broadcast that RTÉ had ever attempted, and required a huge level of logistical and human commitment. But, from the beginning, the RTÉ production was driven by a combative and self-confident approach: 'How do you get an audience of four to five thousand people into a very small town in northwest Cork that has no railway station?' Liam had asked me, and then answered his own question: 'You build a railway station, and you charter trains – that's what you do.'

An entire fleet of new buses was commandeered from CIE – Ireland's national transport agency. Block bookings of hotels in the region were made by RTÉ months in advance of the competition. There were no roads around Millstreet that were capable of accommodating the coaches that would carry international delegates – so the existing ones were widened, straightened and resurfaced. The entire ground level of Noel Duggan's jumping arena was lowered by several feet to allow for the ambitious design of the Eurovision stage.

The population of Millstreet village also became involved: a steering committee was set up, houses were repainted, flower beds were planted, and each of the twenty-five Eurovision entrants was adopted by one of the local businesses. According to the show's producer, Kevin Linehan, this was 'the kind of heroic endeavour that only a public service broadcaster would have the nerve to pull off.'

Kevin, who had been head of the Irish delegation in Malmo, had been appointed producer of the contest at an early stage, and so had the director, Anita Notaro, who became the first woman to fill that role. Anita would later write a number of best-selling novels – some of which are set in an Irish television station, not unlike RTÉ. She died – much too soon – in 2014.

The next decision that had to be made by RTÉ was to choose who would present the Eurovision. The initial idea was to continue the format used in 1988, and use one male and one female presenter. The frontrunner for the male presenter role was Gerry Ryan. His daily radio show was hugely popular with the Irish public, and he was immediately – and typically – greatly enthused with the prospect of presenting the contest.

I regarded Gerry as a highly intelligent, shrewd and creative broadcaster. However, an integral part of Gerry's genius as a performer was the sense of mischief and spontaneity that he was able to bring to the airwaves – and that very quality had made him some influential enemies within RTÉ. Gerry described them to me as the sort of people who held their noses while the station trousered the substantial revenue that his radio show was generating. He was my first choice to present the contest, and I was confident that he would respect the occasion. But there were a number of senior executives in RTÉ who were very apprehensive about his involvement in

1. Ireland's love affair with the Eurovision song contest began in 1965, when Butch Moore became Ireland's first Eurovision entry. His song, 'Walking the Streets in the Rain', finished in a creditable sixth place in the final in Naples, and Butch was greeted as a hero on his return to Ireland. He entered the national song contest on two more occasions, but did not get another chance to sing for Ireland. © RTÉ Stills Library

2. When Muriel Day won the national song contest in 1969, she became the first woman to represent Ireland in a Eurovision final. She was also the first performer from Northern Ireland to do so. Muriel moved to live in Canada for some years, but returned to Ireland and resumed her performing career in the 1990s. © RTÉ Stills Library

3. Dana in the RTÉ studio for the national song contest in 1970. Dana went on to win the Eurovision final in Amsterdam a few weeks later. It was Ireland's first win, and caused great excitement in the country – and some controversy within RTÉ. © RTÉ Stills Library

4. Tina Reynolds pictured in front of the Brighton Pavilion at the 1974 Eurovision. The winner that year was the Swedish group, ABBA. They went on to sell more than 400 million records, and to become the most successful break-out act – both commercially and critically – of any winner in the history of the © RTÉ Stills Library.

5. The Swarbriggs in a scene from the video that accompanied their 1975 Eurovision entry. The video helped to inspire the much-loved 'My Lovely Horse' episode of the sitcom, *Father Ted*. © RTÉ Stills Library

6. Sheeba was probably the most glamorous act ever to sing for Ireland in a Eurovision final. Marion Fossett, Maxi and Frances Campbell performed 'Horoscopes' when Dublin hosted the contest in 1981. Maxi had already represented Ireland in the 1973 final in Luxembourg. © RTÉ Stills Library

7. Brussels in 1987, and Johnny Logan becomes the first and – so far – the only performer to win the Eurovision twice. Johnny also wrote 'Hold Me Now', but his involvement in the song contest was not yet over, and he would write another winning song in 1992. © RTÉ Stills Library

8. This was Linda Martin's ninth attempt at Eurovision glory. She had appeared in the 1984 final, and finished as runner-up with one of Johnny Logan's songs. She was back in the Malmo Eurovision in 1992 singing 'Why Me?', another song written by Johnny Logan. Her win was the first of four that Ireland would achieve in the 1990s. © RTÉ Stills Library

9. This was the moment when Niamh Kavanagh realised that she had won the Millstreet Eurovision in 1993. Niamh later said that she would never enter another Eurovision, but changed her mind in 2010, when she sang in the Oslo final. Sadly, there was not to be a second victory. © RTÉ Stills Library

10. Jean Butler and Michael Flatley rehearsing *Riverdance* in the days leading up to the 1994 Eurovision final. This seven-minute dance routine caused a sensation when it was performed as the interval act in the Point Theatre in Dublin. *Riverdance* was subsequently developed into a full stage show which has enjoyed huge global success. © RTÉ Stills Library

11. A tense moment backstage at the 1994 Eurovision in Dublin. At this point, it was not yet clear that Paul Harrington and Charlie McGettigan were on course to achieve the third successive win for Ireland in a Eurovision final with 'Rock 'n' Roll Kids'. © RTÉ Stills Library

12. Eimear Quinn delivered Ireland's fourth Eurovision win in just five years at the Oslo final in 1996. 'The Voice' had been written by Brendan Graham – who also wrote 'Rock 'n' Roll Kids', the winning song in the 1994 Eurovision. © RTÉ Stills Library

13. Dustin is the only novelty act that RTÉ has entered for the Eurovision. He was also the only act to be booed by an audience in the national song contest. Although RTÉ's hopes were running high, the Turkey failed to qualify for the 2008 Eurovision final in Belgrade. © RTÉ Stills Library

14. John and Edward Grimes are better known together as Jedward. The identical twins first attracted public attention when they appeared on the UK talent show, *The X-Factor*. Jedward represented Ireland in the 2011 Dusseldorf Eurovision. They became the first and – so far – the only Irish performers to appear in two successive finals, when they performed in Baku the following year. © RTÉ Stills Library

15. In the past fifty years, there have been more than a dozen different commentators for RTÉ at the Eurovision finals. But Marty Whelan has provided the Irish commentary more than any other. He is seen here with a group of Irish fans at the 2014 Eurovision in Copenhagen – his sixteenth final.

16. The winner of the 2014 Eurovision, Conchita Wurst, seen with the author. Before the contest, petitions calling for the drag queen to be removed from the contest were circulated in Russia and Belarus. But Conchita still won the Eurovision by a large margin – gaining the most votes from both the national juries and the European public.

the Eurovision. I think they feared that Gerry would not be able to resist his own impulses to subvert what they properly regarded as a prestige event.

At first, it seemed that the perceived problem with Gerry might be addressed by the choice of the female presenter. In this case, the favourite was Cynthia Ní Mhurchú – who was already an experienced and accomplished TV presenter with RTÉ. It was believed that Cynthia and Gerry would bring complementary strengths to the presentation of the Eurovision, and they began to rehearse together. However, as the date of contest drew closer, it became clear that the opposition to Gerry had grown more intense, and that serious objections to his appointment were now expressed at the highest editorial level within RTÉ.

In the meantime, another strong contender to present the contest had emerged. Fionnuala Sweeney was working as a newscaster on RTÉ's 2 FM. She had limited experience of TV broadcasting, but she exuded a good deal of self-confidence and cool authority. Her screen test confirmed her natural ability, and it was decided at corporate level that she would present the Eurovision on her own.

It fell to Kevin Linehan, as the producer of that year's Eurovision, to tell Gerry of RTÉ's decision, but he asked if I would accompany him when the news was broken. We both knew Gerry well, and were acutely aware of just how disappointed he would be. Gerry later described in his autobiography how 'agitated and uneasy' Kevin and I both seemed when we met up with him. Gerry had no idea of the news we were about to break, but had assumed we wanted to talk about some indiscretion of his that had caused difficulties with a government minister, or the RTÉ Authority. It was obvious that Gerry was deeply upset when we told him that he was not going to present the

Eurovision in Millstreet. In his autobiography, he defined it as the moment when he first realised that he could not 'beat the system' inside RTÉ.

It was also a depressing and demoralising meeting for Kevin and myself. However, it was typical of Gerry's professional generosity that he reacted to his personal disappointment by inviting Fionnuala Sweeney on to his radio show to discuss the contest, and even went down to Millstreet to record a special edition of his show. 'It was the final day of rehearsals,' he wrote later, 'and I could see the arena where the show was about to take place.' It was an emotional occasion for Gerry, but he also attended the final, and later praised both the production and Fionnuala Sweeney's performance in the role he had craved.

The focus of the station seemed so firmly fixed on organising the ambitious event in Millstreet that I sometimes felt that everyone had forgotten that Ireland was still supposed to be entering a song in the 1993 contest. I think it was assumed that whoever represented Ireland – in the year that came directly after an Irish win – would only feature as an also-ran. Despite that, there had been a healthy number of songs submitted through the pre-selection procedure, and one of them in particular had caught my attention.

I had listened to Niamh Kavanagh sing before I saw her perform. Bill Whelan had given me a CD of music recorded for the movie *The Commitments*. Niamh hadn't appeared in the hit movie, but she had sung the lead vocal on a number of tracks on the double album. I had admired her interpretation of soul classics – such as 'Destination Anywhere' – and when she appeared on *An Eye on the Music,* an ambitious world music series that Bill was presenting for RTÉ, I was further impressed. When the selection committee gathered in my office in January 1993 to choose the finalists for the national song contest, I was pleased to see that her name was on the long list.

I wasn't disappointed when I listened to her song. Niamh later told me that she had been offered songs for the previous three or four years, but had turned them all down. When she listened to 'In Your Eyes', she felt differently. She liked the song, and its composer, Jimmy Walsh, 'spent forty-five minutes crying down the phone from New York saying that, if I didn't do it, he'd pull the song from the competition. I guess I'm a sucker for a sad story.' The song had been written by Jimmy Walsh with Niamh in mind, and it played to the strength and range of her voice. As I listened to 'In Your Eyes' for the first time, I felt that it was a strong contender to make that year's Eurovision a double win for Ireland. The national final was staged in March at the Point Theatre in Dublin. It was hosted by Pat Kenny, and eight songs competed to represent Ireland in Millstreet.

My belief in the potential of Niamh's song was reinforced that night by her compelling performance. She was dressed with an understated elegance, and barely moved as she sang. The economy of her presence on stage threw the focus onto her exceptional vocal gifts, and I was not surprised when she won the national contest by a large margin. However, at that point, the attention of most of my colleagues was directed towards Millstreet, and there was little expectation of what was to come.

At times, it almost seemed that the production team for the Eurovision had disappeared through some time warp into a different dimension. Every time I visited them at the Green Glens Centre in Millstreet, I was taken aback by the scale of the changes that had taken place. Roads had been laid, the railway station had been built, and RTÉ had turned the inside of Noel C. Duggan's jumping arena into a huge television studio. There were more than a hundred kilometres of cabling and circuits, a hundred microphones, eleven cameras, and forty commentary boxes. It was also clear that all the weeks spent in the small Cork village had given the large crew a strong sense of collective identity. There were almost two hundred RTÉ staff based in Millstreet, and it was as if they had formed their own small, but self-sufficient tribe.

Liam Miller told me later that, for him, every day spent in Millstreet was 'both hell and immensely rewarding'. Many of the others who were involved in the production told me that working on the contest was the best experience of their professional lives. Of course, it wasn't all hard work, and there was an implicit understanding that what happened in Millstreet would stay there. There had been reports that some of the foreign delegates and journalists were apprehensive about spending so much time in a remote location. However, according to John McHugh – who was head of the Irish delegation – they had reckoned without the traditional hospitality of Kerry and West Cork, which worked its customary magic.

Everything seemed to be going so smoothly that I was shocked to receive an urgent call from Kevin Linehan, the show's producer, just a few days before the final. It seemed that the opening act – an Irish star with a global reputation – had decided to pull out of the show at that very late stage. I immediately contacted two composers, Ronan Johnston and Shea Fitzgerald, to see if they could write a musical piece at very short notice. I had worked with Ronan and

Shea before when they had written the signature theme for a series that I produced called *Nighthawks*. Through some technical mix-up, I has listened to that signature piece backwards, and I had liked what I heard – which meant that their theme was played backwards on the show for the next four years. I also contacted Davy Spillane – an *uilleann* piper whose playing I had long admired. Luckily, Davy, Ronan and Shea were all available, and, within a day or so, we were in Shea's small studio in Monkstown, County Dublin, recording the new track that would open the 1993 contest. Davy Spillane was soon on his way to Millstreet – where he would be the first performer to be seen on the Eurovision stage.

Locating the contest in a small rural village was not the only unusual feature of the 1993 contest. Seven Eastern European countries had wanted to make their Eurovision debut in Millstreet. There wasn't room for all of them – so a pre-qualifying contest was held in Ljubljana in advance of the contest, and the top three entries were allowed to perform in that year's Eurovision. One of those three was Bosnia-Herzegovina.

At that time, a bitter civil war was waging in Bosnia, and the airport in Sarajevo was subject to sustained attacks from snipers and artillery emplacements. When the Bosnian delegation tried to leave Sarajevo, their plane came under direct fire while it was still on the runway. As a result, not all of the delegation members were able to board, and the composer and the conductor were left behind on the tarmac. Despite that, the Bosnian act was able to take part in the contest – with Ireland's Noel Kelehan standing in to conduct the orchestra.

Bosnia might not have gained many points at the end of the competition, but their participation was an achievement in itself. It may have been an unlikely setting, but the pain and defiance of a tortured country were on display for the rest of Europe to witness. When it came to the turn of the Bosnian jury to give their votes at the end of the contest, and a voice was heard over a crackling phone line saying, 'Hello Millstreet, Sarajevo calling', the Irish audience broke into spontaneous and enthusiastic applause.

Niamh Kavanagh was the fourteenth act to perform. 'There's a fantastic moment,' she said later, 'when you're sitting in the green room getting ready for the show, and the next thing they play the opening credits, the Eurovision anthem, and a big euphoria sweeps through the whole auditorium.' When she went on stage, to a tumultuous reception, Niamh was dressed in a well-cut deep-red jacket, and a long dark skirt. The look was simple, smart and stylish – and the expressive power of the song still came from her voice.

I thought that the interval act, on the other hand, was rather uninspiring: it featured Johnny Logan and the 'children of Millstreet' performing an anthem in which the audience was encouraged '*to keep love alive*'. The song was obviously intended to be uplifting and inspirational. However, it lacked some of the underlying anxiety that features in most of Logan's best work, and, I thought, suffered as a result. Once the voting from the national juries began, things got livelier. It soon became apparent that the real contest was between Niamh Kavanagh and Sonia, the British entry. According to Niamh, 'The whole night was fun and joyful, right up to when it looked like we might win. Then, it got horrific and dreadful.' She told me later that she felt like she had gone into labour.

I was in the green room for the voting, and felt the tension grow as the lead position swung between Ireland and the UK. There was one awkward moment when Fionnuala Sweeney was distracted by the audience's cheering, and awarded the wrong points to Ireland, and it was only when the last vote was announced that it was clear Niamh had won. Then, in her words, 'The whole place went mental.' In the audience, Albert Reynolds – who had been elected Ireland's Taoiseach just a few months earlier – led a standing ovation, while Niamh made her way back to the stage to perform a reprise of the winning song. Reynolds had once run a chain of dance halls in rural Ireland, and I suspect that he felt at home in Millsreet that night.

Although Niamh told me after the Millstreet contest that she would never enter the Eurovision again, she later changed her mind, and sang for Ireland, with less success, in 2010. Her victory in Millstreet had stunned many of those in RTÉ, who were present in the Green Gables arena that night. The win had simply not been foreseen by those who had been involved in producing the Millstreet contest. Of course, they were delighted by the result, but there was, perhaps, a feeling that their triumph had been slightly upstaged by hers. Given the tremendous resources that had been invested by RTÉ in the 1993 contest, there was some apprehension that the 1994 Eurovision would pale in comparison.

There was also uncertainty about the best approach that should be taken to staffing the next year's competition. A number of options were discussed in the following weeks – including mounting a co-production with BBC Northern Ireland, and keeping the same production team that had worked on the Millstreet event in place for the next twelve months. Before long, both those scenarios were discarded, and it was accepted that a fresh approach to the contest would require a brand new production team. This was to prove a wise decision – and one that led to what is often regarded as the most memorable of all Eurovision contests.

16.
The Interval Act

The Millstreet contest was judged to have been a great success. However, it had also been an expensive commitment for RTÉ. The 1994 Eurovision would take place at the Point Theatre in Dublin, and was designed to be a leaner and more economic operation. The Point had once been a railway depot, but it had been acquired by an inventive developer, Harry Crosbie, and turned into Ireland's leading concert venue. Before its complete renovation, the Point had featured in U2's 1988 *Rattle and Hum* movie. The national contest was held in the University Concert Hall in Limerick, and was presented by Pat Kenny. There were eight finalists, and, as usual, the winner was determined by a regional vote.

Ireland had won the two previous Eurovision contests with female solo singers, but, in 1994, Ireland was represented by two men – Paul Harrington and Charlie McGettigan – performing as a duo. Their song was called 'Rock 'n' Roll Kids', and they would go on to complete a unique hat trick of Irish wins in the Grand Final. The song was composed by Brendan Graham, who had won the national final twice before.

Apparently, there is a belief among some Eurovision fans that 'Rock 'n' Roll Kids' was deliberately chosen by RTÉ because the station did not wish to win the contest for a third successive time. It is true that the song differed from Ireland's previous entries in several respects. To begin with, it was performed by a male duo – a combination that had never won the contest before. What is more, at a time when Eurovision entries had become more elaborate in terms of their staging, Paul and Charlie remained more or less static throughout their performance. The arrangement of their song was also very simple, and consisted solely of Paul's piano and Charlie's guitar accompaniment. No song had ever won the Eurovision before without full orchestration.

I am reluctant to undermine any good conspiracy theory. However, it is quite untrue to suggest that 'Rock 'n' Roll Kids' was chosen because it was considered to have little chance of success. It would be grossly unfair and dishonest to select performers in such bad faith. I chaired the selection committee when the song was first submitted to RTÉ, and, from the start, I believed that it had a good chance of winning the contest – and I hoped that it would. In fact, in the moments after Paul and Charlie's victory had been announced, I can be seen in news footage beside them backstage, and, to the embarrassment of my children, kissing Paul in delight.

It has also been suggested that RTÉ did not want, and was not prepared, to host the next year's contest should the Irish act win for the third time in a row. This is also untrue. It is not compulsory for any country to host the Eurovision even if they win the contest. France, Monaco,

Luxembourg and Israel have all won Grand Finals, and have declined to stage the following year's event. There is also the simple fact that, when RTÉ won the 1994 Eurovision, the station chose to host the 1995 event. I was present at the discussions that immediately followed Ireland's victory, and the idea that RTÉ should decline to host the next year's contest never arose.

In fact, 'Rock 'n' Roll Kids' is generally considered to be one of the event's better entries. It was also the first Eurovision winning song to score more than two hundred points from the international juries. Like many good pop ballads, the back story of 'Rock 'n' Roll Kids' is suggested rather than spelled out in detail. The two singers represent one person who is addressing his romantic partner. The lyrics identify this person and his partner as both approaching their fiftieth birthdays. They can both remember the halcyon years in which rock 'n' roll was born – when they had enjoyed an intimate and carefree relationship. In the present, however, they seem to have lost contact with each other, and it appears that even their children don't want to spend much time in their company.

This lament for the loss of the fire and passion of youth is understated and wistful. But it is also quite poignant, and the bitterness of that loss is offset by the sweetness of the melody. The lyrics may be written from a middle-aged perspective, but the themes – of faded dreams and jaded relationships – are able to cut across demographic barriers, and connect with most age groups. In that respect, the song was well judged for the Eurovision juries.

From an early stage, Moya Doherty had been identified by Liam Miller as the producer of the 1994 contest. This was something of a departure for the station, because, at that time, Moya was no longer a member of RTÉ staff.

However, she had an excellent reputation as a creative producer, and she had recent experience of working on large, live broadcasts. According to Gerry Ryan, Moya had made his involvement as a presenter a condition of her own commitment to the event. I was delighted when it was announced that Gerry and Cynthia Ní Mhurchú would present the Eurovision, and it was clear that they both relished the prospect.

Gerry in particular appeared to savour every moment of the experience. In his autobiography, he admitted that he grew obsessed with the contest, and that, for the best part of a year, he ate, slept and breathed the event. Although he continued to present his daily radio show until shortly before the final, he seemed willing to attend every reception, every rehearsal and every press conference connected with the Eurovision. However, it was not an entirely easy ride for Gerry. He believed that the Director-General of RTÉ, Joe Barry, remained 'extremely ambivalent' about him presenting the final, and it is certainly true that Gerry came close to being kicked off the contest on a number of occasions.

I remember one instance in particular. Joe Barry had been driving back from Cork one morning when he tuned in to Gerry's radio show, and was outraged to hear him joking about the size of his (Gerry's) penis. According to Gerry, Joe drove straight down to the Point Theatre to confront him. The production team assumed that RTÉ's Director-General had arrived to 'look at *Riverdance,* or the set, or listen to the music.' Instead, Joe had come to warn Gerry that, if he mentioned his penis on air again, he would be sacked. In his autobiography, Gerry claimed – accurately – that I had to spend a lot of time over the following weeks 'throwing oil on troubled waters'. As it turned out, the partnership of

Gerry and Cynthia worked extremely well, and I know how much they both enjoyed the contest. However, the 1994 Eurovision is not principally remembered for its presenters, or even for its songs, but for its interval act.

It had become an established practice that some form of entertainment was presented in every Eurovision contest after all the songs had been performed. This provided an opportunity to count and collate the votes that had been cast, and, as more countries joined the Eurovision and the voting procedures became progressively more complicated, the duration and scale of the interval acts also began to grow.

Throughout the history of the contest, there has been an enormous range in the type and quality of these acts: they might feature acrobats, classical musicians, circus clowns, church choirs, trick cyclists, or jazz bands. For Eurovision audiences, the interval act began to generate its own sense of expectation. For the host broadcasters, they came to represent a part of the contest where the production team could make a distinctive contribution, and put their stamp on the event as a whole: the songs were covered – the interval act was created.

Dance had featured in these acts for many years. Sometimes, this had taken the form of traditional folk dancing; sometimes, ballet; sometimes, modern routines – sometimes, a combination of all three. But, when I first heard reports that the interval act in the 1994 Eurovision planned to feature traditional Irish step-dancing, I was both surprised and a little disappointed.

It seemed to me to signal a move in the wrong direction: Irish dancing had, after all, been part of the entertainment provided by the Bunratty Castle Singers when RTÉ first staged the contest back in 1971. I mentioned my reservations to Gerry Ryan, and he was able to reassure me: this act might be based on traditional step-dancing, he said, but it was very different from anything we had seen before. The director of that year's Eurovision was Pat Cowap. He told me that he had listened to Bill Whelan's track for *Riverdance* before he met the dancers, and was immediately impressed. He had seen both of the lead dancers perform, and could well imagine how hard-shoe step-dancing would match the percussive rhythm of Bill's score.

At that time, Pat was not a great fan of Michael Flatley, the male lead: 'He had the reputation of being an incredibly fast dancer,' Pat told me twenty years later, 'but my attitude was – so what? Just because he could dance quickly, it didn't mean he could dance well.' Pat changed his mind when he attended the first rehearsal. 'It was obvious to me then that Michael had something special – star quality, genius, whatever you want to call it – he was amazing.' Some days later, I saw *Riverdance* for the first time in rehearsal, and it was also clear to me that, for once, the interval act would dominate the entire Eurovision show.

Soon after that rehearsal, I attended the weekly corporate editorial meeting in RTÉ. I was the only one of those present who had seen *Riverdance*, and I was asked to describe the interval act to the meeting. I was effusive in my praise, but I recall the expressions on the faces of my colleagues when I mentioned that I thought it had introduced sex to Irish dancing – or words to that effect. One of them burst out laughing, some of them looked confused, and several of them displayed obvious signs of distaste and disapproval. There was a pause after I had finished my enthusiastic but rather incoherent account. Then, one senior manager fixed me with a baleful eye, and asked, 'Could we not find any Irish people that can dance?'

This was a reference to the fact that neither of the leads in *Riverdance* had been born in Ireland. In fact, they were both Irish-Americans. The female lead, Jean Butler, was a New Yorker, whose mother came from County Mayo. From a young age, Jean had competed in Irish dancing championships, and she had won numerous national and regional titles. In 1993, she had performed in *Mayo 5000.*

This was intended to mark the (supposed) anniversary of the birth of that Irish county, and Moya Doherty and her husband, John McColgan, had produced a gala concert in Dublin to celebrate the occasion. It was attended by the Irish President, Mary Robinson, who had been born in Mayo. The concert featured a new musical piece by the composer Bill Whelan. It included choral pieces by the Anúna group. It also starred the dancers Jean Butler and Michael Flatley – although they did not perform together. All of these artists would play a central role the following year in *Riverdance.*

In 1994, Jean Butler was completing her studies in Theatre and Drama at the University of Birmingham in the UK. Because of her American background, Jean knew nothing about the Eurovision Song Contest. When I interviewed her some years later, she told me how she was first approached to take part in the event: 'I hadn't a clue what it was about. I got a phone call asking me to perform, and I just said, "How much?"' When she told her flatmates of the offer, they were horrified: 'They fell around the place laughing. They said, "You can't perform in that. Don't touch it. It's horrible."' But Jean had her university fees to pay, so she decided to accept the offer.

As far as Jean was concerned, once she arrived in Dublin, 'The dance really took over from the event. It was about what was happening in rehearsal, in the studio, in the space. And really the whole concept was intriguing, and fascinating, and very exciting.' The Eurovision contest was always of secondary importance to her. In fact, Jean told me that 'it never even came into my mind.'

The male lead dancer, and her partner in *Riverdance,* was Michael Flatley. He had been grown up in Chicago, but, like Jean, he had a strong connection with the West of Ireland – where both his parents had been born. Some years earlier, Michael had become the first non-Irish resident to win the World Championship for Irish Dance. He had toured with the acclaimed traditional folk ensemble, the Chieftains, in the previous decade, and had also danced solo as part of the Mayo celebrations in 1993. Indeed, footage from the Mayo event reveals striking similarities to the steps he later used in *Riverdance.*

But Michael's skills were not confined to the dance traditions of Ireland. He was also extremely accomplished at tap, and even held the world record for tapping speed. In addition to that, he was an award-winning flautist, and a champion boxer. All of these different aspects of his life – artistic, athletic and technical – seemed to feed directly into his bravura performance in *Riverdance.* What is more, he brought huge personal presence to the stage of the Point Theatre, and an extraordinary ability to electrify an audience. I met Michael a few days before the contest, and told him that watching the rehearsals had reminded me of the movie *Strictly Ballroom* – in which the hero breaks out of the narrow constraints imposed on his dancing techniques by literal-minded officials. 'Story of my life,' he replied.

Shortly before the live transmission of the final began, Pat Cowap experienced an alarming attack of nerves. 'I'd been pretty calm during all the rehearsals – and then I suddenly felt really frightened. I had to clear my head, so I left the OB unit, and went for a walk by myself.' By chance, Pat bumped into Declan Lowney, who had directed the Eurovision in Dublin in 1988. 'In some ways, he was the last person I wanted to meet – because I knew what a great job he had done,' Pat told me. 'But he turned out to be the best person I could have met. He was very supportive, and he helped calm me down.'

Riverdance began with a choral sequence performed by the Anúna ensemble. Jean Butler was the first of the dancers on stage. She was wearing a short, black, lacy dress, and performed a delicate slip jig. It was an appealing and elegant routine, and it worked more or less within the existing conventions of Irish dance. Then, Michael made his entrance, the stage lighting turned red, and those conventions seemed to explode.

There was a time – in the fairly recent past – when Irish dancers were trained to keep their arms immobile and rigid at their sides: only the lower half of their bodies were supposed to move in a frantic rhythm. From the moment that Michael bounded on to the Eurovision stage, his arms raised in a gesture of gladiatorial triumph, there was the unmistakable sense that a cultural threshold had been crossed. Michael's hard shoes beat out what seemed like a call to arms. At times, it was difficult to tell whether his steps were traditional Irish or American tap, but when the chorus line of black-clad step-dancers moved in unison towards the audience, like the front wave of an advancing army, the *coup-de-theatre* – and the collective thrill it induced – were sheer Broadway.

For me, the defining moment of *Riverdance* was a tracking shot along the row of dancers. Pat Cowap later told me that this had been influenced by a similar track used by Francesco Rosi in his high-voltage 1984 film of Bizet's opera, *Carmen*. For Pat, the turning point of the dance came when Jean returned to the stage to engage with Michael: her movements seemed feline – almost predatory – and they were charged with sensual energy. Pat had marvelled at the strength of commitment and self-discipline that Michael Flatley brought to the act. 'He drove the rest of the troupe extremely hard, and he never seemed to sleep,' Pat told me. 'He was the first there in the morning, and the last to check out at night.' The precision of Flatley's steps also took Pat by surprise. 'We had to patch the stage shortly before the Grand Final. Michael hit exactly the same spot so many times in rehearsal that he had worn down the surface.'

Some of my colleagues may have expressed prior reservations about the American background of Michael and Jean. But the two Irish-Americans brought a sense of drama to the interval act that would have been difficult to introduce without them. When I interviewed Jean Butler, she was clear that 'if two Americans hadn't led *Riverdance* from a creative point of view, I just don't think it would have made the impact that it did.'

I had tried to describe the interval act to my wife and some of my friends in the hours before the contest, but my words had proved inadequate. It is equally difficult to describe the visceral impact of this performance on the audience in the Point Theatre that night. However, it would be no exaggeration to say that it produced a heady mixture of astonishment, pride and undisguised joy. As I looked around the arena, I saw a number of people weeping with emotion. 'Good grief!' said Terry Wogan in his BBC commentary. 'That brought back the folk memory – small hairs rising on the back of every Irishman's neck.'

Pat Cowap was directing the show from an outside broadcast unit that was located beside the Point Theatre. He had not anticipated the storm of applause that burst out a few seconds after *Riverdance* had finished. 'You could feel the unit rock with the wave of sound,' he told me. 'The noise was so loud, at first I thought it was a shower of hailstones hitting the roof.' One of the cameramen offered Pat a shot of Ireland's President, Mary Robinson, in tears, but he declined to take it. 'I thought it would be a cheap shot, and I've never regretted that call.' Back on stage, Gerry Ryan could hardly contain his excitement. He called the routine 'the most spectacular performance you have ever seen' – and there were few in the auditorium that night who would have disagreed with him.

Of course, the impact was not confined to the Point Theatre – or to Irish viewers of the Eurovision. *Riverdance* had made a huge impression wherever the contest was being broadcast. However, in Ireland, this represented an iconic moment in our cultural history, and one that seemed to lead to a surge of national self-confidence. Pat Cowap felt the secret of the act's success lay in its dramatic structure. 'The music is constantly building throughout the piece,' he told me. 'The dance has a strong erotic dimension, and, by the end, the momentum has become irresistible.' According to Tom Inglis, one of Ireland's leading cultural critics, the dance represented the victory of 'the modern over the traditional'. It was as if Irish viewers felt that they were no longer bound by inherited shibboleths, but were free to pick and choose which traditions they wanted to retain, and which they wanted to drop, or adapt. In that respect, this seven-minute dance led to a genuine sense of liberation.

'Rock 'n' Roll Kids' enjoyed some solid chart success across Europe, but the reaction to *Riverdance* went into the stratosphere. In Ireland, the single of Bill Whelan's score stayed at the number one slot in the charts for eighteen weeks, selling more than 150,000 copies – an extraordinary number that has never been equalled. Elsewhere, the reaction was so powerful that it did not take long before the idea of basing a whole stage show on the seven-minute act was floated. It was not surprising that RTÉ was asked to invest in this production, or that the station – and Liam Miller in particular – was more than willing to do so.

I attended a meeting at which the level of the station's investment was discussed. Everyone around that table wanted RTÉ to make a very substantial commitment to the forthcoming spectacular. However, it was pointed out by one of RTÉ's legal executives that we would have to seek official approval from the Department of Finance if we wanted to make a commercial investment beyond a relatively limited amount.

I remember someone asking how long it would take to be given such approval. One of our financial executives shook his head wearily: he estimated that it would probably take many months before we were informed of the Department's decision. Since the timetable for the *Riverdance* stage show could not afford that sort of delay, we chose to proceed immediately with the maximum investment that RTÉ was permitted by law. Over the following years, that modest sum proved to be the best commercial investment that the station ever made. In fact, the dividends from the station's financial commitment to *Riverdance* more than paid for the cost of all four of the Eurovision contests that RTÉ produced in the 1990s.

The stage show of the seven-minute interval act was developed in the months that followed the contest, and it eventually became a worldwide phenomenon. However,

Michael Flatley left the production in 1995, due to disagreements with the producers over issues relating to creative control. The next year, he devised, produced and directed a new show called *Lord of the Dance*. It opened at the Point Theatre – the scene of his earlier triumph – in July of 1996, and also became a huge global hit.

The remarkable impact of *Riverdance* has sometimes obscured other impressive features of this final. In reality, the entire show was extremely well produced – and at a fraction of the cost of the Millstreet event. The theme of the river – which was central to the interval act – had been introduced at the start of the contest, and was developed unobtrusively but consistently throughout the rest of the show. The sense of drama that infused the production included the entrance of the two presenters, who arrived on stage from a bridge that descended in unexpected fashion – and to Gerry Ryan's great anxiety – from the roof of the theatre. The stage, which had been designed by Paula Farrell, was four times larger than the one at Millstreet, and made highly effective use of a changing night sky backdrop.

Because so many countries wished to participate in the 1994 contest, the EBU had ruled that the five lowest-placed countries from the preceding year's contest could not take part. This meant that Belgium, Denmark, Israel, Slovenia and Turkey were all excluded. However, that did not mean that there was no innovation in the ways in which votes were cast. For the first time in Eurovision history, voting was done via satellite – instead of by telephone – which meant that viewers could actually see the spokespersons onscreen.

When the voting began, the Hungarian singer won the maximum of twelve points from the first three juries, and it looked as if Hungary were on the way to victory in its first Eurovision appearance. However, this turned out to be a false dawn, and it soon became obvious that Paul Harrington and Charlie McGettigan would romp home and win by a hefty margin – and that Ireland would become the first country to win the contest for a third successive year.

More than twenty years have passed since the 1994 Eurovision, but *Riverdance* and *Lord of the Dance* are both still on the road – and both shows are still able to draw huge and adoring audiences. Irish dancing is no longer confined to Ireland or even to the Irish diaspora, but has taken a firm root in new territories – such as Argentina, Japan and Russia. Moya Doherty and Michael Flatley may have gone their separate ways since they worked together in Dublin's Point Theatre – but the creative vision and courage they both displayed back then has been thoroughly vindicated, and continues to inspire.

17.
Still There

Following three consecutive victories, the 1995 contest was once again held in Ireland. Soon after the 1994 Eurovision, I was appointed Assistant Director of TV Programmes – which meant that I had less involvement in Ireland's participation in the next contest. I also left the EBU's Eurovision Steering Committee. I was more than happy at that point to move on, and felt that I had played my part in helping to change the way in which RTÉ approached the Eurovision. However, that does not mean that I was able to resist maintaining some connection with the event: there is an addictive quality about the Eurovision that can make it hard to break away from the contest for good.

I was not involved in the selection of the Irish entries for the 1995 national contest, which took place in the Opera House in Cork, and was presented for the fifth year in a row by Pat Kenny. There were eight acts, and ten regional juries. The winner was Eddie Friel, who came from Belfast. The two composers also came from Northern Ireland. The

155

song they had entered was a ballad called 'Dreamin'' – and the lyrics were relatively unusual in that they did not refer to any sort of romantic relationship. Instead, the song was about exactly what was suggested in its title. Eddie Friel sang about being in a dream, and how much he enjoyed the experience of dreaming.

This was not a power ballad, or any kind of showstopper, but a slow air that was gentle and inoffensive. Eddie Friel also seemed a pleasant and likeable performer, but not one who looked to me like a potential winner of the Eurovision. In fact, the only real media attention that Eddie or his song attracted before the contest was when its writers were accused of plagiarism.

The American folk singer-songwriter Julie Felix had enjoyed great success in the UK in the late 1960s and early 1970s. One of the songs she had written and performed in those years was called 'Moonlight'. Within a few days of Eddie winning Ireland's song contest, Julie Felix's song was being played on radio alongside 'Dreamin'' – and the similarities of melody, theme and lyrics seemed obvious. This raised an acute dilemma for RTÉ, since we had to determine if we would allow the song and its singer to remain in the contest.

We asked RTÉ's Head of Music, Gareth Hudson, to provide a forensic analysis of the two compositions. He reported back that the number and sequence of identical notes in both songs meant that Julie Felix could claim with some reason that 'Moonlight' had been plagiarised. We also met the two songwriters of 'Dreamin'', who assured us that they had no intention of copying Julie Felix's song. As they pointed out, it had not been a major hit, and was almost a quarter of a century old. They told us that they couldn't recall ever having heard 'Moonlight', and we found them credible and convincing.

The conclusion we reached was that the similarities between the two ballads were so fundamental that the writers of Eddie's song might have been influenced – even if unconsciously – by the prior composition. When she was interviewed, Julie Felix was adamant that the song Eddie Friel was performing in the Eurovision was one that she had written. However, she also made it clear that she did not propose to take any legal action in advance of the contest. This meant that, if any pre-emptive move were to be made, it would have to be at RTÉ's initiative. Our reasoning was that Julie Felix would only sue if 'Dreamin'' won the Eurovision. In the professional opinion of both Liam Miller and myself, it was unlikely that Eddie would win the contest, so we decided to let his entry go ahead.

After the enormous success of the 1994 Eurovision, it was almost inevitable that the following year's final would seem like something of an anticlimax. Indeed, RTÉ indicated to the EBU that, in the event of yet another Irish win, the station did not intend to stage the final. That did not mean, however, that RTÉ had selected a song that was designed to fail – or that the production team did not give the final the same level of commitment as in previous years. It was also untrue that staging three Eurovision finals in a row had bankrupted RTÉ. Apart from the revenue from RTÉ's ownership of the video rights to *Riverdance*, all of the three contests had received substantial commercial sponsorship, as well as subvention from the EBU.

The 1995 Eurovision was again located in Dublin's Point Theatre, and the first voice heard was that of Mary Robinson, the Irish President, in an extract from her speech at her inauguration in 1990. She quoted some of the poet Yeats' most famous lines: 'I am of Ireland', she recited, 'Come dance with me in Ireland.' In the montage that followed, we were reminded that – for the first time in several decades – the guns of both loyalists and republicans in Northern Ireland were silent, and the island was at peace. The Eurovision was presented that year by Mary Kennedy – who had first auditioned for the same role in the 1981 final. She welcomed the audience to what she described as having 'almost become the annual Eurovision Song Contest in Ireland.' Mary did an excellent job – perhaps, that was because she looked as if she were thoroughly enjoying every moment.

The first Eurovision had taken place in 1956, which meant that 1995 marked the fortieth staging of the contest. The EBU had decided that this would also mark its fortieth anniversary – which struck me as a little strange, and rather like celebrating the new millennium in 1999, rather than 2000. At any rate, the occasion was celebrated in the opening of the show with a four-minute montage of memorable moments from previous years, in which the Irish victories featured prominently. Two of Ireland's winners were in the audience that night: Dana and Johnny Logan. It was Johnny's birthday, and – in a rather embarrassing gesture – the audience were persuaded to sing 'Happy Birthday' to him. Eddie Friel was the second act to perform, and, when the voting got underway, it soon became clear that RTÉ was unlikely to encounter any legal action from Julie Felix: Eddie ended up in fourteenth place with just forty-four points.

After the phenomenal impact of *Riverdance*, there was great anticipation of the interval act. John McHugh was the producer of the contest, and he was acutely aware that, as far as the Irish audience was concerned, staging the Eurovision had lost some of its novelty value. 'Millstreet was the first final to be staged outside Dublin, and the *Riverdance* show was the first to be staged in the Point Theatre', he told me, 'So there was a definite sense that we were following in their footsteps.' In order to avoid direct comparison with *Riverdance*, John was determined that the interval act would not include dancing of any description – which I think was a very wise decision. Instead, the plan had been to feature an Irish singer-songwriter of international renown. However – as in Millstreet – the intended artist chose to withdraw without explanation and at a relatively late stage.

RTÉ responded by commissioning the distinguished composer Mícheál Ó Súilleabháin to write an original piece of music, and this was performed by the station's concert orchestra. It also featured some traditional musicians – as well as Brian Kennedy and Moya Brennan as soloists, and a number of Benedictine monks from Glenstal Abbey in County Limerick. The name of the piece was '*Lumen*' – the Latin for 'light' – which seemed a somewhat ironic title, since the stage remained shrouded in semi-darkness for most of the performance.

In many respects, '*Lumen*' was a wonderful composition, but it was debatable whether it was well suited to the occasion. Eurovision interval acts are part of a popular entertainment show, but where *Riverdance* had been exhilarating and rousing, the mood of '*Lumen*' was sombre and reflective. Perhaps it also strove for cultural significance a little too earnestly.

The Swedish entry had been the favourite to win the contest, but it was the Norwegian group, Secret Garden, that ended up with the most points. Their entry was the only song ever to win the Eurovision with what was essentially an instrumental piece: it only contained twenty-four words – twelve at the beginning and twelve at the end – and the central melody of the performance was carried by a solo violin. Secret Garden included a strong Irish dimension, since the group's violinist, Fionnuala Sherry, was Irish – in fact, she had once been a member of the RTÉ Concert Orchestra – so there was a strong sense that Ireland was still part of the winning act.

After Eddie Friel's relatively poor result, there was further speculation that Ireland had deliberately entered a weak song because the station did not want to win the contest. This theory also cropped up in several subsequent years, and even formed part of a plotline in a very funny episode of the sitcom *Father Ted*. It is, of course, very flattering to RTÉ to believe that the station could win the Eurovision every year if it only chose to do so, and that Ireland's failures must be part of some deliberate conspiracy. But, sadly, it is quite untrue.

In truth, RTÉ's revenues were never higher than in the first decade of this century – and the station had never been in a better financial position to host the contest – but that decade also coincides with Ireland's worst-ever results. In any case, the Eurovision in Oslo – the year after Eddie Friel's entry – provided concrete proof that RTÉ had not yet lost the will to win.

18.
The Last Hurrah?

Brendan Graham had written 'Rock 'n' Roll Kids' – the winner of the 1994 Eurovision. Two years later, he was back with another song submitted for the national contest. This one was called 'The Voice', and it was written in a very different musical idiom to his previous winner. While 'Rock 'n' Roll Kids' had been a bitter-sweet pop ballad, 'The Voice' sounded as if were a track from a New Age album. While the lyrics of 'Rock 'n' Roll Kids' had suggested a fading relationship, those of 'The Voice' were more abstract, and did not carry any hint of a romantic affair. The instrumentation of the first song had worked within the framework of modern pop music. The second one involved traditional Irish instruments – such as the *bodhrán* drum, the tin whistle and the fiddle. One song was set firmly in the present; the other identified itself as timeless. When I first heard 'Rock 'n' Roll Kids', I thought that it had a very good chance of winning the Eurovision: when I first heard 'The Voice', I was not so sure.

Brendan had submitted a demo recording of his new song, which featured the traditional folk group, Dervish, and the song had been selected as a finalist in the national contest. However, there was no obligation on the composer to use the same performer in the national final, and it was not uncommon for changes of personnel to be made. Shortly before the national contest took place, Brendan Graham attended a Christmas performance by the Anúna chorale. On this occasion, Brendan was greatly impressed by Eimear Quinn, one of the ensemble's members. Anúna had been part of the *Riverdance* interval act in 1994, but Eimear had not been part of the group at that time. After hearing her sing 'Winter, Fire and Snow' – a song he had written, and which had already been recorded by Anúna – Brendan decided she was ideally asuited to performing 'The Voice.'

She did so in the national final in the Point Theatre – on the same stage where 'Rock 'n' Roll Kids' had won. Eimear's performance was extremely simple, but highly effective. She hardly moved during the song – which threw the audience's attention onto her vocal delivery. Eimear clearly possessed great talent, and made an immediate impression. She was also a very good-looking young woman, and, when it came to the regional voting, it was no surprise that she won the contest by a considerable margin, and would represent Ireland in Oslo.

For several years, the EBU had been struggling to find a system of selection for the Grand Final that would meet the wishes and needs of all its members. There was general agreement that the final could not last much more than three hours. Agreement had also been reached that the maximum number of countries that could participate was around twenty-two. Since more than that number wished to take part, the EBU had tried to devise a method of eliminating some of them in advance of the Grand Final. Over the next few years, several different systems were tested and found wanting, but perhaps none of them proved less fit for purpose than the one that followed in 1996.

Audio tapes of the twenty-nine countries who had submitted entries to the Eurovision were sent to juries in each of them. From those tapes, each jury selected the ten songs that it thought deserved to compete in the final. When the jury votes were collated by the EBU in Geneva, they determined which twenty-one other countries would join Norway – which had automatic entry as the host nation – in the Grand Final. It is hard to imagine that this method of selection had been devised by people with any previous experience of broadcasting.

In effect, this selection system meant that several artists – who had gone through the painful process of national selection – had their hopes of competing in the Eurovision snuffed out by a phone call. These acts had already won their own national contests, but they were not even given the opportunity to perform in front of any jury. To make matters worse, the precise results of the juries' votes were neither televised, nor revealed to the general public – since it was believed this might influence the result of the Grand Final. In other words, for seven of the countries competing, the method of selection was not only deeply disappointing, but had been conducted behind closed doors. It all seemed unfair and undemocratic – and its impact was profoundly anticlimactic.

Germany was particularly aggrieved by its abrupt elimination from the contest since it was not only one of the Eurovision's most loyal members – but one of its major financial contributors. In fact, it was the fear of losing German and other major subventions that led the EBU to drop this system of selection from all future contests. It was, in any case, almost inevitable that the results of the juries' deliberations were leaked. This established that Eimear Quinn had polled extremely well; in fact, her song had rated second among the international juries. Since their votes had been based on audio recordings, the visual impact of Eimear's performance was also likely to ensure that 'The Voice' would be a strong contender in the Grand Final the following month. Indeed, from this point I thought it likely that Ireland would win the Contest for the fourth time in just five years.

The Norwegian staging of the Eurovision saw an attempt to introduce some new elements to the contest. One of these was a short 'good luck' message delivered to each national act by a political leader or state official from their native country. In the case of Ireland, Taoiseach John Bruton delivered the message. Other well-wishers included the Secretary of Education in the Netherlands, the Spanish Ambassador to Norway, and the Speaker of the Finnish Parliament. I found this eclectic collection of apparatchiks an unfortunate innovation. For the most part, they were unknown to the contest's viewers, and – with their mirthless smiles, and wooden deliveries – they seemed likely to remain that way. I am glad to report that this Norwegian experiment has never been repeated.

Eimear sang seventeenth in the final. Her dark dress from Ireland's national contest had been exchanged for a flowing white gown, which added to the ethereal feel of her performance. Once again, it was hard not to be impressed by the purity and conviction of her voice. The UK entry – Gina G with 'Give A Little Bit More' – was at the other end of the spectrum. Her song was old-school disco, and there was no need for its singer to emulate Eimear's outstanding vocal gifts. Gina G and her backing singers wore extremely short miniskirts, and their dance routine had an explicit erotic dimension. That sort of sexual display has seldom worked well with a Eurovision audience – at least, in terms of votes – and this contest was no exception: Gina G only managed to finish in eighth place.

Eimear, on the other hand, polled well from the outset. Indeed, some spectators began to leave the stadium early once the result seemed a foregone conclusion. Eimear ended up winning the contest by a large margin, and was awarded the maximum of twelve points by seven of the national juries. However, there were some complaints afterwards that the juries – which were mainly composed of those working in the music or entertainment industries – were not representative of the European public. In that context, it might be worth mentioning that, while Gina G's song might not have appealed to the Eurovision juries, it turned out to be extremely popular with pop music fans across Europe, and became a major international hit. This was the last time that the result of the contest was determined solely by juries. In the years that followed, the EBU sought to balance the role played by national juries with the introduction of public televoting.

Since winning the Eurovision, Eimear has enjoyed a successful recording and performing career, and has appeared on television many times. There was one other unexpected bonus from the Eurovision: she later married Noel Curran – the head of the Irish delegation in Oslo.

By 1996, Ireland had won the song contest a record seven times – and four of those wins had taken place in the space of five years. In the aftermath of the Oslo contest, BBC News ran a report which suggested – with heavy-handed irony – that this sequence of victories had become something of an embarrassment to RTÉ, and to Ireland. A series of vox pops conducted on the streets of Dublin gave the impression that the Irish public as a whole was sick and tired of winning the Eurovision. On the basis of this report, there seemed to be a national consensus that it was time to 'give someone else a go'. If those people genuinely wanted RTÉ not to have to stage another final – which I doubt – they did not have much more to endure.

19.
Goodnight from Dublin

The 1997 Eurovision was the fourth contest that RTÉ had hosted in the course of just five years, and there was undoubtedly some sense of fatigue inside the station. This was caused less by the financial demands that the final incurred than by the demands it made in terms of creative talent, personnel and equipment. In future Eurovisions, much of the technical support needed to stage the contests would be outsourced to independent suppliers. Should Ireland ever win another Grand Final, RTÉ would have to follow a similar route – there are no longer any suitable outside broadcast units in the station – but, in 1997, RTÉ still planned to produce the event out of its own internal resources. Of course, the station was also committed to making a memorable Eurovision, and to continue its tradition of developing the contest as a major entertainment event.

Ireland's national contest was held in Limerick. Once again, there were eight finalists, and a similar number of regional juries. The winner was Marc Roberts singing an up-tempo number called 'Mysterious Woman'. The song tells a story – not only of unrequited love, but of undeclared love. The singer apparently saw a woman at an airport, with *'a ticket in your hand'*, and was instantly attracted to her.

In the era of iPhone apps, he might have been able to contact her and arrange some sort of hook-up. But back in 1997, he could only speculate about the sort of person she might be. However, even by the standards of 1997, his guesswork was rather naive. He wonders if she comes from an exotic location, such as *'the streets of Paris'*, or *'the coast of Italy'* – or even *'the gulf of Araby'*. As the song ends, the *'mysterious woman'* has been called to board her plane, and the singer is left alone in the terminal, with his *'bitter-sweet'* memories. In a curious way, the lyrics echo the rather more complex themes of 'Terminal 3' – Linda Martin's song in the 1984 contest.

After the debacle of the previous year's pre-selection process, the EBU had introduced a new system of elimination. It might have been less arbitrary – and less cruel – than that used in 1996, but it was not without its own problems. The goal was still to contain the contest within a duration of three hours by limiting the number of countries competing in the final. Under the new arrangement, those countries with the lowest average scores over the previous four years would be excluded from the 1997 contest, and those with the lowest averages over the previous five years would be excluded from the 1998 contest. However, some exceptions would be made so that every country excluded for one year would automatically be allowed to participate in the following year's contest.

It was not – to put it mildly – the most elegant of solutions, and it was one that I found difficult to explain in casual conversation. In some ways, it was characteristic of the bureaucratic nature of the EBU – some of whose members had little direct experience of TV production. However, it did achieve its primary objective, which was to hold the number of finalists to an agreed limit.

There was the usual intense debate within RTÉ about who should present the 1997 Eurovision. From an early stage, there was strong support for Carrie Crowley. Carrie had started her TV career working on one of the station's children's programmes. She had fluent Irish, and worked with the (future) comedian Dara Ó Briain on Irish-language editions of the series *Echo Island*. Later, she had starred in a preschool series called *The Morbegs*. In many ways, she seemed like a safe pair of hands: she had a warm and attractive presence on screen. She was experienced in live performance, and she was also not one of the more predictable choices.

Presenting the Eurovision would form something of a watershed in Carrie's career – but, in several respects, it proved to be a mixed blessing. In the aftermath of the contest, she became overexposed on television: a recurring weakness of RTÉ's when dealing with new talent. Carrie starred in what seemed like a rapid succession of health, cookery and chat shows – as well as working regularly on RTÉ radio. Eventually, she distanced herself from her work in television to follow an acting career – even describing herself as an 'accidental tourist' on Irish TV.

It had also been decided at an early stage that Carrie would work with a male co-presenter. But there was some internal debate about who that person should be.

The producer of the 1997 Eurovision was Noel Curran – later to become the Director-General of RTÉ – and he was in favour of using the pop singer Ronan Keating as the co-host. In 1997, Ronan was already famous in Ireland and the UK as the lead singer of the boy band, Boyzone. He had also started to take his first steps in establishing a successful solo career.

There was little doubt that Ronan would prove a popular choice of presenter. However, I was also aware that, when his name was first proposed, Ronan was still a teenager. At the time of the contest, Carrie was in her early thirties. She was not only older, but taller than Ronan, and I wondered how their combination might work on screen. It would, of course, have been wrong simply to conform to the expectations of gender stereotypes, and it was pointed out to me by Noel and Liam Miller that RTÉ wanted to attract new and younger viewers to the show, and that Ronan Keating was more than likely to achieve that goal. I was also reminded that Ronan was mature for his years, with a wealth of experience of performing in front of large audiences, and that he would not be overawed by the occasion.

It is true that Ronan proved to be remarkably self-possessed when it came to presenting the contest, and it is also true that his involvement brought a new dimension and new viewers to the event. However, I still feel that the combination of Ronan and Carrie was not entirely successful – though not for reasons of age or height. There was little on-air chemistry between them, and I don't believe that their interaction worked greatly to either's advantage. Ronan also wrote and performed the song featured in the interval act in the 1997 contest – when he was joined by the other members of Boyzone. Overall, this was a spectacular production, with a stunning set, and it rated alongside the previous finals that RTÉ had staged.

This was also the first contest in which televoting contributed directly to the final result. Even though this only applied to five countries in 1997, it would soon become an integral feature of the Eurovision – with significant consequences for the event. The results of this first exercise in televoting were revealing – since, in some cases, the public vote was very different from the points awarded by the traditional juries. In the case of Iceland, for example, sixteen of its eighteen points came from the five countries whose populations had voted by telephone. For the first time, Germany awarded Turkey its top score of twelve points, and this was attributed to the large number of Turkish *Gastarbeiter* who had voted by phone for their native country.

Marc Roberts finished as runner-up in the final – which was a better placing than many, including myself, had expected. However, it was not a close contest: unusually for a runner-up, Marc only received one top score of twelve, and he finished a full seventy points behind the winner. The voting was dominated from the very beginning by Katrina and the Waves, an American band representing the UK, with their anthem 'Love Shine A Light'. The British entry scored an unprecedented 227 points. It received votes from all the participating countries – including ten sets of the maximum points – and is still regarded as one of the most successful of all Eurovision winners.

There was some relief within RTÉ that Ireland had not been faced with the prospect of staging another contest in 1998. There was also pleasure that Marc Roberts had done so well, and an implicit confidence that it would not be long before the station was hosting another Grand Final. The question was not so much 'if?' as 'when?' The sad reality is that no Irish entry has equalled Marc Robert's result in the two decades that followed the 1997 contest.

20.
Back to the Future

RTÉ's 1998 national song contest took place, once again, in the studios at Montrose, and was presented by Pat Kenny. Eight acts participated, and the favourites to win were the Carter Twins – an act managed by Louis Walsh. The Carters' song had been written by Ronan Keating – from Boyzone – whom Louis also managed. However, Louis had to wait for more than a decade before another pair of identical twins that he managed would perform on the Eurovision stage.

In 1998, the regional juries voted for Dawn Martin, a young singer from Dundalk, County Louth, and her song posed an enigmatic question – 'Is Always Over Now?' The song was a ballad, sung from the perspective of a woman at the end of a relationship. She reminds her former lover – in a tortured use of syntax – that in the past, '*Always, you said, was me and you*', before posing her unanswerable question: '*Is always over now?*'

At the time of the national contest, Dawn was working as a hairdresser, and she was dismissed by Louis Walsh as 'an amateur'. There was further minor controversy when RTÉ decided that Dawn's two backing singers needed to be replaced before the final in Birmingham. Instead, the station chose two more experienced singers to back her – including Paul Harrington, the co-winner of the Eurovision in 1994. Some people believed that singing in English would be an advantage for Dawn – since this was the first year that the result of the contest would be determined largely by televoting.

It was also the first time that the use of an orchestra was optional, and seven of the twenty-five competing countries chose, instead, to use full backing tracks. Of greater significance was the breaking of a basic sexual taboo. For the first time, a transsexual performer, Dana International, was on stage: she represented Israel, and her song was called 'Diva'. Almost as much media attention was given to the German entry, Guido Horn, who was known for his unorthodox and extravagant stage performances. Many of his German fans even travelled outside their own country so that they could vote for Horn in the televote, and his involvement may also explain why the 1998 contest set record-breaking audience figures in Germany.

At the close of voting, Dawn Martin had received sixty-four points, and finished in ninth place. It was a close contest, but the 1998 Eurovision was won by Dana International – to the dismay and disgust of some Orthodox religious Israelis. She was crowned with a gold and silver trophy made by the Birmingham School of Jewellery. For her reprise performance, Dana had a change of outfit: she wore a revealing feather dress – which ensured her picture was on the front page of most European newspapers the following day. In his live commentary for RTÉ, Pat Kenny caused some controversy when he referred to her as 'he, she or it'.

Nineteen ninety-nine was another eventful year for the Eurovision, and saw some important changes in the rules of the contest. Following the limited introduction of public televoting the year before, 1998 saw a big expansion of that system of voting with almost every country adopting this method of awarding its points. Only those countries not technically able to use such a system continued with juries.

The obligation for every country to sing in one of its own national languages was also scrapped. Although Ireland's 'first official language' is Irish, only one entry in the previous thirty-four years had been in Irish. Instead, Ireland had been one of just three countries – the others were the UK and Malta – that were permitted by the EBU to sing in English. Over the years, some countries had tried to find ways in which they could work around this prohibition: using nonsense words, or claiming that some expressions – such as 'rock 'n' roll' – could no longer be considered as strictly English, since they had gained an international currency.

How much of an advantage the use of English had given Ireland is open to question. Eurovision lyrics – in any language – are often only memorable for their crass and clichéd sentiments. In that context, it may even be beneficial for the audience not to understand all of the words. Nonetheless, since this rule was abolished, the majority of Eurovision-winning songs have been written and sung in English.

Perhaps of greater importance was the EBU's decision that some countries would automatically be allowed to participate in the Grand Final every year. The 'Big' European countries – France, Germany, Spain, the UK, and, on occasion, Italy – are also the highest-paying members of the EBU, and it was considered unrealistic for them to continue to pay unless they were sure of a place in the televised event: as Terry Wogan drily commented, 'music and money talk'.

However, there was also a widespread belief among EBU members that the status of the Eurovision would be seriously undermined if some of the larger countries decided to withdraw from the contest. This was particularly true of the UK – not only because Britain was the only European country – with the exception of Ireland – whose popular music has genuine global appeal, but also because of the near-veneration in which other European public service broadcasters tend to hold the BBC.

The option of a live orchestra in the final was also closed. The first country to follow this change in the rules was Israel – the host nation in 1999. Since then, no live orchestras have been used in any of the Eurovision finals. Instead, all entries have been performed to pre-recorded backing tracks. This change was criticised at the time by Johnny Logan, who suggested that the lack of an orchestra would turn the event into a 'karaoke contest'. However, it seemed that the absence of an orchestra made little practical difference to the Eurovision, and it probably went unremarked by most viewers.

In fact, the removal of the orchestra from the Eurovision stage was to have a significant and long-term impact on the contest. Until then, set designers had been compelled to accommodate the presence of a large number of musicians, and this usually meant that the orchestra shared the stage with the performing acts. That limited the space available both for the acts and for the set designers. Once the orchestra had been removed from the equation, it meant that the designers had more space to play with, and this in turn encouraged the acts to fill the space by including other types of performers. Before long, these included dancers, mimes, acrobats, gymnasts and even trapeze artists.

This change in the Eurovision rules also meant the end of the involvement of Noel Kelehan in Ireland's Eurovision entries. Noel had conducted twenty-nine Eurovision songs – of which twenty-four were Irish entries. No one has ever participated on more occasions in the Eurovision contest than Noel, and it is highly unlikely that anyone ever will. He conducted five winning songs – another record – but Noel was also an accomplished jazz musician and composer. He had a dry and acute sense of humour. I had invited him to serve on the pre-selection jury for Ireland's national song contest, and his contribution over several years was always shrewd and succinct – and often very funny.

The 1990s had seen a decade of extraordinary success for Ireland in the contest. The run of winning acts was not the only source of pride for RTÉ: the national station had staged four of the world's biggest entertainment shows with consummate professional skill, creative flair and technical innovation. The image of Ireland that had been presented to the rest of Europe was one of a self-confident and sophisticated nation – at ease with its traditions, and not afraid to engage with the future.

The songs that had won four victories for Ireland were very different from each other – but they had all seemed part of the fabric of modern Irish society. Even 'Rock 'n' Roll Kids' – whose underlying impulse was clearly nostalgic – viewed the recent past from a contemporary perspective. So it may seem strange that, as Ireland entered the new millennium, the Irish Eurovision entries seemed to hark back to a bygone era.

In 1999, the winners of Ireland's national song contest were two sisters from Northern Ireland called the Mullans.

'When You Need Me' was a fairly gloomy ballad written by Bronagh Mullan. It was told from the viewpoint of a woman whose lover had ended their relationship. In the song, she pleads for him to let her *'feel his pain'*: an appeal which, I imagine, most men would find all-too-easy to resist. The rather bleak theme of the lyrics was accentuated by the low vocal pitch of the lead singer. Despite the despairing scenario expressed in the song, there was a surprising lack of emotion – or animation – in the performance of either of the two sisters.

The Mullans both wore dresses that were long, black and shapeless: the visual impact was downbeat, depressing and dated. When they performed in the Eurovision Final in Jerusalem, their shapeless black dresses had been exchanged for shapeless silver and gray ones – but the sisters' synchronised movements onstage still seemed extremely stilted, and their performance was still lacking in energy and emotional commitment.

The sense of constraint in the Mullans' performance appeared to be reflected in their attitude towards their fellow competitors. They were quoted in Irish newspapers as having said the Swedish entry, Charlotte Nilsson, looked like a 'porn star' – from which it can only be assumed that the Mullan sisters had led somewhat sheltered lives. Ms Nilsson responded in kind – claiming that the Mullans looked like a pair of 'pregnant nuns'. Perhaps she found further satisfaction when she won the competition – while the Mullans ended up in seventeenth place, with a miserable eighteen points gathered from just four countries.

Karen Mullan later claimed that they had been convinced by everyone in RTÉ's delegation that they were 'shoo-ins' to win the Eurovision. Her sister Bronagh agreed: suggesting that they had been 'pumped up to believe we'd win' by RTÉ, and that those false assurances made it harder to accept their crushing defeat. She reckoned that it had taken them 'about three months' to recover from the shock of getting so few votes. In this instance, I think the sisters' criticism of RTÉ is unfair: members of the Irish delegation, after all, were unlikely to tell the Mullans that they had little chance of winning the contest.

The Mullans were succeeded as the Irish entry in the 2000 contest by Eamonn Toal, singing 'Millennium of Love'. Given the year, there was an obvious topicality in the theme of his song, and this may have worked to Eamonn's advantage with the televoters in Ireland's national song contest. In fact, his song turned out to be the only entry in that year's Eurovision to make any reference to the new millennium. That could have been because no one else had thought of it – or it could have been because writing about the millennium had seemed too predictable, corny and stale.

It is doubtful, in any case, that the lyrics of the Irish song could have won it many votes. Even by the woeful standards of some Eurovision entries, the words were extremely weak – indeed, it was hard to believe that they had been written by someone whose first language was English. Eamonn lamented man's inhumanity to man, and urged us to celebrate a new millennium *where our footprints leave a harvest for the children'*. As Terry Wogan pointed out, in his laconic BBC commentary, this was rather a 'difficult concept to grasp'.

Eamon had previous form, so to speak, in the Eurovision: having sung backing vocals for Eddie Friel, Ireland's entry in the 1995 contest. His father – Tommy 'Fat Sam' Toal – had also been involved in Ireland's showbiz scene, and his legacy was clearly of great importance to his son. When he competed in Ireland's national song contest, Eamonn said he had felt his dad sitting on his shoulder. He had kept his father's photograph in his pocket throughout the contest, and he later attributed his success to its presence. He promised that his father's photo would also be in his pocket when he sang in Stockholm, and he reckoned that he had 'a big chance of winning'.

As it turned out, Eamonn managed to finish sixth in the Stockholm final. This was the best result that Ireland was to achieve in course of the following decade, but it was noted that only twelve of the ninety-two points that Eamonn scored came from countries that had formerly been part of the Soviet bloc. The apparent failure to appeal to Eastern European voters was to preoccupy RTÉ in the years ahead.

Despite the rather old-fashioned feel of Eamonn Toal's performance, RTÉ was reasonably happy with the outcome. After the Mullan sisters' wretched result, it seemed that the station was back on track as far as the Eurovision was concerned. However, this hope proved to be misplaced. The next year's national song contest took place in RTÉ's studios in February 2001, and was hosted by Louise Loughman. Seven songs were presented, and a new and complicated system of regional televoting was used to select the winner.

This voting system led to a surprising and – to many – an unfair result. The act that received the most votes from the Irish public was a boy band called InFocus – with 13,356 votes. An all-girl band called Fe-Mail came second with 12,271 votes. Third was Gary O'Shaughnessy – who had polled 11,653 votes. However, the final result was not calculated simply on the basis of numbers. Instead, those numbers were adjusted to fit a regional breakdown. On this reckoning, Gary O'Shaughnessy was declared the winner.

Gary had previously competed in Ireland's national song contests in 1997, when he had finished third, and in 1999, when he had placed fifth. This time, his winning song, 'Without You', was a ballad – like most previous Eurovision entries from Ireland. It had been written by a bus driver from Northern Ireland, and the lyrics were a fairly standard collection of love song clichés: the gist of which was the impossibility of the singer *'going on'* without the love of his partner. The 2001 contest was held in the Parken Stadium in Copenhagen, where more than 38,000 spectators watched the final – a record number in Eurovision history. Later, some of the audience protested that that they couldn't see the stage properly, and some of the performers also complained that they had felt dwarfed by the huge size of the arena.

The two hosts of the final delivered all of their commentary in English rhyming couplets – a humorous approach that ran out of steam (and humour) very quickly. This may help to explain why Terry Wogan, in his BBC commentary, made caustic remarks about the presenters throughout the show – referring to them repeatedly as 'Dr Death and the Tooth Fairy'. The Danes were so offended by this that the BBC eventually had to issue an apology. When it came to Ireland's turn to perform, Gary was introduced by Wogan as a 'lawnmower salesman', adding, with measured understatement, that 'the odds on this one are a little long'.

Whatever about the odds, there can be no doubt that Gary O'Shaughnessy gave the song his full commitment: if anything, he seemed rather overexcited, and appeared to struggle at times to stay in key. When it came to the voting, the Mullans' result suddenly began to seem quite respectable: Gary only scored six points, from just two countries – at that time, the worst-ever Irish performance – and Ireland finished in twenty-first place. This was, of course, a great personal disappointment for the singer and the composer of the song, but it also had implications for Ireland's immediate future in the Eurovision.

It had been decided in advance of the 2001 contest that the qualifying scheme used since 1997 would be dropped. Under that scheme, the criterion used to determine which countries could participate in the Eurovision had been based on their average score across the previous five years. Under the new rules, only the countries placed in the top fifteen in the final would qualify for next year's event. The other slots in the 2002 contest would be filled by the 'Big Four' – Germany, France, the UK and Spain – and by those countries that had been excluded from competing in the 2001 contest under the previous rules.

It was clearly a complicated and inadequate solution to some of the problems that the rapid expansion of the Eurovision had created – and it was bad news for Ireland. Under the 'five-year average' method, Ireland would have qualified for the 2002 contest. Under the new rules, Gary O'Shaughnessy's low score had ensured Ireland's elimination. The only crumb of comfort was that Ireland had been guaranteed a place in the 2003 Eurovision Song Contest.

It took some time for all of this to sink in with the Irish public, but there was an immediate response from Louis Walsh. He claimed that RTÉ had abnegated its responsibilities, and had simply lost interest in the contest. He believed this was why RTÉ had 'allowed people to enter who have no previous television exposure'. As it happened, Louis believed he had the answer to the station's problems. 'Bryan McFadden,' he claimed, 'had written a song that would have been perfect for the Eurovision.' At that time, McFadden was a member of Westlife – the boy band managed by Louis.

For the previous three years, the method of selection of Irish acts for the Eurovision had been unimaginative – to say the least – and, perhaps, that was reflected in the quality of those who were chosen by the Irish public to take part in the contest. It was clearly time for RTÉ to rethink, and the method of selection was about to be moved in a very different direction. Sadly, it was a path that would lead the station back to much the same impasse.

21.
Reality Bites

In a sense, 2002 was Year Zero for RTÉ as far as the Eurovision Song Contest was concerned. It is true that the national station had not entered a song for the competition in 1983, but, on that occasion, the decision had been taken by RTÉ itself, and of its own volition. This time around, Ireland's non-participation was not voluntary: the reason for exclusion was entirely due to the dismal performance of the Irish entry in the 2001 contest. Inside Ireland – and RTÉ – there were feelings of dismay and even disbelief.

In the previous decade, Ireland had been a major force in the Eurovision. The Song Contest had become one of the few international events that Irish people had grown accustomed to winning. Of course, fun was often made of the Eurovision – but, if the truth were known, very many Irish men and women felt some degree of pride in the number of times that their small island had carried off the Grand Prix. Given that history, not even to be allowed the chance to compete in the Eurovision was a kind of ignominy. It had been a sorry start to the new millennium, and RTÉ's executives were determined that Ireland would not be excluded from any further contests.

The last years of the twentieth century had seen the birth of a new genre in television entertainment. The wave of reality shows that hit our TV screens appealed to broadcasters for fairly obvious reasons: they were able to draw large audiences, and, since they featured amateurs, they were usually relatively cheap to make. It did not take too long before Irish production companies began to develop their own reality series. At first, these were either direct or indirect copies of formats that had already been proven to work on UK or other foreign channels. But Irish producers soon began to adapt these to the tastes and needs of Irish audiences. Initially, RTÉ had been slow to embrace the new genre, but, in time, the station would do so with the zeal of the convert.

One of the first reality shows to establish an international franchise had begun its TV life in New Zealand. In several respects, *Popstars* was a traditional talent show. However, it was presented as a kind of observational documentary. The original series had followed the formation of a pop group – all the way from open auditions to the release of its first single. To begin with, there was no public vote, and the final composition of the group was determined solely by a panel of expert judges – then it was realised how much income could be generated by involving the audience in telephone voting.

The format of *Popstars* was sold all over the world, and the Irish version was made for RTÉ by ShinAwil, an independent production company. The show proved hugely popular, and the first single released by the winning Irish group – Six – sold over 100,000 copies. Only Bill Whelan's *Riverdance* has sold more in Ireland's musical history.

Following the success of *Popstars*, ShinAwil adapted its format to produce a new and different type of national song contest. The new series was called *You're a Star*, and, over a period of twenty odd weeks, thousands of young and unknown singers competed for the opportunity to represent Ireland in the 2003 Eurovision contest in Riga. Auditions were held all over the country, and the finalists – who came to Dublin to perform live – included some who had been voted for by the public, and some who had been selected by a panel of judges.

The series was fronted by the (then) leading presenter of Today FM radio, Ray D'Arcy. The first judging panel was made up of the veteran composer Phil Coulter; the former member of the girl band, Atomic Kitten, Kerry Katona; and a successful independent TV producer, Darren Smith. The series aired at peak time on Sunday nights, and the finals were broadcast live from the Helix Theatre in Dublin City University.

In most respects, the format of *You're a Star* seemed very close to many other reality talent shows. However, there were also some important distinctions. From the beginning, the show's producers actively encouraged regional support for each of the different finalists. In effect, they were tapping into the culture of rural Ireland, and the importance of localism and county loyalty to organisations such as the Gaelic Athletic Association. By harnessing local identity to the selection process, the support for individual singers became more passionate, and the competition grew more intense. By the time the final stages of the contest were reached, the show had taken on some of the fevered atmosphere of an All-Ireland hurling or football final.

All of this led to a well-produced and dynamic television series, which gained a large and enthusiastic audience, and was of clear strategic value to RTÉ's weekend schedule. There was understandable delight within the station at the success of the series. But, in all the excitement, some of its more problematic features seem to have been overlooked. The Eurovision, after all, was still supposed to be a song contest, and the purpose of *You're a Star* was – as its title proclaimed – to find a future star. In fact, the songs that were competing to be Ireland's entry in the Eurovision were not introduced to the voting public until the last few weeks of the TV competition.

In other words, the Irish public was primarily voting for the singer, and not for the song that would go to the final of the contest. The singers were only introduced to their songs in the final stages of the series. Indeed, the eventual winner, Mickey Joe Harte, later told me that he almost walked away from his chance at Eurovision glory because he did not warm to the song that he had been given to perform.

The majority of the singers taking part in this talent series were young and inexperienced. Harte was one of the oldest contestants – at nearly thirty – and one of the few with a professional background in the music industry. He had even taken part in two of RTÉ's earlier talent shows in the previous decade, and he later claimed to have entered *You're a Star* without knowing how it would differ from the previous models.

The most devoted fans of reality TV shows tend to be found among younger viewers – who often watch with their smartphones at the ready – and the voting process seems to have a particular appeal to teenage girls. However, that demographic is not typical of the viewers who usually vote in a Eurovision Final. The profile of those voters is not so strongly gender-based, and it crosses many age groups.

In other words, the Eurovision contest appeals to quite a different constituency to a reality show, and is likely to produce a very different result.

RTÉ's new talent show also tended to attract amateurs to compete. Many professionals felt, with some reason, that they had too much to lose by competing in such an open contest. The impact of this was obscured when amateurs were competing with amateurs, but the underlying lack of experience was to be cruelly exposed when the winners of RTÉ's reality show came up against more seasoned performers in the actual Eurovision. It could be argued that the failure by RTÉ to foresee this outcome inflicted some personal and professional damage on some of the performers who managed to qualify for the Eurovision.

None of those factors affected the runaway success of the reality TV contest. As the final approached, public excitement in Ireland seemed sky-high. In the light of this mass enthusiasm, RTÉ decided to extend the voting window for the contest's final show from one to three hours. The station said that this decision had been taken following the 'unprecedented response' to the semi-final: 'Last weekend,' an RTÉ press release explained, '635,000 votes were registered in the 1-hour voting period, and an even greater response is anticipated for the final.'

The final ran across two successive nights, and RTÉ reported that more than 1.3 million votes had been cast. To put the size of that vote in perspective, when Gary O'Shaughnessy won the contest to represent Ireland just two years earlier, the total number of votes cast by the Irish public for all of the acts had barely reached 50,000.

This time, the huge public response ensured that Mickey Joe Harte would defeat Simon Casey, who had also competed unsuccessfully in the previous season's

Popstars show. Harte's song rocketed to the top of the Irish charts – where it stayed for many weeks – and it became the best-selling single of the year. According to the *Sunday World*, Harte had gone from being an 'unknown singer-songwriter on the chicken-and-chips circuit to becoming one of the most talked-about entertainers in Ireland.'

Harte was accorded a civic reception by Sligo County Council. Its chairman stated proudly that there was 'no reason to believe that Mickey Joe will not emerge as the next in a distinguished line of Eurovision winners'. Against this background, it would be hard to overestimate the public enthusiasm when Mickey Joe Harte departed for Riga. The motto that Latvia had chosen for their first Eurovision was *Magical Rendezvous* – which seemed to match the level of expectation in Ireland that Mickey Joe would return from Riga in triumph.

'We've Got the World' – the winning song that he had initially been reluctant to sing – was a relatively upbeat number. It was true that the lyrics were fairly conventional – and involved Harte assuring his lover that she was the reason his world turned on its axis – but they seemed to work well enough within the context of Eurovision. Harte was the third act to perform in the final – normally considered a good position – and he gave a polished and confident performance. His act had hardly changed since the *You're a Star* final – though he had now acquired a smart black suit, and a colourful T-shirt. Back in Ireland, many of the hundreds of thousands of those who had voted to send Harte to Riga must have believed that another Irish win was on the cards.

There was great disappointment, therefore, when Ireland finished halfway down the field of entries – in equal eleventh place with Germany. At the time, this result was considered a demoralising anticlimax after all the months of competition. A few years later and it would have been viewed as quite satisfactory, but in 2003, it was as if a bubble had suddenly been burst.

In retrospect, it is clear that Harte's chances of success in the contest had been misjudged, or seriously overhyped by RTÉ. The reality of Harte's disappointing result could have been an opportunity for the station to reassess whether or not *You're a Star* was the best vehicle to identify a strong contender for the Eurovision. But it was highly unlikely that RTÉ would abandon the format that had been developed in the first season of this reality show: the size and composition of the viewing audience it had delivered must have seemed too important and too desirable to be given up after just one shot, and just one apparent failure. Instead, RTÉ reaffirmed its commitment to select the Eurovision entry through the same method and the same show.

One of the judges in the second series of *You're a Star* was Louis Walsh. Before the new season began, he gave a typically direct assessment of what he wanted: 'People who look good, and who aren't controversial.' He was equally forthright about the future he envisaged for the two finalists in the previous season. 'There's a chance,' he said, 'that Mickey Harte 'could do OK in the UK. It'll be tough for him though.' He was more dismissive of Simon Casey's future career: 'He might be a local hero, but that'll be it. He's not marketable abroad.' He admitted that he had no interest in managing either singer: 'I don't think they will sell many records, and each of my acts has to have the potential to be really successful.' For some, this seemed a harsh assessment, but, sadly, it proved to be shrewd, and well-judged.

The second series came on air in November 2003. This time, thirteen singers competed in the Dublin finals. Ten of these were chosen through regional audition heats, and the judging panel gave 'wild cards' to the remaining three. Once again, the final was held in Dublin's Helix Theatre. On this occasion, it featured a head-to-head contest between Chris Doran – whose song had been written by Bryan McFadden, a former member of Westlife – and James Kilbane. There were a few complaints when it was revealed that Doran's track had been recorded by some of the leading figures in Ireland's music industry – while Kilbane's song had been produced by *You're a Star*'s in-house arranger. This certainly led to a marked difference in the technical quality of the two tracks, but may not have affected the outcome.

When the votes for the national final were announced, Chris Doran was the clear winner. His success had a special significance within Ireland, and represented a particular achievement on his part. Chris came from a large family in the Travelling community – a group that has been subject to systematic discrimination over many years by mainstream Irish society. Chris had won awards in his youth as a kickboxer, and had worked as a builder before becoming a singer. In the national contest, he had delivered a reasonably pleasant ballad, simply and quite effectively, and it had ensured his passage to Istanbul.

Because of Mickey Harte's performance in Riga, Chris did not have to compete in the semi-final when he arrived in Turkey a few months later, but went straight into the Grand Final. However, when he performed in that final, his lack of experience became all too obvious: he appeared nervous and uneasy on stage, his vocal performance was uncertain, and, at times, his tuning seemed off-key – which, it was later claimed, was due to faulty monitoring equipment.

When the votes were recorded, it was clear that the Irish entry was not going to win that year's contest. In fact, Chris's song only received points from one of the countries that were eligible to vote that night, and finished in twenty-third place – out of twenty-four. This was the lowest number of points that an Irish song had ever been awarded in the Eurovision, and, once again, there was a profound sense of anticlimax back in Ireland. After months of auditions, heats and finals – and hundreds of thousands of votes – the end result was that Ireland's entry for that year's contest had led to further, and even greater, disappointment. There was also the unwelcome consequence that Ireland would now have to compete in the 2005 semi-final in order to get a chance to appear in the Grand Final.

RTÉ reacted to this result by announcing that they were examining the future development of *You're a Star*. It was now clear to some within the station that the talent show format could only mean diminishing returns as far as the Eurovision was concerned. However, it also became clear that RTÉ remained committed to using the reality series as the means of selecting Ireland's Eurovision entry; the continuing ratings success of the show meant that its place in the schedule was secure. As a kind of compromise, RTÉ announced a number of changes in the series for the coming season.

The most significant of these changes was that entry would no longer be limited to solo singers. From then on, bands or groups with no more than six performers would also be allowed to take part. RTÉ believed that this would not only broaden the talent pool available in Ireland, but would also increase the appeal of the winning acts across Europe. Ironically, it was this change that led to the end of *You're a Star* as the method of selecting Ireland's Eurovision entry.

Once again, auditions for the talent show were held at regional centres all over Ireland. Among those taking part in the Waterford auditions were a brother and sister from County Westmeath, who performed the popular hymn 'Amazing Grace'. Joe and Donna McCaul were both very young at the time they sang in Waterford – Joe was only fifteen years of age, and Donna was just a few years older – but they advanced steadily through the later stages of the competition. In the semi-final, Joe and Donna sang 'Love?' The romantic song might seem a little inappropriate to be sung as a duet between a brother and sister. Nonetheless, it took the McCauls through to the final – which they won the following week.

There were some who felt that the McCaul siblings were likely to find themselves out of their depth in a Eurovision Final. But there were also some in RTÉ who had high hopes for them. One of these was Julian Vignoles, who had worked as the station's executive producer on the two previous series of *You're a Star*, and was already known as RTÉ's 'Mr Eurovision'. At that time, Julian was also the commissioning editor of a series I was producing for RTÉ, and I was very surprised at the level of confidence that he expressed to me in the ability of Joe and Donna to make an impact on the Eurovision stage. He told me on several occasions that he was convinced their youth and innocence would be loved by viewers all over Europe, and would be welcomed as a change from the slickness, the cynicism and the extravagance of some of the other acts. Indeed, according to Julian, the McCauls had a real chance of winning the Grand Final, and bringing the contest from Kiev back to Ireland.

Before they could compete in the Eurovision Final, the McCauls had an immediate priority. Because of Chris

Doran's poor result in Istanbul, Joe and Donna had first to compete in a semi-final – and finish in the top ten – if they were to qualify for the Grand Final. The McCauls were the first Irish act ever to have to compete in this round, and it was assumed by many in Ireland that they would automatically sail through.

That was an unjustified assumption: the attrition rate in the semi-final was extremely high – in fact, the majority of those taking part would not go through to the next stage of the contest. When the McCauls took the stage, it seemed that some attempt had been made to add production values to their song after they had won Ireland's talent show. Joe and Donna were joined on stage by four dancers, and even attempted to join them in some of their moves.

Although their performance was lively and eager, brother and sister both appeared to lack the basic stagecraft that usually only comes through a combination of good direction, innate talent and practical experience. I watched their performance on TV in Ireland, and, in the middle of their act, one of my daughters turned to me and said she felt sorry for them. I understood what she meant, but sympathy is seldom enough in a Eurovision contest, and few can have been surprised when the McCauls failed to get past the semi-final round.

Reaction in Ireland to their failure cut to the heart of the problem. According to Louis Walsh, Ireland had failed because it had sent 'two amateurs'. The former Eurovision winner, Linda Martin, said the McCauls were 'childish and inexperienced', and without any 'star quality'. RTÉ's commentator, Marty Whelan, was more considerate of the feelings of the two teenagers involved: 'They had worked their socks off,' he claimed, and were devastated by the outcome. Not surprisingly, the failure to qualify seems to have affected the McCauls badly. It was reported that Joe had locked himself in his hotel bedroom after the result had been announced, and had refused to come out to be comforted.

It was now abundantly clear that *You're a Star* could no longer be used as the means to select Ireland's Eurovision entry. However, RTÉ continued to value the viewing figures that the show was able to provide. The series stayed in the station's schedule for several more seasons – but winning the competition no longer ensured a place in the Eurovision. Perhaps the acid test for any talent show that aims to create new stars is the number of winners who have gone on to establish successful careers in show business. By that reckoning, the success rate of the Eurovision acts that emerged from *You're a Star* is not very impressive.

Mickey Harte had a number one hit in Ireland with his Eurovision single. He also released an album in the aftermath of the contest that sold extremely well. Mickey had a performing career before *You're a Star*, he is still a working musician, and has recently been described, in a press release by his management company, as a 'mainstay of the Irish acoustic scene'.

Following his win in *You're a Star*, Harte signed a valuable recording contract with Sony, but that deal came to a premature end. 'I'd be a liar if I told you I had no regrets,' he said a few years ago. 'I think I did make bad decisions. Myself and my manager were like rabbits caught in the headlights. We were young, and we didn't really know what we were doing.' Harte's most recent album received good reviews, but only surfaced briefly in the lower reaches of Ireland's charts. Apart from continuing to play around Ireland, Harte has appeared in *Celebrities Go Wild* – another of RTÉ's reality shows.

He also wrote some of the music used in *Brian and Pippa Get Married*, an RTÉ reality documentary about two of Ireland's minor celebrities.

Following his Eurovision performance, Chris Doran came back to Ireland to perform in an open-air concert in Waterford City. His Eurovision song was number one in Ireland in the run-up to the contest, but soon fell out of the charts following his performance in the final. Chris released a number of other singles over the next few years, with a steadily declining rate of success. His last record was released in 2008, and failed to chart in Ireland.

In 2013, Chris was arrested – along with seven others – by a police armed response squad after an affray in County Tipperary. Chris was ordered to observe a curfew from 11pm to 7am each night. For the time being at least, his show business career seems to have stalled, or been put on hold.

Joe and Donna's 'Love?' was the only single from the reality show's three Eurovision performers that failed to reach the number one slot in Ireland. Given their youth, it seems unfair that the McCauls became the target of ridicule in their native country following their elimination in the Eurovision semi-final. They appeared on RTÉ's satirical series, *The Podge and Rodge Show*, to promote the follow-up single to 'Love?' However, just as they began to sing, the show deliberately cut to a commercial break. It was very funny – and very cruel. A clip was also shown on the same show of their performance in the Eurovision, after which one of their hosts asked himself, with heavy irony, 'I wonder why they didn't win?' A few years later, the McCauls appeared – perhaps, inevitably – on yet another of RTÉ's reality shows.

In 2011, Donna performed as one of the backing singers in the Maltese pre-selection for the Eurovision, but the song failed to qualify. The following year, she featured in Ireland's national song contest – but, once again, her song failed to make the final cut. In 2015, she auditoned for the US version of *The Voice*. Her brother had been working in amateur musicals around his home town of Athlone, but in 2012 he entered another reality TV talent show. Joe managed to make it through the first few rounds of the UK's talent show, *The X-Factor*, before being eliminated.

In 2014, it was revealed that Joe McCaul had been diagnosed with Multiple Sclerosis. Although he had found it hard to accept that he had developed MS at such a young age, Joe showed exemplary courage in facing his illness. With the support of his mother, he said he was determined to come to terms with MS. 'I can either lie down under it, or get up and go,' he told one Irish journalist. 'When people say to me, "But you've got MS," I say, "But MS hasn't got me".' Joe appeared on RTÉ's *Saturday Night Show*, where he was interviewed by Brendan O'Connor. He spoke openly and bravely about his future with this progressive disease, and, in the process, convinced many viewers that there was a lot more to this young man than a failed Eurovision adventure.

You're a Star had been a resounding success as a TV show. It had been produced to high professional standards, had delivered consistently large audiences to RTÉ, and had proved especially popular with younger viewers – normally considered the most elusive target for broadcasters to reach. But, as a way of choosing Ireland's entries for the Eurovision, the talent show had been a fairly comprehensive flop. After three seasons, RTÉ decided they had no option but to abandon this selection procedure and resort to a method that was perhaps less exciting, but appeared to offer a better chance of success.

22.
Cry Me A River

After the chastening experience of Donna and Joe McCaul in Kiev, RTÉ announced in November of 2005 that they had decided to break with what was described as the 'tradition' of linking the contest with a youth-oriented reality TV talent show. Instead, they announced that Ireland's song in the 2006 contest would be performed by Brian Kennedy.

This was the first time in more than thirty years that RTÉ had chosen the act that would represent Ireland in advance of the song being selected. The choice of Brian Kennedy as Ireland's entry also represented a radical departure from the priorities of the previous three years. Instead of using the contest to showcase new young talent, RTÉ had decided to opt for a man in early middle age who was, in the words of the station's press release, 'one of the most respected and popular singers in Irish music.' It was claimed by RTÉ that Kennedy's involvement provided concrete proof of the station's 'determination to return Ireland to the forefront of the Eurovision Song Contest'.

Brian Kennedy had first come to public attention as one of Van Morrison's backing singers: the purity and sweetness of his voice had proved highly effective in counterbalancing the roughness and edge of Morrison's vocal performance. Kennedy was subsequently signed by RCA records, and released a debut album. It included some self-penned songs, and was well received by critics, but was not a great commercial success.

Kennedy had his first real involvement with the Eurovision in 1995 when the contest was staged in Dublin's Point Depot. He sang the lead vocal for '*Lumen*' – the interval act – accompanied by a group of monks from Glenstall Abbey. It was an accomplished performance, but – perhaps inevitably – half-a-dozen chanting monks lacked the dramatic impact of a chorus line of feisty young Irish step-dancers, and '*Lumen*' was overshadowed by the spectacular triumph of *Riverdance* in the same theatre the previous year.

Despite that, Kennedy began to achieve some solo success in the years that followed the 1995 Eurovision. His singles started to feature in both the Irish and British charts, and he won several industry awards in Ireland – including the Best Irish Male Artist in the late 1990s. It seemed that Kennedy was poised for a definitive breakthrough as a solo performer. However, his career seemed to falter just as it had appeared to be on the verge of taking off, and his third solo album was considered a commercial flop. In 2000, Kennedy was dropped by his record company, and his career took a new direction when he joined the cast of *Riverdance* on Broadway.

In the years leading up to his Eurovision entry, Kennedy's career became even more diverse. In 2003, he presented a BBC Northern Ireland TV series in which he visited some of Ireland's best-known locations to perform some of Ireland's most familiar songs – such as 'I'll Take You Home Again, Kathleen', and 'Danny Boy'. The series clearly had greater appeal for an older audience, and it seemed that Kennedy was moving into the middle of the road, in career terms, and embracing a more conservative style of music.

However, he had also been active in a very different creative area, and in 2004, his first novel, *The Arrival of Fergal Flynn*, was published. It appeared to have been inspired by his own life and experiences, and it told the story of a youth growing up on Belfast's Falls Road during some of the worst years of the Northern Irish Troubles. In Kennedy's novel, the central character is seen struggling to come to terms with his talent as a singer, and with his homosexuality.

Apart from his performance on stage in the 1995 Eurovision, Kennedy had also worked with Secret Garden – the Norwegian winners of the 1997 contest. He had sung on their recording of 'You Raise Me Up' – a hugely successful ballad co-written by two composers who were both double-winners of the Eurovision. Kennedy had also recorded a single with Ronan Keating – the co-presenter of the 1995 contest in Dublin. Given this background, it did not seem so surprising that Brian Kennedy was happy to become involved in the 2006 Eurovision. Indeed, he made it clear in interviews with the Irish press that he was a genuine fan of the contest, and that he intended to commit himself wholeheartedly to securing another Eurovision victory for Ireland.

Kennedy gave an unexpected but revealing explanation for the reasons why representing Ireland in the contest meant so much to him. 'Coming from somebody who was as deeply unpopular as I was at school,' he told the BBC, 'it is quite an irony to be selected for something so important.' This comment suggests a degree of personal insecurity that may also relate to other aspects of Kennedy's work: he might have possessed a wonderful talent, but his career had sometimes seemed to lack a degree of focus and definition.

Almost from the start, controversies seemed to dog Ireland's 2006 Eurovision entry. The deadline that RTÉ had set for submissions of songs was only five weeks after the station had launched the competition. Some songwriters felt this meant there was simply not enough time to compose material with Kennedy in mind. Eventually, RTÉ agreed to accept submissions for several further weeks – but it was claimed this left those who had already submitted songs to meet the original deadline at a distinct disadvantage. Despite these issues, an unusually large number of songs were submitted to RTÉ. Irish songwriters were no doubt attracted by the prospect of an artist of the calibre of Brian Kennedy performing and recording some of their material.

For the previous three years, the selection process for the Eurovision had been strongly oriented towards young people: it was principally teenage girls who had used their mobile phones after each edition of *You're a Star* to call or text support for their favourite act. In 2006, RTÉ swung to the other extreme. The station chose to set up a small judging panel to select four songs that would go to the national final. Initially, there were just three members of this panel – all of whom were men, and all of whom were in their sixties.

One of these was Paul Brady – a highly regarded singer-songwriter who had spent most of his career performing folk and traditional music. Brady is widely admired for his musical integrity, but he struck many as having little in common with the type of songs associated with the Eurovision. Also on the panel was Shay Healy, who had written a winning Eurovision song more than a quarter of a century previously, and Brendan Graham – who was one of the few songwriters to have won the Eurovision twice. The three men were later joined by Juliet Turner. Like Brady, Turner was a gifted singer-songwriter – but, once again, she was not someone associated with the sort of power ballads or pop songs that normally feature in the Eurovision.

There was further controversy when RTÉ announced the four songs that had been shortlisted. All of the four songwriters chosen had established reputations, but one of them was Brian Kennedy – who had been permitted by RTÉ to enter and sing one of his own compositions. There was nothing in the Eurovision rules that prohibited artists from performing their own song – in fact, it was not an uncommon occurrence in previous contests. However, *The Irish Times* journalist, John Waters, felt this represented a fundamental conflict of interest.

Waters went on Joe Duffy's popular radio show, *Liveline*, to complain at length about the unfair advantage he believed this would give Kennedy. He also claimed that extending the song submission-process had given an advantage to some composers by allowing them extra time to work on their material. It transpired that Waters had himself submitted material for consideration by the panel – which had not been selected for the national final.

The four shortlisted songs were supposed to be featured on RTÉ's *Late Late Show* – where the winner would be decided by a televote. However, before that could take place, one of the songs was withdrawn. RTÉ issued a press release stating that 'Strong Enough', by Barry Walsh, had been found to be ineligible for Eurovision selection because it had already been released commercially in 2002. There was a well-known and long-standing stipulation in the rules of the contest that all Eurovision entries had to be original compositions with no previous history of recording or release, and it is only surprising that the implications of this regulation for Walsh's song were realised at such a late stage. Had the song competed and won the Irish televote, it would later have been disqualified from the contest.

The first entry to be performed on *The Late Late Show* was Jimmy McCarthy's 'The Greatest Song of All' – a title that seemed to invite a sceptical response. This was intended as a celebration of nature's beauty, and was apparently inspired by Vivaldi's famous 'Four Seasons' suite. McCarthy had written some iconic Irish songs over the years, but they were mainly in the folk genre, and they were not of obvious appeal to a Eurovision audience. The second song had been written by Don Mescall, and focused on the innate wisdom that adults can supposedly learn from children. Mescall was also an experienced songwriter, but, once again, his work was not normally associated with the musical genres that have proved popular with Eurovision audiences.

The last song Brian Kennedy performed that night was his own composition. It may be true that this gave him an initial advantage over the other two competitors – in that he had been able to write a song that matched the strengths of his own voice. However, 'Every Song Is a Cry for Love' was not only the most compelling of the three finalists, but it was also the one that was best suited to the Eurovision contest. Perhaps its most obvious weakness was the overly sentimental lyrics – but soppy sentiments have often been a feature of the Eurovision. In any case, since the vast majority of viewers watching the contest do not speak English, the words of Kennedy's song were likely to be of secondary importance.

Ireland had failed to qualify for the Grand Final in Ukraine – so the first obstacle that Brian Kennedy had to overcome when he arrived in Athens was getting through the semi-final of the competition. On this occasion, there were four automatic qualifiers for the Grand Final: France, Germany, Spain and the UK. In addition, the countries that had finished in the top ten in the 2005 Eurovision would qualify. Lastly, those countries that finished in the top ten of the 2006 semi-final would also pass through to the final. The rest would be eliminated – just as Joe and Donna McCaul had been the previous year.

Twenty-three countries were taking part in the semi-final, and this meant that the majority of those competing would not feature in the final. Ireland was the fourth country to perform, and, as it happened, this resulted in Brian Kennedy singing the 1,000th song to be performed in the history of the contest. It soon became clear that very little had changed in the staging of the Irish act since it had first been chosen as Ireland's entry.

Kennedy's hair seemed to have been slightly restyled; he was wearing a slightly different dark suit; and the string section that accompanied him in the national contest had been replaced by three backing singers. The lack of enhanced production values stood in striking contrast to several of the other acts – notably the Finnish entry, Lordi. This was the first time that a hard rock number had featured in the Eurovision, but the song's unusual genre was nothing compared to the appearance of the Finnish band and the level of commitment they brought to their performance. Apart from the mild shock of hearing a type of heavy metal music played on a Eurovision stage for the first time, the physical impact of Lordi was immediate. They all wore a kind of gothic body armour, with grotesque makeup and horror masks. It was no surprise to learn that their first single had been called 'Would You Love A Monsterman?'

Despite their gruesome appearance, Lordi's song had a definite and appealing melodic line; their stage act was extremely entertaining; and – perhaps above all – they conveyed a strong sense of genuinely believing in what they were doing. In comparison, Brian Kennedy looked as if he were about to make his first Holy Communion. The lyrics of Lordi's song – which were in English – also turned out to be prophetic: '*Who dares, wins*', Mr Lordi sang. '*The jokers will soon be the new kings.*'

The votes cast in the semi-final were not released until after the Grand Final, but it later emerged that the Irish entry had ended up ninth out of the ten countries to qualify. It was not exactly a ringing endorsement of Brian Kennedy's song, but he was caught on camera backstage mouthing 'Thank God!' when Ireland's place in the final was announced. He was not the only one to feel relieved. RTÉ had chosen to play it safe by selecting this type of singer to perform this type of song: to have taken so few risks and still to have failed to qualify would have caused considerable embarrassment within the station's Entertainment Department.

It might also be worth pointing out – for those who claim that the contest had been, in some way, compromised by Eastern European voting pacts – that half of the countries eliminated in the semi-final round came from the former Soviet bloc, including Bulgaria, Slovenia, Belarus, Estonia, Albania and Poland.

Ireland was the twenty-first country to perform in the Grand Final two nights later, and Brian Kennedy seemed, understandably, to be rather more nervous than he had appeared in the semi-final. But, if anything, it was the lack of production – and the absence of any real imagination in the staging of his song – that was more apparent on second viewing. There was minimal contribution to the presentation from either the backing singers or the accompanying guitarist. Instead, the weight of the performance was carried entirely by Kennedy – and that seemed too substantial a burden for him. The title of his song was 'Every Song Is a Cry for Love', and, in the final, the emphasis fell heavily on 'Cry'.

It is true that the sentiment of the lyrics was somewhat lachrymose, but his performance might have been more successful if Kennedy had worked a little more against the grain of his own words. Instead, he appeared to milk the emotion – seeming on the brink of tears throughout the song. And, of course, the more he over-emoted, the less convincing his act became.

In visual terms, the climax of the song came when Kennedy knelt at the beginning of the second verse. This was reminiscent of Johnny Logan's move in Brussels in 1987, when he had bent down to reach for the key change that would bring his song to its resolution. Logan's move was unexpected, it was dramatic, and it was full of barely contained emotion. It also made sense within the musical structure of his song. Kennedy's move lacked any of those conditions. It appeared calculating and premeditated: he went down on one knee at the start of the second verse, and rose promptly – as if on cue – once that verse was over. In a small but telling gesture, he even hitched up one of his trouser legs before he began to kneel. The overall impact was counterproductive, and only drew attention to the contrived nature of the staging.

When the voting results came in, they revealed that Lordi had won by a very large margin. In fact, the band had received the highest tally of votes ever recorded in a Eurovision. Mr Lordi described winning the contest as a 'victory for rock music, and a victory for open-mindedness' – and it was hard to argue with his assessment. Brian Kennedy had finished in what RTÉ's press office termed a 'respectable' tenth place. However, in several ways, this result was a disappointment: Kennedy is a fine singer, and he had delivered a well-crafted song that was ideally suited to the range of his voice. Both he and RTÉ could reasonably have hoped that the Irish entry would have rated higher – which it might well have done if his performance had been better produced. However, RTÉ was still pleased with the result – the run of exceptionally poor Eurovision results seemed to have been stopped in its tracks.

Brian Kennedy had performed well – though not quite as well as one member of the Irish government appeared to believe. In a statement posted on his Department's website soon after the result had been announced, Ireland's Minister for the Arts, John O'Donoghue, praised Kennedy for his performance. The minister wished to express his 'congratulations to Brian on his marvellous win for Ireland in the Eurovision Song Contest in Athens tonight.' Kennedy had given a 'wonderful performance', the Minister continued, 'and in the process extended Ireland's record number of Eurovision wins to eight.' The minister urged the entire Irish nation to share in his own excitement: 'Everyone should be proud of Brian,' he concluded, 'and his excellent achievement.' It was clear that nobody had checked which statement from the Minister was to be released to the press.

I had lunch a few weeks after the event with a senior executive from RTÉ who had been centrally involved in the contest, and he told me of his relief that the whole Eurovision 'situation' had now been stabilised. He believed that Brian Kennedy's performance had not only been credible, but had helped set the station back on the road to future success. As we were talking, Kennedy came into the restaurant, and he joined us briefly. I congratulated him on his performance, and told him – truthfully – that I thought he had deserved to be placed higher. I was reminded that, thanks to his efforts, Ireland would not have to take part in the next year's semi-final, and this was regarded as an important achievement – both for himself and for RTÉ.

In the aftermath of the contest, Kennedy did not regret his decision to participate: 'I take away from it good things,' he told one journalist. He also claimed that his involvement had made him better known in countries such as Slovenia and Belarus. Later in 2006, Kennedy presented a ten-part TV series for RTÉ with the ungainly title of *1 to Remember with Brian Kennedy*. It was the sort of deal with which the station tended to reward – or entice – each year's Eurovision entry.

In this instance, the format of Kennedy's series seemed as if it had been cobbled together without much thought. *1 to Remember* tried to appeal simultaneously to older and younger audiences. On one hand, Kennedy revived chart hits from the past – on the other, he asked viewers to use their mobile phones to call and text their votes for the songs they wanted him to sing. He even pleaded with the Irish public to come out 'in their droves' to vote. 'They couldn't vote for me in the Eurovision Song Contest,' Kennedy explained, 'so I'm begging them – vote now.' Despite his begging, the series seemed to fall between two stools, and failed to please enough old or young viewers. It was not re-commissioned for a second series.

In the years that followed his Eurovision entry, Kennedy was seen on a number of Irish TV programmes. These were often based on Reality formats: he was a judge on the first season of *The Voice*, and took part in the first season of *The Hit*. He also appeared on a celebrity version of *Come Dine With Me* – where he threw a glass of red wine over another guest in what seemed like a fit of pique. Kennedy has continued to take an interest in the Eurovision, and has sometimes used social media to express critical views of those taking part. In 2012, after he had seen the Jedward twins on *The Late Late Show* – where they won Ireland's national song contest – he tweeted: 'Boring song. Four backing singers? Surprise, surprise. Scarlet is all I have to say. Poor Jedward. No amount of jumping will be enough. Morto.'

As things turned out, Jedward were higher placed in the previous Eurovision than Brian Kennedy had been six years earlier. Kennedy's comments also drew a withering riposte from Louis Walsh, who had been a judge on *The X-Factor* – the reality talent show that had first featured the twins – and he had subsequently managed them. 'I really hope that Jedward don't end up like Brian Kennedy,' Walsh told one journalist. 'Bitter, without a recording deal, and taking any silly reality show that comes their way.' The problem with Brian Kennedy, he continued, was that 'it's all over for him, and no one seems to have told him.' Walsh added, in a final stinging putdown, 'I used to like Brian – when he was one of Van Morrison's backing singers.' Since then, Kennedy has continued to sing in front of appreciative audiences, and he has also issued several albums on his own record label – which he says allows him greater creative control.

In the context of the previous years of lamentable results, RTÉ executives were right to feel that Brian Kennedy had performed with some credit in Athens. He had also raised the morale of those in the station's Entertainment Department. However, the conclusions drawn by RTÉ from the 2006 Eurovision proved to be badly flawed, and the station was unable to build upon Kennedy's relative success. Indeed, by the end of the following year's contest, Ireland's search for another Eurovision winner seemed to be back at square one.

23.
From Lissadell to Latvia

In 2007, RTÉ decided to follow the same selection procedure that they had used in 2006. Although Brian Kennedy had only achieved a relatively modest success, he had at least ensured that Ireland would not need to compete in the semi-final the following year, but could advance straight to the Grand Final. The strategy of choosing a single act to perform all the shortlisted songs was therefore deemed by RTÉ to have been something of a triumph, and the station decided to continue to select the Irish act through an internal process.

Several names were said to be in contention to represent Ireland in Helsinki – and, perhaps inevitably, the frontrunner was rumoured to be Johnny Logan. In an interview on RTÉ's *Tubridy Tonight* chat show, Logan fuelled speculation by saying that he would like to represent Ireland in the contest if 'everything was right,

211

and everyone was in agreement'. Despite some preliminary discussions, a deal with RTÉ was not agreed, and Logan was not chosen to compose or sing for Ireland. According to Johnny, he had learned from the press that he was not to be included in the station's plans, and he felt aggrieved by what he regarded as this unprofessional treatment.

Other names had also been mentioned, and it seemed that RTÉ was inclined to look to the past for current inspiration. The station was said to be considering Linda Martin, who had won the Eurovision in 1992, and Ronan Keating, who had co-presented the contest in 1995. However, in November 2006, RTÉ surprised most observers by announcing that the traditional Irish folk group, Dervish, had been chosen to represent Ireland in Helsinki. There was little evidence to suggest that traditional, folk or ethnic acts had ever performed well in the contest. Indeed, none of the winners of recent contests belonged in that category – which may explain the somewhat defensive press release issued by RTÉ in an apparent attempt to justify its choice.

According to RTÉ, Dervish was a 'critically lauded' band from the west of Ireland that had 'enthralled' audiences around the globe. In 2006, it was noted, the band had even accompanied an Irish government delegation on a trade mission to China. Although Dervish were 'deeply devoted to traditional Irish music in its purest form', RTÉ's press release continued, the band was also committed to 'pushing the boundaries', and was apparently famous for its 'interpretation of a wide range of modern songs'. It was claimed that Dervish was noted both for its 'wild and swirling' performances, and its 'deep and spiritual' musical values. Prospective songwriters were offered a unique opportunity to write for a band that was 'extraordinarily tight', and yet 'warm, strong and versatile'.

According to RTÉ, Ireland's victory in the 1996 Eurovision had proved that 'ethnic song styles' were popular with European viewers. It might be stretching definitions to describe Eimear Quinn's winning entry as a traditional Irish composition – and none of the contests in the following decade had been won by anything that could fairly be described as an 'ethnic' song. Nonetheless, the press release argued that, in the context of an increasingly complex competition, Dervish's 'exciting performances' made them an 'exciting proposition' for the Eurovision stage. Shane Mitchell, one of the musicians in Dervish, responded to RTÉ's offer by saying, 'We are honoured to accept [the] invitation to represent Ireland at Eurovision 2007, and look forward to raising the roof of the "Areena" in Helsinki.'

Would-be and established songwriters were instructed that all songs had to be submitted to RTÉ by 5.30pm on Monday, 8 January 2007. They were also advised that the songs submitted would need to be suitable for both Dervish and the Eurovision contest. In effect, this meant that all songs had to be compatible with a musical arrangement that included traditional Irish instruments – such as the tin whistle, fiddle and *bodhrán*. Given the limits that this form of instrumentation would impose on any composer, it remained to be seen just how many 'modern songs' would be entered for the national competition.

RTÉ had also decided that all entries held to be eligible would be judged by a panel of six experts. They would reduce the number of songs to just four, and these would be performed live in a televised national final. The judging panel once again included Shay Healy, who had written Ireland's winning Eurovision song twenty-seven years previously.

More than two hundred songs were submitted to RTÉ for consideration, and the four shortlisted songs were subsequently performed by Dervish on Ireland's premier entertainment series, *The Late Late Show*, in February of 2007. The show also featured several previous winners of the Eurovision contest – Dana, Eimear Quinn and the Brotherhood of Man – as well as the somewhat bizarre inclusion of Dmitry Koldun, who provided a 'sneak preview' of the Belarusian entry for that year's contest. This was 'only the fourth' time Belarus had taken part in the Eurovision, the show's presenter told his mystified audience.

The first two songs performed by Dervish in the national contest were both mournful and forgettable ballads. There was little evidence in either of Ireland's 'ethnic song style' that RTÉ had claimed to be seeking. That was not entirely surprising since the composers of the two songs were both Scandinavians. There was also little sign of the 'wild and swirling' style of performance that RTÉ had also promised; perhaps the station's press office had confused Dervish with a troupe of Sufi dancers.

The Dervish musicians all wore sombre black clothes, and hardly moved a muscle for the duration of either of the first two songs. Instead, they stood or sat around their lead singer, Cathy Jordan, who was wearing a plain dark-purple dress, and who also seemed frozen in front of her microphone stand. The band's total lack of animation might have been anticipated by RTÉ – since, like many Irish traditional musicians, Dervish normally preferred to let their music speak for itself.

The third song they performed that night – 'Until We Meet Again' – was a little more upbeat, but the band remained static throughout its performance. This song had somewhat more of an Irish flavour. Cathy Jordan played the spoons, and the chorus included a version of the traditional – if rather hackneyed – Irish blessing, 'May the road rise up to greet you!'

The fourth and last song was better tailored to the stated aims of RTÉ. 'They Can't Stop the Spring' included a plaintive introduction on the tin whistle – of the sort that is invariably described as 'haunting'; the musical break featured a traditional fiddle; and, halfway through the song, the lead singer played the *bodhrán*. There was even a small amount of physical movement on stage – though this was confined to the singer's arms, rising and falling with the music. The song began slowly, but it picked up speed as it progressed, and, unlike the other entries, built to something approaching a musical climax. In such a weak field, it came as little surprise that the winner of the national contest – as the result of a televote – was 'They Can't Stop the Spring'. It was, to put it simply, the best of a pretty bad bunch. What was more surprising to many viewers was the identity of one of its writers.

John Waters had the reputation in Ireland of being not only a very serious journalist, but also someone who took himself very seriously. He was known as something of a contrarian, but also as a principled and, at times, courageous writer, who had been prepared to risk unpopularity by campaigning for a number of causes – such as the legal rights of fathers. His involvement in an event that might seem as ephemeral and frivolous as the Eurovision Song Contest was hard for some observers – and, particularly, for some journalists – to comprehend. There was, after all, something of a consensus in certain sections of the media that the perennial value of the Eurovision was its capacity to supply material for knocking copy.

The key to the apparent contradiction in Waters' involvement appeared to be that he took the Eurovision just as seriously as he seemed to take everything else in his life. In the years leading up to 2007, a religious impulse had become increasingly apparent in his writing, and he had become identified with the radical wing of conservative Catholicism. Later in 2007, he would publish an autobiographical book called *Lapsed Agnostic*, in which he related his 'journey from belief to un-belief and back again'. It would seem that he was imbued with a comparable sense of spiritual commitment when he entered the Eurovision contest.

Waters had submitted material for Ireland's national song contest the previous year, but it had not been accepted for the final. He had appeared to take this rejection badly, and had publicly criticised the fact that RTÉ had allowed Brian Kennedy to enter and perform his own composition – claiming that this gave Kennedy an unfair advantage over the other songwriters.

When he won Ireland's national final in 2007, Waters' view of the significance of the contest had grown positively transcendent. The Eurovision, he had decided, was 'about human desire, in all its complex reality.' The contest represented 'desire as fantasy, but also desire for something real, substantial and inspirational.' In its mix of 'lightheartedness and solemnity', he believed that the Eurovision was reaching towards 'a new level of cool and self-consciousness, as though experimenting with what might be acceptable inside the outer boundary with excess'.

Although only three of the Eurovision contests in the previous ten years had been won by countries from the former Soviet bloc, there was a widespread belief in Western European broadcasting circles that some sort of seismic shift towards Eastern Europe had taken place. Waters appeared to share that opinion, echoing the view expressed by Julian Vignoles – RTÉ's 'Mr Eurovision' – some years previously that the 'centre of gravity' of the contest had 'drifted to the east'. For Waters, the 'central questions' raised by the Eurovision now 'gravitated around the cultural implications of the still relatively recent collapse of the Berlin Wall.'

As might be evident from the above, Waters was not given to understatement – or known for the lightness of his touch. He did, however, bring his customary sense of personal mission to the lyrics that he had written for this Eurovision entry. Initially, its title and theme might have appeared to be reminiscent of several other songs. The American rock band The Flaming Lips had released a track called 'Can't Stop the Spring' a few years earlier, and Tom Waits had also previously recorded a song called 'You Can Never Hold Back Spring'. It would be unfair, however, to accuse Waters of plagiarising or borrowing either of those compositions, since they all shared the same source of inspiration – and that could be found in the recent history of Eastern Europe.

In 1968, Alexander Dubček had become the First Secretary of the Communist Party of Czechoslovakia, and had ushered in a period of political reform that became known as the 'Prague Spring'. Dubcek had tried to dismantle the most repressive aspects of the existing regime, and to create 'socialism with a human face'. As his reforming programme gained momentum, the Soviet leadership of the Warsaw Pact tried to limit the changes that Dubček was planning to introduce. Eventually, Soviet troops – accompanied by other Warsaw Pact forces – entered Czechoslovakia, and seized control of the country. Dubček was compelled to concede to Soviet demands, but was quoted as saying that, while Russian tanks might have been able 'to crush the flowers', they 'can't stop the Spring'.

Waters claimed that the 2007 Eurovision contest represented in some sense the true 'flowering' of the political vision offered by Dubček in 1968. He also seemed to think that his song was in tune with the underlying zeitgeist of the new millennium – pointing out to the *Sligo Champion* newspaper that he and his co-writer had actually written their song 'before we learned that the Czech Republic [was] entering Eurovision for the very first time.' Waters drew attention to what he regarded as other significant coincidences. 'This year,' he told the *Champion*, 'as well as being the 50th birthday of the European Union, is also the 30th anniversary of Charter 77, the protest movement that led to the eventual Czechoslovakian revolution of 1989.' Waters described his song as a 'Celtic celebration of the Eastern European revolutions and their eventual outcome.'

The Prague Spring may have inspired Waters, but his lyrics referred to slightly more recent events in European history – namely, the fall of the Iron Curtain and the breaching of the Berlin Wall. Indeed, the opening lines of his song informed all those who were still unaware of the historic events. From now on, Waters assured Europe, *'from Lissadell to Latvia, we're singing as one clan.'*

In an attempt to connect with the experience of Eastern European countries, Waters was not only inviting the audience to celebrate events that had taken place almost two decades previously, but he was also claiming that those events enabled him to consider Eastern Europeans as part of an Irish 'clan'. Such sentiments might well have seemed naive and patronising in those countries that had managed to endure and overcome decades of repressive totalitarian rule.

For the most part, the lyrics of 'They Can't Hold Back the Spring' fell awkwardly between two diverging idioms. On one hand, there was a genuflection towards rock music, and the rebellious use of double negatives *à la* Pink Floyd: '*We don't need no party*', the singer declared. '*Just a party band.*' On the other hand, there was a self-conscious straining for poetic effect: '*The archipelagic icicles have melted like the cage*'. This was not the easiest of lines for any singer to deliver – let alone understand – but the reference is apparently to the magnum opus of the Russian dissident writer, Alexandr Solzhenitsyn. In his later years, Solzhenitsyn became an ardent supporter of Vladimir Putin's foreign policies – which might not have made him a popular figure in some countries that had once been part of the Soviet bloc.

Much of the initial reaction in Ireland to Waters' song winning the national contest was negative. Indeed, he became the target of some ridicule in the Irish press. Journalist Fiona Meredith claimed that the 'obscure literary flourishes' of Waters' overblown lyrics had led to 'snorts of derision', and voiced the suspicion that RTÉ had deliberately chosen 'a rubbish act' to represent the country because the station did not want to shoulder the expense of hosting the contest again. The same journalist predicted that Waters' 'winsome' composition would not even gain as many votes as the Belgian novelty act, the Krazy Mess Groovers. Sadly, the accuracy of that prediction was never tested: unlike the Irish entry, the Belgian Groovers had to compete in the semi-final of the contest – and were promptly eliminated.

Despite such criticism, the *Sligo Champion*, at least, was supportive of Ireland's song, and was keen to make the most of its local provenance, noting proudly that the lyrics mentioned the county's 'historic landmark', Lissadell (the country estate that had once been the home of Countess Markiewicz, the Irish aristocrat and revolutionary dilettante). The newspaper also pointed out that both John Waters and his co-writer, Tommy Moran, had 'strong Sligo connections'. Tommy Moran was quoted as saying that he hoped their song would help to promote tourism in Ireland's northwest region.

By then, it was known that Dervish would be performing fourth out of the twenty-four entrants in the Eurovision Final. Moran believed that this position could work to the band's advantage because be presumed that 'people's concentration levels are highest at either the start or the end of the contest'. Moran hoped that Ireland's song would therefore be 'freshest in people's minds when the voting began'. Cathy Jordan, Dervish's lead singer, was quoted in a sister newspaper, the *Roscommon Champion*, as being confident that Dervish would do well in the Eurovision. Their brand of Irish traditional music, she claimed, was 'loved all over the world', and this would prove to be their 'trump card' in Finland.

The 2007 contest was the fifty-second Eurovision, and it was staged in Helsinki's Hartwall Areena. The previous year was the first time the contest had been won by Finland – after forty-five failed attempts – and a record number of forty-two countries were participating in the Finnish event. Since the Lordi band had won Eurovision with a hard-rock number, it was perhaps inevitable that several countries sent other rock songs to the contest. The bulk of entries, however, still fitted into the usual pop or ballad genres. The only entry written in an 'ethnic song style' was that of Ireland.

In the weeks that had passed since 'They Can't Hold Back the Spring' had won Ireland's national song contest, some attempt had been made to present the song in ways that might make it more appealing to a mass European audience. Cathy Jordan's new dress was more stylish and contemporary, and there was now a flower in her hair. Although the Dervish musicians were still dressed in sober black outfits, one of them now sported a light-grey polo neck.

The maximum number of performers on stage permitted by the Eurovision rules is six – and, since there were six members of Dervish, this meant that their routine could not be enhanced by the addition of dancers, or mime artists, or acrobats, or suchlike. RTÉ had tried to address this issue by extending the instrumental break in the middle of the song to allow for a greater degree of movement on the part of the band. They now bobbed up and down on the stage with varying degrees of enthusiasm throughout their performance, and, at one point, two of them even swapped places in the line-up for no apparent reason.

The backing track now featured the *uilleann* pipes – arguably, Ireland's only indigenous musical instrument – and Cathy Jordan moved through the musicians with her *bodhrán*. It was clear that the band had also been told to look a bit more cheerful – because they grinned, gurned and winked at each other relentlessly through the song.

Dervish might have convinced themselves that they were having a good time – but their performance did not persuade the Eurovision audience. The attempts to generate some sense of traditional Irish *craic* on stage could not disguise the fundamental weakness of the song – or its unsuitability for the contest in which Ireland was competing. Cathy Jordan's vocal performance was to attract a good deal of adverse comment – with some critics claiming that it was flat and expressionless. But, in truth, the composition of the song did not allow the singer to display her real vocal abilities.

As the votes began to come in, it soon became apparent that the Irish entry was not going to win the contest. In fact, it was soon quite clear that Ireland's song was going to do very badly. Voting was by telephone and SMS, and all forty-two countries were eligible to vote in the final. It was the largest popular constituency in the history of the Eurovision, but Ireland did not gain a single point from the first thirty countries that voted. The thirty-first country to vote was Albania. For technical reasons, Albania had been unable to run an electronic voting system – so its vote had been decided by a small jury in a TV studio in Tirana. They gave 'They Can't Hold Back the Spring' five points. They proved to be the only points that the song received that night, and Ireland finished last in a Eurovision Final for the first time in its history.

The following day an RTÉ spokesperson announced that the station planned to review the Eurovision entry selection procedure in the light of Ireland's disastrous showing. 'We will definitely be having a sit-down,' she told the press, 'and looking at our geographical position, and going through the whole process.' The need to look at Ireland's 'geographical position' may seem puzzling – even RTÉ, after all, cannot physically relocate the island. In reality, this reference carried an oblique suggestion that there had been an unfair 'hijacking' of the Eurovision by the countries of Eastern Europe.

It was, surely, ironic that the country which had entered a song which purported to be a 'Celtic celebration of the Eastern European revolutions' should end up trying to blame Eastern Europeans for its abject failure in the contest. Serbia – the winner of the 2007 contest – may have received high points from its neighbouring countries, but, then, so too had Finland in 2006. And Serbia also received high votes from Western European countries – such as Sweden, Switzerland, the Netherlands, Austria, and the host country, Finland.

Ireland was not the only country all too ready to believe that Eastern Europeans were ganging up on the West. The UK had also shown a marked tendency to explain Eurovision voting patterns in terms of sinister foreign intrigues. One of the principal exponents of the notion of a 'Balkan conspiracy' was Terry Wogan. He became convinced after the 2008 contest that the future prospects for Western European participants in the contest were very poor. Indeed, he suggested that they would have to decide 'whether they want to take part from here on in'. Terry Wogan had already made up his mind, and chose to withdraw from any further involvement with the Eurovision. Since then, his dire predictions have proved to be unfounded.

The eagerness to detect signs of conspiracy in Eastern Europe's voting patterns has seldom been accompanied by a comparable scrutiny of similar patterns in the West. For decades, the Scandinavian countries have awarded consistently high points to their neighbours – and the Nordic voting bloc increased in size and influence with the advent of the Baltic states in the 1990s. When Lordi won in 2006, they scored seventy-eight points out of a possible maximum of eighty-four points from their Scandinavian and Baltic neighbours. When Loreen won for Sweden in 2012, her song gained maximum points from Iceland, Norway, Finland, Denmark, Estonia and Latvia. In neither case was there any outcry about bloc voting. The record also shows that, across the past five decades, Ireland has been given the highest number of points from our nearest neighbour – the UK. The UK, in turn, has been given the most points by its closest neighbour – Ireland. However, this long history of mutual support had never seemed to concern Sir Terry Wogan.

In 2014, a detailed analysis of Eurovision voting patterns was published in *The Journal of Applied Statistics*. The finding of this research was that there was no evidence to support media claims that that the Song Contest was compromised by prejudice or voting pacts. The research established that, in the vast majority of cases, the tendency of European countries – East and West – to vote for their neighbours could be explained more credibly by reference to culture, geography, history and migration. The analysis concluded that, in any case, the effect of countries voting for their neighbours was not substantial, and had never had a decisive impact on any performer winning the contest.

In 2008, the RTÉ spokesperson exonerated both the band and the song from any criticism. She emphasised that they continued to have RTÉ's full support, and were not to blame for the flop. 'We were really proud of them. They performed really well on the night, and we were happy with the song.' She added that 'it just wasn't our night.' John Waters admitted that all those involved in Ireland's entry were deeply upset. 'In football manager's speak,' he said, 'I am gutted.'

One member of the Irish entourage was quoted as saying that Ireland's 'ethnic' song was not 'what the masses, particularly in Eastern Europe, wanted to hear'. Once again, the impulse was to blame Eastern Europe – and its 'masses' – for Ireland's dismal showing. In reality, the only votes that

'They Can't Hold Back the Spring' managed to obtain came from Albania – in Eastern Europe – and none of the Western European countries chose to give the song a single point.

After they arrived back in Ireland, Dervish announced that they would continue to play traditional music. They reminded the Irish public that their music was about 'heart and soul – and not about votes'. Later that year, the band recorded an hour-long TV special for RTÉ. This might have been part of the package that had convinced Dervish to accept the invitation to enter the Eurovision contest in the first place – or perhaps it served as a form of compensation for the embarrassment of the band finishing last. RTÉ's press release for the TV special promised Irish viewers 'stirring renditions of great tunes' and 'jaunty melodies'. No mention was made of the band's participation in the 2007 Eurovision; it seemed to have been airbrushed out of existence. Since then, Dervish has returned to its previous musical circuit – where the band continues to please its committed fans.

In 2010, RTÉ announced that John Waters was again attempting to represent Ireland at the Eurovision contest, with the song 'Does Heaven Need Much More?' Once again, he had co-written the song with his childhood pal, Tommy Moran. The news that Waters had reached the final of the national song contest for a second time was greeted with some dismay in the Irish press. Dublin's evening newspaper, the *Herald*, headlined the story: 'Heaven Help Us! Waters is back to give us another Eurovision ear-bashing'. This time, his song had been written in a more recognisable pop idiom, but the lyrics still retained an underlying sense of Waters' religious preoccupations: not many pop songs mention Jehovah by name, or speculate about the nature of Eternity. '*Will every step be Perfect Truth?'* Waters wondered, *'as we trip out the Light Fantastic?'*

The song was performed by Leanne Moore – who had won a reality TV talent show on RTÉ in 2008 – about whom Waters enthused with a characteristic lack of inhibition. He claimed that the singer was able to 'possess a song' and could 'breathe herself into it'. Waters thought that she would give European viewers the 'sense of a future Ireland' – one in which 'we can start dreaming again'. On a less exalted plane, he added that the singer also looked 'amazing'. However, his prediction that Irish viewers would 'just want her to go wherever she wants to' was not realised in the national final: the popular vote ran against Waters and Moran – and they finished in second-last place.

Despite his Eurovision setbacks, Waters continued to appear regularly on RTÉ – across a wide range of documentaries and chat shows – in the years that followed. In one of these programmes, he uncovered the fate of an earlier John Waters – a relative who had died in the Great Famine – with whom the current John Waters could identify in emotional terms. In another documentary, he stripped off to be painted in the nude. His belief in a synthesis between popular music and transcendent religion remained unabated, and, in 2012, he curated an exhibition called *Rock 'n' Roll as a Quest for the Infinite* – a title that verged on self-parody. Waters continues to take an interest – and to comment – on the Eurovision, and it is possible that he will enter more of his songs in future.

In the aftermath of the 2007 contest, Julian Vignoles announced that the station would be reviewing their strategic approach to the Eurovision. A special 'consultative Committee' was soon established – whose stated purpose was to explore ways in which Ireland could launch 'a serious challenge for victory'. As a result of its protracted deliberations, the committee reached the conclusion that the Eurovision was 'a performance contest as much as a song contest'.

This was hardly a profound or an original insight: it is difficult – if not impossible – to think of any previous Eurovision where the artist's interpretation of his or her song has not been of some importance. Indeed, earlier in 2007 RTÉ's own press office had drawn explicit attention to the 'exciting performance' it promised Dervish would deliver in Finland.

One of the concrete recommendations of RTÉ's committee was apparently based on its discovery of the value of visual performance. Songwriters were therefore 'encouraged' not only to enter songs, but also to provide DVDs that could 'demonstrate the potential performance of their songs'. This struck me as a most unfair request: there is, after all, no reason to suppose that gifted composers or singers are also talented visually – and the ability to make effective DVDs tilted the national contest strongly in favour of those who had some experience of television or film production. In any case, it was surely the responsibility of experienced RTÉ personnel to evaluate the visual potential of the songs submitted, and determine how they could be properly produced and staged effectively on television.

RTÉ's committee issued new and detailed guidelines for aspiring songwriters, and the shift of emphasis was further spelled out by Julian Vignoles. RTÉ's focus, he explained, was now on the 'visual and stage appeal of the act as well as finding a show-stopping song'. As it turned out, in the attempt to meet both those goals, RTÉ ended up achieving neither – and the

227

following year's contest in Belgrade was to prove, in several respects, an even greater debacle for Ireland than Helsinki.

24.
Enter the Turkey

There are always some crazy guys competing in the Eurovision contest: novelty acts or eccentric performers. They tend to come from the Nordic countries – which seem determined to prove that they are not the sober and industrious types we believe them to be, but have got an unconventional and fun side to their national characters. The presence of these wacky acts on the Eurovision stage can always be cited as proof that there is room in today's Europe for individualists and nonconformists, and that – for all our seriousness and modernity – we can still enjoy a jolly good laugh at ourselves.

Eurovision's novelty acts usually garner a reasonable share of the votes – which may explain their persistence. However, even their most precious asset – their strangeness or novelty value – soon begins to wear thin, and they have seldom built successful careers in the aftermath of the contest. Perhaps we collude as viewers in their participation because we fear we will be accused of having no sense of humour if we confess that we do not regard the madcap antics of these clowns as remotely amusing.

For me, the role of Eurovision jester was epitomised by Guido Horn – the wild man of the Rhineland-Palatinate rock scene. Guido represented Germany in 1998, and, unusually for a rock musician, played the cow bells. He also rushed about the stage – and into the audience – in erratic moves that were clearly designed to give the impression of a deranged but creative spontaneity. By 1998, Herr Horn was already very popular in Germany: perhaps his dishevelled appearance and zany stage persona seemed to offer a welcome inversion of the national stereotype. I suppose the name of his backing group – the Orthopaedic Stockings – gave the rest of us some clue as to what we might expect. Guido did not win the 1998 contest, but he did not disgrace himself – at least, not in terms of the number of votes he received.

In Copenhagen in 2014, it was Iceland's turn to provide the novelty. 'Pollapönk' consisted of four bearded musicians who were joined by two backing singers for the TV performance. These two backing singers were both large men with thick beards, and they both wore dark shades. They were dressed in vivid orange and purple jumpsuits and matching baseball caps – weirdly reminiscent of the outfits worn by the Islamic jihadists detained in Guantanamo Bay. They stood impassive and immobile throughout most of the performance; their brooding presence on stage was deemed enough to signal just how mad they were.

The Icelandic band had turned up for the Copenhagen contest's red carpet event wearing brightly coloured women's dresses. They told the assembled press this was a gesture to show their solidarity with women – 'girls, mothers and grandmothers' – everywhere. As it happened, the eventual winner of the Copenhagen contest was a genuine drag queen, and she also wore a beard. That was more or less where the similarities between the two sets of beards ended. Conchita Wurst's beard was immaculately groomed: in fact, it looked as if it were the only fake part of her manicured appearance. The Icelanders, on the other hand, boasted real men's beards. They were full and bushy – though still quite neatly trimmed. Just in case there were any lingering doubts about their sexual orientation, they also wore men's trousers under their flaming chiffon frocks.

The name of Pollapönk suggests that these Icelanders saw themselves as heirs to the rebellious punk tradition in rock music. But it was no surprise that the mildly transgressive nature of their costumes proved to be cosmetic. At heart, they were still your archetypal socially responsible and earnest Scandinavians. In fact, the band had been founded by two schoolteachers – and their ambition had been 'to make music that appealed to both children and adults alike, [and] which the whole family could enjoy together'. One of their earlier songs had dealt with the harrowing experiences of a young boy who stammered. According to the band's press release, they had hoped this would help place the problems that people with speech impediments face 'firmly on the agenda'.

Pollapönk 2014 entry was called 'Without Prejudice', and its lyrics pleaded for greater tolerance of Europe's minorities: '*Let's do away with prejudice*', they sang. '*We've got to get together on this.*' It was, once again, an admirable sentiment, but hardly a controversial message. It transpired that one of the band's crazy backing singers was an elected member of the Icelandic parliament – which may have been carrying the joke a little too far. I suppose that, by voting for the Icelanders, Eurovision viewers were not only showing that they cared about the sort of world they were creating for their children, but also that they had a keen – and an appealingly quirky – sense of humour.

Ireland does not have a tradition of entering novelty acts in the Eurovision: for most of the past half-century, we have taken the contest too seriously to go down that road. It might also be the case that, unlike our Nordic cousins, we have little to prove to the rest of the world as far as madness is concerned. However, there has been one notable exception to this general rule: in 2008, Ireland became the first country to enter a puppet in the competition.

Dustin was the name of a puppet turkey who had first appeared regularly on an RTÉ afternoon children's programme called *The Den* in the early 1990s. Originally, he was merely the sidekick to two other puppets called Zig and Zag. They had originally planned to eat him for Christmas, but, when it was revealed that Dustin was half-vulture, his life was spared, and his future with RTÉ TV was assured. When Zig and Zag were signed by a British TV channel and moved to the UK, it was time for the Turkey to shine, and, over the years, he established himself as a lead character in his own right. He spoke with a pronounced Dublin accent, and expressed himself in the irreverent vernacular – and fabled wit – of the city's streets. Children loved him because of his cheekiness to his adult co-presenters, but Dustin also managed to acquire a substantial audience outside the young people's demographic.

He frequently appeared on mainstream TV shows – where he specialised in the unmerciful 'slagging' of Ireland's home-grown stars and celebrities. There was – to say the least – a dearth of satirical humour on Irish television for most of this period, and Dustin served, in part, to fill that vacuum. The hapless butts of the Turkey's jokes tended to freeze in his company: rictus smiles fixed on their faces as they were subjected to protracted ridicule from Dustin. They clearly felt unable to respond in kind because it might indicate to the public that they lacked a robust sense of humour. The Turkey took full advantage of the license this afforded him, and his comedic shtick was often pointed; sometimes, acerbic; occasionally, wounding.

One of Dustin's favourite targets was Pat Kenny – the host of RTÉ's flagship series, *The Late Late Show*. It became something of a tradition on *The Late Late*'s annual Christmas show for Pat to stand and smile while he was roundly abused by the Turkey. 'You're so wooden you could get two tables, four chairs and a hat stand out of you', was a fairly typical jibe.

Over the years, the Turkey became something of a cult figure in Ireland – and, as the decades passed, his public career was able to diversify. In 1997, he announced his intention to stand for the Irish Presidency, and, in the subsequent election, Dustin received a surprisingly large number of (spoiled) votes. He also released a number of records – with over a dozen singles, and half-a-dozen albums. These featured vocals from many well-known Irish stars, such as Ronnie Drew, Bob Geldof, Boyzone and Joe Dolan. Most of the recordings were parodies of Irish folk songs, or old chart hits, and a large part of the humour was provided by Dustin's jarringly discordant voice. The Turkey's ventures into popular music proved very successful, and, on one occasion, he even held the coveted Christmas number one slot in Ireland.

The success of these records may have emboldened Dustin to enter the Eurovision contest. But there might also have been the feeling that the Turkey's TV career was flatlining, and needed something of a boost. In 2008 Dustin entered the national song contest designed to find Ireland's entry for the Eurovision, and his entry was accepted by RTÉ.

The producers who made that decision must have been aware that the chances of Dustin winning the national contest were extremely high. Dustin was, after all, a well-known and very popular figure who had been a constant presence on Irish TV screens for almost two decades. By contrast, most of the other contestants were unknown to Ireland's viewing public – their odds of beating the Turkey were slim to zero.

Puppets are not expressly forbidden in the Eurovision rules. However, RTÉ had several options when considering Dustin's submitted song. The station had the right to determine that puppets were disbarred from entering Ireland's national song contest. RTÉ could also have rejected Dustin's entry for its lack of musical appeal. But RTÉ chose to do neither, and to accept the Turkey's entry as bona fide, and it may be worth considering why that decision was made.

To begin with, the station was still smarting from its abject defeat in Helsinki, and were looking for a clear and empthatic change of direction. At that time, almost no one who had been part of the run of Eurovision victories in the 1990s was still working in RTÉ's TV Entertainment Department. For the most part, they had either left the station, or were employed in different capacities. Perhaps those in charge in 2008 also wished to make it clear that they had moved on from the previous decade. 'They wanted to show that they were part of a new generation,' one producer told me, 'and that they could bring a fresh perspective to the event.' In the past, Ireland's Eurovision offerings had sometimes been painfully sincere; this time,

RTÉ would enter the contest with explicit and self-conscious irony. Perhaps it was believed this represented a more sophisticated approach to the contest – and one that was more in keeping with Ireland's (then) current status as a thoroughly modern European state, with a booming 'Tiger' economy.

In that context, it may seem surprising that RTÉ reverted to the selection format that had been followed in Ireland's national song contests throughout the 1990s – as a standalone show – with the same system of televoting and SMS that had been adopted in the previous decade. That was, however, the recommendation of the special 'Consultative Committee' that had been set up following Ireland's humiliating performance in the 2007 contest. What is more striking is that the song eventually chosen to represent Ireland was, in musical terms, also something of a throwback – since it was clearly based on the techno-dance tracks that were a feature of the 1990s.

Ireland's 2008 national song contest was broadcast live from the University of Limerick's Concert Hall. Apart from Dustin, there were five acts taking part, but well before the event had taken place, the media – inside and outside Ireland – had focused its attention on the Turkey. On the morning of the competition, Dustin appeared on Sky News. He was interviewed by a TV anchor with the sort of mock-seriousness that was intended to signal that he too 'got' the joke: 'Do you regard yourself as something of a diplomat for your country?' he asked Dustin, and smirked at the irony of his own question. Later that evening, Dustin also appeared on BBC's *The One Show*. It seemed the British were delighted to have found someone who appeared to be even more cynical about the Eurovision contest than they were. The British certainly seemed more enthusiastic about Dustin than some of those in the University Concert Hall that night.

The other performers had good reason to feel apprehensive. On the morning of the national contest, the Turkey had received a generous endorsement from Bob Geldof – which was headlined on the front page of the *Irish Times*. By the time the contest commenced that evening, Dustin was the red-hot favourite to win – with odds at 2/9 on. The Turkey was the second act to perform, and, for the first time in the history of the event, a contestant was booed – even before he had arrived on stage. It was not hard to see why Dustin had provoked and angered some of those present. Many of them were friends or relatives of the other artists – to whom the chance of competing in the Eurovision meant a very great deal. The sheer presence of the Turkey – whose recording career was based on his apparent inability to sing in tune – seemed to ride roughshod over their hopes and dreams.

In musical terms, the Turkey's song – deliberately misspelled as '*Irelande – Douze Pointe*' – was principally distinguished by its thumping bass line. The satiric edge of the song was fairly blunt, and there was an obvious attempt to appeal to a prospective European audience: '*Do you like Irish stew?*' Dustin asked. '*Or goulash as it is to you?*' It was clear that Dustin's sights were already set beyond Limerick's Concert Hall. As it happened, the lyrics hardly mattered. The song was belted out by Dustin at such breakneck speed that there was little time for the audience to comprehend – let alone be amused by – what he was saying.

What was unavoidable, however, was the strident manner in which Dustin's song was staged. The Turkey was wheeled out in a supermarket shopping trolley; three semi-naked male dancers threw themselves about the stage; while two women, strutting around in grossly unflattering costumes, provided the backing vocals. The overall impact managed somehow to seem both incoherent and knowing at the same time. Given the musical bombardment, the scrambled lyrics and the anarchic staging, it was clear that the chief thing going for Dustin that night was his familiarity and popularity with the Irish public.

In some respects, Dustin's song might be understood as a reaction to the bland musical arrangement, the lack of production values and the lyrical pomposity of Ireland's previous entry. 'They Can't Hold Back the Spring' had combined traditional Irish instruments with sentiments that strained for significance – in a naive attempt to construct some sort of pan-European liberation anthem. But, risible as Ireland's entry for the 2007 contest may have been, Dustin's attempt to reach out to other European countries was also to prove ineffective.

It was, of course, obvious from the outset that the Turkey's song was intended as a parody, but it was not clear to me precisely what was being parodied. Put simply, the satire of the song seemed to lack a sharpness of focus. The dominant musical idioms in the past half-century of Eurovision contests have been pop songs and power ballads, not disco. Perhaps the real target of the Turkey's satire did not lie in continental Europe, but closer to home. In one of the verses of his song, Dustin apologised to his fellow Europeans '*for Riverdance*'. The lyrics also referred rather dismissively to Michael Flatley – the charismatic star of *Riverdance* – as '*a Yank*'. Halfway through the Turkey's performance, the male dancers and backing singers came together briefly to form an Irish step-dancing chorus line – and, once again, the obvious point of reference was Eurovision's 1994 interval act.

A panel of commentators had been assembled beside Limerick's Concert Hall stage. They were not there to vote, but to give their opinions of the songs, and, as it turned out, their views proved to be prescient. The first to speak after Dustin's performance was Dana – Ireland's first Eurovision winner. She claimed to 'respect' Dustin, but believed his entry was 'not a song for Eurovision'. In the weeks that followed, Dana's hostility to the song became more emphatic.

The next member of the panel was the previous year's Eurovision winner, Marija Šerifović. According to a press release, Marija's performances were characterised by her 'strong emotion, specific colour and strength of voice'. She was also the first Eurovision winner to declare herself openly as lesbian. It would have been interesting to learn her views on the Turkey's act, but she seemed genuinely puzzled by 'the duck', as she called Dustin. Perhaps she felt that, as a guest in Ireland, it was not her place to venture an opinion. Her only comment was a plaintive and enigmatic: 'What can I say?'

Last to express an opinion was Louis Walsh, who had considerable experience and knowledge of the Eurovision contest. His view of the song was: 'I don't think they'll know what to make of it in Europe.' Louis Walsh had been the good-natured victim of Dustin's ridicule on many prior occasions, and he clearly enjoyed telling the Turkey that it was 'good to see you booed for a change – since you normally are booing others'.

None of this seemed to bother the viewers at home, and, when the results of the popular vote were revealed, it was clear that Dustin had won a landslide victory. He returned to the stage of the Concert Hall to reprise his song at the end of the TV show – and, once again, he was greeted by a considerable amount of booing from the audience. However, in the weeks that followed, it seemed that Dustin had indeed become 'something of a diplomat' for Ireland. He was interviewed extensively by the foreign press, and on St Patrick's Day represented his native country on British breakfast television, where the ever-cheerful presenters appeared to find him hilarious – always a worrying sign.

As the contest approached, it seemed that some senior figures in RTÉ had come to believe their own publicity. When I spoke to one of those with special responsibility for the Eurovision entry, he was convinced that Ireland was on the brink of another famous victory. He believed that the Irish entry would be welcomed across Europe as 'something different', and confessed that he had even begun to check out possible venues where we might host the following year's contest. He thought that Dustin's song would send out a message that 'the Irish don't take themselves too seriously'. Whether or not anyone wished – or needed – to hear such a message was a question that did not seem to have troubled him.

RTÉ's Julian Vignoles believed Dustin's entry showed that the station was prepared 'to move with the times'. He defended the puppet and the anarchic staging of his song. 'Something that makes an impact on the stage,' he claimed, 'is as likely to win as a well-crafted song.' It was a candid – if somewhat jaundiced – assessment of the contest. But Ireland's partners in the European Broadcasting Union were inclined to take a much less favourable view of the Irish entry. Many of them were shocked and appalled by the song – which they believed made a mockery of everything that the contest stood for. It was even suggested by some that Ireland should be excluded from that year's event on the grounds that the Irish entry would bring the Eurovision into disrepute.

There were other more specific complaints: the Greeks objected to Dustin's mention of 'Macedonia', since it was EBU policy that this state would always be described as 'The Former Yugoslav Republic of Macedonia': a name that is, admittedly, difficult to work into the lyrics of most popular songs. The number of Irish performers on stage was also queried: Eurovision rules only permitted six of these, but the Irish act now numbered seven – if one included the Turkey. RTÉ argued that, since Dustin was confined to a shopping trolley, he was not technically on stage – and the EBU conceded the point.

Ireland had finished last in the previous year's contest, so Dustin had to compete in a semi-final in order to qualify for the Grand Final. There was little doubt in the minds of the Irish delegation that this was a mere formality, and that the Turkey would sail through to the main event. However, Darren Smith, one of the song's composers – was aware that this should not have been considered as automatic. 'The voters in the semi-finals tend to be dedicated fans of the contest,' he told me, 'and they were probably less appreciative of Dustin than the typical audience for a Eurovision final.'

Dolly Parton famously once remarked that you need to spend a lot of money to look really cheap, and Ireland's Eurovision entry for 2008 seemed to confirm the wisdom of her words. The Irish entourage that arrived in the Serbian capital that May was the largest ever, and the staging had been considerably enhanced since the original performance in Limerick. The guiding principle seemed to have been that less is . . . well, less. Dustin was still in his trolley, but was now dressed in a sparkling silver suit. There was a profusion of feathers, gold and glitter on stage. The dancers looked as if they belonged in a low-rent leather bar, and their moves had become more frenzied. Heavy make-up and plumed headdresses made the backing singers look even more like drag queens. The overall visual impression for me was chaotic and confusing.

It seemed that the extravagant staging of the Irish act marked some attempt to engage with a camp aesthetic – and, perhaps, to win the votes of the contest's large number of gay fans. Camp has been an integral part of the Eurovision contest for many years, but it had seldom been presented on stage with such indiscriminate vigour. By comparison, Conchita Wurst – the 'bearded lady' who won the contest in 2014 – would seem to be a model of restraint. Of course, she could also sing.

In several respects, the Turkey would seem a most unlikely icon for the Eurovision's gay constituency – given his dreadful dress sense, and predilection for belching and farting on screen. Setting Dustin in such a camp context might have worked if it had been presented with a greater degree of sophistication. As it was, combining Dustin's rough and ready persona with the hyper-camp staging of his song simply did not seem credible, and the interaction between Dustin and the rest of the Irish performers was non-existent. The problem was not that television viewers were unable to grasp the satiric intentions: the problem was that the overproduced staging allowed those intentions to come across as simply too crude and blatant.

'Eastern Europe – we love you!' Dustin roared in the closing stages of his song. He went on to name sixteen of the countries that had once been part of the Soviet bloc.

No doubt, such open soliciting of votes was meant to be ironic, but, at the end of the competition, Dustin really *did* want Eastern European votes. The implicit condescension of this appeal does not seem to have been lost in Eastern Europe: only three of the countries he had name-checked gave him any votes. As it turned out, this lack of support from the East was to prove decisive in Dustin's rapid ejection from the contest.

There was considerable shock in Ireland when the Turkey failed to make the cut for the Grand Final. There was even a sense of national embarrassment; it seemed that nobody had found Ireland's little joke as funny as the Irish did. One of the members of the Irish delegation told me how, on the flight back to Ireland, he had the first inkling of the hostile reception they were about to encounter. 'That day's Irish newspapers were on the plane,' he told me, 'and the first one I opened had a review of our performance that could only be described as savage.' It seemed as if Dustin's act was no longer regarded by the Irish media as a harmless bit of fun, but as something approaching a national disgrace. Questions were raised in Current Affairs programmes on RTE, and even in Dáil Éireann. Not surprisingly, the station seemed anxious to evade any responsibility for what had occured in Belgrade. It was pointed out to me by several of those involved in the selection procedure that Dustin's song had been chosen by a popular vote. If anyone were to blame for the selection, it could therefore only be those members of the Irish public who had voted for the Turkey.

This argument strikes me as rather disingenuous. It was, after all, quite predictable that a popular figure – who had appeared frequently on RTÉ television over many years – would win any vote when he was competing with performers who lacked any significant degree of public recognition. For me, the primary responsibility for the failure of the Turkey's Eurovision venture does not lie with Dustin, or with any of those in his team. Instead, his selection represented a error on the part of RTÉ – and a lack of understanding of what the contest is about.

In the immediate aftermath of Dustin's defeat, RTÉ claimed to have been delighted with the Irish performance. The station also announced that it had major plans for the Turkey's future broadcasting career. Work had already begun, it was claimed, on a new series for Dustin: one that would be aimed at a 'more mature audience'. A pilot version of a new show was eventually produced, but the promised series never materialised. The Turkey was also dropped from his long-standing TV slot on *The Den*. Dustin later claimed that it had taken 'four or five of us' to create *The Den*, and 'about fifty-five RTE managers to knock it down.' The trace of bitterness in his comments seems understandable. 'I suppose the Eurovision fiasco was a tipping point,' one RTÉ producer told me. 'After that type of exposure, he couldn't really go back to what he had been doing. It just wouldn't have been appropriate.'

On his return to Ireland, Dustin launched his own campaign against the ratification of the Lisbon Treaty of the European Union. He was frank about his motives: 'They didn't vote for us,' he said. 'Now, we can get them back.' Perhaps the Turkey found some consolation when the Irish public rejected the EU Treaty in a referendum the following month – though, perhaps, the Irish Government's blundering 'Yes' campaign also contributed in large measure to that result.

Dustin's performance in the Eurovision may have damaged his career within Ireland, but it seems to have opened some doors for him elsewhere, and he has no apparent regrets about participating. Neither does Darren Smith – one of the composers: 'The song was a joke that started in a pub,' he told me, 'and perhaps it should have stayed there. But I'm glad it didn't.' Although Dustin seldom appears on Irish TV these days, he can still be found on social media and he continues to be regarded with great affection by many of his fans.

Other European countries are still bewildered: they cannot understand why Ireland should have sought to denigrate an event to which it had been so committed – and so successful – in the recent past. They are also puzzled by Ireland's criticism of *Riverdance* – a cultural phenomenon that is widely regarded as one of the outstanding creative achievements in the history of the contest.

In some respects, it is tempting to view Dustin's Eurovision adventure as one of the last hurrahs of the Celtic Tiger. When the Turkey won Ireland's national song contest, Bertie Ahern – the man whose freewheeling style and 'light touch' approach seemed to embody Ireland's boom years – was still taoiseach. When Dustin arrived in Serbia, Ahern had already been replaced by Brian Cowen – the man who, over the next few years, would sleepwalk the country into economic misery.

Three months after Dustin's failure to qualify for the Eurovision Final, it was announced that Ireland had officially entered economic recession – for the first time since 1983. Later in the same month, the Irish Government decided – in chaotic circumstances – to offer a €400 billion guarantee to prevent the collapse of the Irish banking system. Ireland is still paying the price for that rushed and ill-considered decision – and will continue to do so for some years to come.

Since 2008, it has become apparent that the degree of national self-confidence that Ireland's economic boom had helped to generate was gravely misplaced. There is now ample evidence that supervision of the Irish financial system was hopelessly lax and wholly inadequate. The high degree of confidence − some might say, the hubris − with which the Irish travelled to Serbia in the spring of 2008 also proved to be ill-founded. But pride, as they say, often precedes a fall.

25.
The Road to Nowhere

After the debacle in Belgrade, it was rumoured that, once again, RTÉ producers were talking to Johnny Logan about the possibility of him writing and singing for Ireland. According to one Irish newspaper, RTÉ had offered Logan a deal that would include a substantial lump-sum payment, as well as his own 'prime time music show'. It was claimed this was similar to a deal that had been struck with Brian Kennedy in 2006. But, once again, agreement was not reached between the singer and the station.

Given the grim economic scenario that was unfolding in Ireland, there was speculation that RTÉ might withdraw from the contest entirely – or, at least, try to save money by making an internal selection. Instead, RTÉ chose to revert to the format that had been used in 2007 – and made the national song contest part of a special edition of *The Late Late Show*. Six acts would be chosen by a new judging panel to compete in the final of the national song contest, and the winner would be decided by a mixture of regional juries – in Dublin, Sligo, Cork and Limerick – and by a televote. Unusually, the judging panel did not contain any editorial representatives of RTÉ television.

Selection of the act that would travel to Russia took place in February 2009. The host, Pat Kenny, asked the RTÉ commentator, Marty Whelan, and the former Eurovision winner, Linda Martin – who had served as chairperson of the judging panel that had selected the six finalists – to assess each of the songs. The third person asked to assess them was rather more unexpected: Jerry Springer. Although RTÉ's press office drew attention to his recent work as the host of a US talent series, Springer's principal claim to fame was still the lurid TV talk show that he has presented for many years. He was polite, but seemed somewhat bemused throughout the *Late Late*.

Some of the songwriters competing in Ireland's 2009 national contest came from other European countries – and so did one of the artists. The song performed by Kristīna Zaharova had been submitted to the Latvian national contest as well as to the Irish – and had been selected for both national finals. It was clearly impossible to take part in both, so the composers decided to withdraw from the Latvian event, and to participate in the Irish final. It was a decision they may have regretted later – since Kristīna only finished as an also-ran in Dublin.

The winner of the 2009 national song contest was Sinéad Mulvey and Black Daisy, whose song 'Et Cetera' received thirty-eight out of forty points from the four regional juries, and the maximum forty points from the televote. Both Sinéad and Black Daisy had been separate competitors in previous seasons of *You're a Star* – although neither had won that competition. It had been RTÉ's idea to combine the two acts – in the process, excluding one of the existing members of the band, and relegating its lead singer to a supporting vocal role.

After their win, Sinéad Mulvey described the song as 'modern', 'new' and 'funky', and promised that she and the band were going to 'rock Moscow' in the 2009 Eurovision. However, the song seemed closer to mainstream pop than rock, with a marked similarity to the sort of material produced by the *American Idol* winner Kelly Clarkson in the previous decade.

'Et Cetera' had been written by a multinational team of Irish, Swedish, Italian and Danish composers. The team included Jonas Gladnikoff. Jonas is perhaps best known for his role in writing 'I Wanna Dance the Go Go' for the Technicoloured Roses – a three-piece combo in which he also plays. He had already begun to specialise in entering the national song contests of many of Europe's peripheral countries: Moldova, Albania, Bulgaria, Lithuania, Romania, Latvia, Hungary and Iceland. However, it was only Ireland that selected his songs as entries in the Eurovision. Over the next few years, Jonas would be involved in writing no less than three of Ireland's entries – though, alas, not with any great success.

Because Dustin had failed to qualify for the Eurovision Final in 2008, Sinéad Mulvey and Black Daisy had to compete and qualify in a semi-final before they could appear in the Grand Final. In rehearsals, it soon became clear that a number of changes had been introduced to the staging of their song. When they had performed on *The Late Late Show*, they were accompanied by two backing singers. By the time they reached Moscow, the backing singers had been dropped. Sinéad's hair had also been restyled, and the overall appearance of the band had been sharpened to make them look more like archetypal rock chicks.

The biggest change, however, was in the visual direction of the song. For obvious reasons, the director of the Eurovision semi-final had many more cameras, and other technical equipment at his disposal than the director in RTÉ's Studio 1 back in Dublin. As a result, the pace of cutting and the speed and fluidity of camera movement had been greatly enhanced from the Irish national contest. This certainly accentuated the modern feel of the song, but the use of sophisticated technology also tended to shift the focus away from the band – and to an extent undermined their central role in the performance of the song.

The viewing – and voting – audience needs to connect at some level with each act, and it is obviously harder for them to do so if the cameras only rest fleetingly on each of the performers. Insofar as they could be heard or understood, the lyrics were also rather downbeat and unromantic – telling of a young woman's growing disillusion with the serial infidelity of her partner.

Once again, there was genuine surprise in Ireland when the Irish entry failed to qualify for the Grand Final. There was dismay, in particular, in RTÉ's Entertainment Department – since this was the second year running that Ireland had not been able to enter the final. Once again, the station announced that it was planning to hold a review of future strategy. Once again, there was speculation that RTÉ might choose to withdraw from the next Eurovision due to the dire economic climate in Ireland.

However, in October 2009, the station confirmed that Ireland would continue to participate in the contest. Indeed, the station seemed determined to approach the following year's Eurovision with a renewed sense of purpose. After the disappointing result in the 2009 contest, RTÉ had set up another internal review of the selection procedure, and had decided on what it termed 'some important and necessary modifications'. The station claimed to have listened closely to the 'comments and conclusions' of the 2009 expert judging panel.

Not only had RTÉ listened closely to those 'comments and conclusions', but, 'based on their work on Eurosong 2009', the station had decided to reappoint the same panel for the 2010 contest. This might seem rather a strange decision – given the failure of that panel to identify a song that was able to reach the Eurovision Final in 2009. In this context, it was revealing that the five-member panel still did not include a TV producer – or, indeed, any member of RTÉ's Programme Division.

In fact, RTÉ had decided to give the 2009 panel even greater control over the selection of Ireland's 2010 Eurovision entry – or, in the words of the station's press release, to give its members 'more flexibility' in relation to the 'pairing of songs and performers'. According to the press release, 'serious and detailed deliberation' was required by the judging panel of 'all the possible options' so that Ireland's performance could be dramatically improved.

RTÉ also announced details of new rules for the national song contest. Once again, the station not only asked for original songs, but for the proposed performance and staging details. RTÉ had decided that the judging panel would be 'entitled to engage in discussions with any songwriter or performer or combination of these in respect of any entry with a view to selecting the strongest possible combination of song and performer.' This not only gave the panel the right to select the performer – it also allowed its members to attach the performer of one song with another entry. There were clearly very high expectations of the panel's capacity to deliver, but, in delegating its editorial role, it seemed as if RTÉ's Entertainment Department had lost some confidence in its own professional judgment.

In February 2010, RTÉ revealed the names of the five finalists in the national contest, and it turned out that the allegedly radical strategy devised by the judging panel was, in reality, thoroughly conservative. The line-up of finalists included some very familiar names, such as Mikey Graham, a member of Boyzone, and Niamh Kavanagh, who had won the Eurovision in 1993. Leanne Moore, who had won the last season of the reality talent show, *You're a Star*, was also in the final, and so was Lee Bradshaw, who had competed in the previous year's national song contest.

The songwriters selected by the panel also featured some familiar names: John Waters and Tommy Moran – who had written Ireland's failed entry of 2007 – were back in the reckoning, and so were some veteran composers from other European countries. Marc Paelinck, from Belgium had written Eurovision songs for Belgium's national final on two occasions, and also for Malta in the previous year – although none of his songs had performed well in their respective finals, and they had all failed to appear in the Eurovision. Among the other songwriters was Ralph Siegel – who was something of a legend in Eurovision circles. He had written many previous Eurovision entries – for Germany, Switzerland, Montenegro and Luxembourg – and had even won the Eurovision on one occasion. His writing partner, Bernd Meinunger, preferred to use the *nom de plume* of John O'Flynn when he and Siegel entered the Irish contest.

Jonas Gladnikoff was the Swedish composer who had been part of the writing team responsible for Ireland's previous entry, when Sinéad Mulvey and Black Daisy had failed to qualify for the final. This time, he was part of the team who had written Niamh Kavanagh's song.

The national song contest was again staged on a *Late Late Show* special, which was hosted by Ryan Tubridy – who had now replaced Pat Kenny as the resident host. The show featured performances by Dana and Johnny Logan – as well as one from Michael Ball, the British runner-up in the 1992 final. Dana and Logan were joined by RTÉ's Eurovision commentator, Marty Whelan, to assess each of the competing songs. Given the context, it was hardly surprising that their remarks were uniformly bland and non-committal. The songwriters were also asked to explain the meaning of their work to Tubridy. Since most of them had entered the contest on previous occasions, they were almost all asked if they were 'gluttons for punishment' – a question that might have been better addressed to the studio audience.

Six regional juries and a public televote determined that 'It's for You', sung by Niamh Kavanagh, was the winner of the national contest – gaining the maximum points from both the regional juries and the public televote. Once again, Niamh would represent Ireland in the Eurovision – this time in Oslo – and, for the second year running, Jonas Gladnikoff was part of the winning songwriting team.

Niamh's performance in the national contest had seemed at odds with RTÉ's prior claim to be concerned with the impact of the staging and production of the Irish entry. Her winning song was performed with the utmost simplicity: there were no special effects, dancers, mime artists or acrobats. Instead, she was accompanied by two backing singers and a whistle player – whose presence on the stage was almost subliminal. When she performed in Oslo, the only significant change to the production was that Niamh was now wearing a long dark-purple dress. The original design chosen for her had been dropped by RTÉ in favour of a more conservative look. Not surprisingly, the original designers were deeply upset: they accused RTÉ of shoddy, unprofessional treatment. They claimed that the original dress had been commissioned by RTÉ at a fraction of their usual fee, and that they had been 'led up the garden path' by the station.

Certainly, the dress that Niamh wore in Oslo did her few favours, since it looked bulky and lacked definition on screen. However, by all accounts, Niamh Kavanagh was popular among spectators and journalists in Oslo. She was not only regarded as friendly and unpretentious – but also as one of the best vocalists ever to have taken part in the Eurovision contest. And, as a former winner of the contest, she was treated with respect by the other artists.

Because of Sinéad Mulvey and Black Daisy's poor result in 2009, Niamh had first to compete in a semi-final in order to qualify for the final. There were now two semi-finals, and Niamh sang in the second of these. The EBU had decided that the voting system would change from previous years to balance televoting with national juries. This change had been introduced to offset what was perceived to be the 'Easternisation' of the contest. It was believed that selected juries – with a background in the media – would be more receptive to the style of Western European performers. RTÉ believed that this change would also benefit Niamh, and there was considerable relief among the Irish delegation when she managed to become the first Irish act in several years to reach the Grand Final.

Niamh was not the first Eurovision winner to return to compete in the contest. However, in general, those who have been drawn to the contest for a second time have not fared as well as they had hoped. In fact, Johnny Logan is still the only Eurovision winning performer to score a second victory – and, in his case, both the song and his performance were widely considered to have been stronger than on his first appearance. In 2010, Niamh Kavanagh showed that she was still an excellent singer, but neither the lyrics nor the melody of her song were as appealing as in 1993, and they did not allow her to display the same vocal and emotional range. At the end of the night, she scored a total of just twenty-five points – and finished twenty-third out of twenty-five entries.

Niamh Kavanagh took her low score with characteristic equanimity. She believed that she had performed the song to the best of her ability. 'If I hadn't sung well,' she said later, 'I'd have been disappointed. But I felt I did everything I could and did it well, so I'm happy with that.' She was also aware of her role in the continuing story of the contest. 'Once a winner of the Eurovision, always a winner,' she claimed. 'Once you win, you're forever part of the club.'

There was obvious disappointment in RTÉ at the result. This was not only because members of the Irish delegation had believed that Niamh deserved a better place. It was also because it meant that the Irish entry in 2011 would, once again, have to compete in the semi-finals, and that Ireland's place in the Grand Final was not secure. Beyond that, the poor result cast further doubt on the capacity of the judging panel to identify a strong contender for the contest – and, perhaps, also on RTÉ's own naivety in placing repeated faith in their judgment.

Once again, RTÉ had to go back to the drawing board, and come up with a new plan – and, once again, that plan would entail moving the responsibility of producing an Irish winner outside the station. On this occasion, RTÉ's decision would result in Ireland being represented by twin brothers that were – to say the least – not highly regarded for their singing abilities, but who still proved able to deliver Ireland the best result in a decade.

26.
Double Exposure

The failure of the judging panel in 2009 and 2010 to identify a successful Eurovision act had led RTÉ to consider a new selection process. The new procedure involved choosing five professionals in Ireland's music industry, who would develop and mentor five separate song entries for the national song contest. The five mentors were given the right to source and commission both the song and the performer. The winner of the national contest would be chosen from a combination of public votes and regional juries, and would represent Ireland in the Eurovision semi-final in Dusseldorf, Germany.

According to RTÉ's Julian Vignoles, it was the station's duty to see what method could improve Ireland's chances of winning on the Eurovision stage. He believed that Ireland had a vibrant and successful music industry which could be harnessed to find the best performer. In that context, he continued, RTÉ had decided to 'suspend the open call for entries', and instead to 'harness the skills and experience of professionals' to source both the 'talent and the song'.

This marked a radical shift in the selection of Ireland's national entry: in effect, it ended the policy of open access to the contest, and also transferred significant creative control to a number of individuals outside the station. The five chosen mentors only included one who had any background in professional entertainment production: Caroline Downey, who had a track record of staging highly successful events.

The composer, Ronan Hardiman, who had written the score for Michael Flatley's *Lord of the Dance* – mentored the singer-songwriter Don Mescall, who had written an unsuccessful Eurovision entry in 2006. Hardiman had also co-written the song for the national contest with Mescall. David Hayes, a music arranger, mentored Nikki Kavanagh – one of the former Eurovision winner's backing singers – with a song that had been written by a team that once again included Jonas Gladnikoff. Willie Kavanagh – the chairman of EMI Music in Ireland – mentored Patrick Mahoney. Liam Lawson, another composer, mentored the Vard Sisters – who had also written their own song.

Finally, there was Caroline Downey, who mentored John and Edward Grimes, better known together as Jedward. They were not her original choice of act, but she was turned down by the first two singers she approached. Then, Louis Walsh suggested that she consider the Grimes brothers. She told me that she was apprehensive at first, since she was aware of their vocal limitations. However, once she had decided to mentor Jedward, Caroline brought both her professional nous and personal determination to the task in hand.

She listened to dozens of possible songs before settling on one that had been written by a multinational writing team – which included two members of Deekay, a Danish production and song-writing house. Deekay had an established reputation for providing songs for a wide range of artists. However, it is unlikely that any of their previous work had been written for such an eccentric act as Jedward.

The Grimes brothers had first attracted public attention when they appeared on the sixth series of the UK's reality talent show, *The X-Factor,* in 2009. This series is, in essence, an old-fashioned singing competition, and part of the reason that John and Edward stood out from the crowd of other entrants was due to their obvious lack of musical ability. But there were other reasons for their appeal to the viewing public: the brothers were identical twins; they seemed utterly self-confident; they were possessed of what appeared like demonic energy; and they seemed to be geuinely *strange.* Perhaps above all, they were recognisable by their upright and rigid hair – otherwise known as the 'Viagra' style.

The ways in which the brothers mirrored each other's actions, their apparent compulsion to 'vogue' for the camera, and the bewildering speed with which they could free associate – both on and off stage – seemed to suggest that the Grimes boys came from a different planet. The twins appeared able – simultaneously – to mock and endorse the underlying ethos of *The X-Factor.* It was also possible for the series' viewers to have it both ways, and to vote for Jedward to win the competition with some sense of subversive irony.

The performances of the twins as they progressed through the various stages of *The X-Factor* were notable for their enthusiasm rather than their talent. Despite being described by Simon Cowell as 'not very good and incredibly annoying', Jedward still managed to finish in the final six. They were subsequently managed by Louis Walsh, who had been their champion on the TV show.

In the aftermath of the series, the brothers became one of the most financially successful of all former *X-Factor* contestants: signing record deals, releasing hit singles and albums, appearing on many TV programmes, and embarking on extensive tours of Ireland and the UK. I filmed Jedward for a charity project in 2010. The twins were just beginning their *Planet Jedward* tour, and I was struck both by their anarchic vitality, and by the remarkable devotion of their young fans: indeed, their popularity in Ireland was such that it was compared by one Irish journalist to that of Beatlemania.

Given the extent of Jedward's popularity, there was concern among the other performers and songwriters that Ireland's national contest would turn out to be a one-horse race. There were also suggestions that Jedward's song had been given an unfair advantage by its early release as a single, and there were moves by the other mentors to have the brothers disbarred from the contest. RTÉ responded by agreeing to deduct 20 percent of Jedward's share of the public vote – so that the balance was shifted towards the regional juries. It seemed like a clumsy solution, but it was enough to pacify the other entries and ensure that they would continue to participate.

Louis Walsh, the Grimes brothers' manager, reacted angrily to rumours that RTÉ did not want the twins to win the national contest. In his typically outspoken manner, he told the Irish press that Jedward had 'a lot of shite to deal with', and that RTÉ executives had staged a 'dirty tricks campaign' in an attempt to stop them representing Ireland in Dusseldorf. If there had been a 'concerted attempt' to damage the twins' chances, as Louis claimed, it was to prove unsuccessful. Although the regional juries voted for Nikki Kavanagh's song, the public's votes were overwhelmingly for Jedward – even after 20 per cent of them had been discounted – and that was enough to tip the count in the brothers' favour by the narrow margin of just two votes.

The song that had clinched the win for Jedward was called 'Lipstick'. It was a catchy and appealing pop tune – with lyrics that were decidedly undemanding. '*Here I come, here I come*', the twins sang, '*Dum da dum da dum da dum*'. The brothers were supported by backing singers, and the song worked within their vocal limitations. It allowed them ample opportunity to exercise their genuine gifts: the ability to leap around on stage, and create a palpable sense of fun and excitement.

'Lipstick' was the twins' first single that was not a cover version, and it was soon to reach the number one slot in Ireland's charts. Jedward already had a sizeable fan base in the UK – thanks to *The X-Factor* – and they were also reasonably well known elsewhere in Europe. In the weeks before the Eurovision, Caroline Downey had arranged for the twins to be trained by one of Ireland's leading voice coaches. 'It wasn't simply a question of teaching the brothers to sing,' Caroline told me, 'they had to learn to control their breathing – so that they would be able to jump around the stage, as well as sing.' The twins would also be accompanied by four backing singers – including one of the song's composers – who would help to augment the vocal performance of the song.

When they arrived in Dusseldorf, Caroline's first objective was to ensure that the twins were noticed. She decided that they needed two complete changes of outfits for each day – to increase their chances of featuring in media coverage. That meant they arrived in Dusseldorf with no less than fifty-six different stage costumes. It seems that Caroline need not have worried. 'The media fell in love with them,' she told me, and the twins were inundated with requests for interviews. Caroline restricted the twins' interviews to those newspapers, magazines, radio and TV stations which she knew could command specific audiences. In particular, she focused on the Eastern European media. Some doubt had been expressed in advance of the contest that Eastern European viewers would be able to understand the twins. As it turned out, there were no such difficulties: Jedward's physical enthusiasm was infectious, and proved well able to transcend Europe's linguistic and cultural boundaries.

In Ireland, the participation of Jedward in the Eurovision seemed to give the country a welcome respite from its economic gloom. The Grimes brothers began the week in Dusseldorf with Irish bookmakers reckoning the chances of them winning the Eurovision at 25:1. By the end of the week, the odds had shortened dramatically to 9:2. Paddy Power, the leading bookmakers in Ireland, revealed that, if Jedward won the contest, the company would suffer greater losses than had ever before been incurred on one single event.

During rehearsals, it became clear that the production values of Jedward's song had been greatly enhanced since their appearance on Ireland's national song contest. The backing singers were visually less prominent, and the twins were more clearly the focus of the entire performance. Their costumes had become much more extravagant, with extra-large shoulder pads and an abundance of sequins. The twins' movements on stage had also become tighter and more stylized: Caroline had employed Jerry Reeve, a choreographer with *The X-Factor,* to work on their steps. The visual impact was intensified by the use of large background graphics. These had been produced and designed by the Dublin post-production house, Tangerine, and they followed the same dramatic red and black colour scheme as the costumes worn by Jedward and their backing singers. The graphics were arguably the most sophisticated and effective of any seen that night, and they made a considerable impression.

Whatever their early reservations might have been, RTÉ made a greater financial commitment to this entry than in the preceding few years. However, Caroline had also made her own contribution to the costs incurred: she paid both for the choreographer and for the background graphics. RTÉ would regard their own investment as money well spent once the first viewing figures were revealed. In order to qualify for the Eurovision Final, the twins first had to compete in the second semi-final of the contest. Over one million Irish viewers watched Jedward perform 'Lipstick' in the Dusseldorf Arena. The viewing figures peaked when the twins – alongside nine other successful acts – were confirmed as having won through to the Grand Final. This compared to an average viewership of just over 440,000 for the semi-final, in which Ireland had competed the previous year. Jedward were elated by the news: 'We can't thank our fans enough,' they were quoted as saying. 'We want the whole of Europe to know how brilliant Ireland is.'

A few days later, they were the sixth act to perform in the Grand Final. Before it began, Jedward received good luck tweets from Robbie Williams and Jonathan Ross, as well as a phone call from the Irish President, Mary McAleese. In the subsequent voting, they received maximum points from several countries: the first time that Ireland had received any top scores since 1997. The twins finished eighth out of twenty-five competing countries – which was the best result Ireland had achieved for eleven years. It also marked the highest Irish viewing audience for the Eurovision contest in fifteen years. The three and a half hour final was watched in its entirety by an average of well over a million Irish viewers – and even more tuned in to watch the final hour, when votes came in from all over Europe.

After the Eurovision, 'Lipstick' charted in several European countries – reaching number three in Austria. It even proved to be a hit as far away as South Korea, and was used in a Hyundai car advertising campaign throughout Southeast Asia. A few weeks after the contest, Jedward performed their song in front of an ecstatic audience of 60,000 people at College Green in the centre of Dublin, singing just before a speech given by the visiting US President, Barack Obama. After his speech, President Obama is alleged to have told the brothers that he liked both the song and their hair styles.

Jedward began their second tour with a series of dates across Ireland, and, in the following months, they appeared on TV shows in Ireland, the UK and elsewhere in Europe. The twins ended the year by starring in a Dublin panto – *Jedward and the Beanstalk* – for which all the performances were sold out.

It was clear that taking part in the Eurovision contest had been a good career move for Jedward, and had raised their profile throughout Europe. It was perhaps inevitable then that they should wish to return to the contest for a second time. It also seemed inevitable – though questionable – that RTÉ would seek to reproduce the formula that had led to the most successful Irish Eurovision entry in over a decade. The mentoring initiative seemed to have worked, and in

RTÉ's view there was no need to change it. This time, however, Jedward were not mentored by an experienced producer like Caroline Downey. 'I didn't want to do it again,' she told me, 'and I don't think Jedward should have either. It would have been better for them to have gone out on a strong performance.' RTÉ might have been better advised to have made a similar decision – since the station seemed to have overlooked the pivotal role that a producer had played in Jedward's success.

In November 2011, the station confirmed that the selection process for the 2012 Eurovision would again involve mentors. Once again, there were to be five of them – and each would choose both a song and a performer. Once again, only one of those mentors could be described as an experienced producer. The other four were a choreographer, two singer-songwriters, and the former Eurovision winner Linda Martin.

Linda Martin was a long-time associate of Louis Walsh, so it was not surprising that the act that she chose to mentor in the national contest was none other than Jedward, whom Louis managed. Linda had also appeared in a number of pantos with the Grimes twins – including *Jedward and the Beanstalk* – and knew them well. Once again, the team that had written Jedward's song was multinational. On this occasion, however, only two writers were involved: a Swedish composer and a veteran American songwriter who was also based in Sweden.

All of the other songs had been written, or co-written, by the mentors of the other acts in a further – and questionable – extension of their role in the selection process. It soon became known that the other acts, and their mentors, believed they were at a distinct disadvantage in having to compete in the national contest against Jedward.

They may have had good reason to think so: the twins had only managed to stay ahead by a few points in 2011; in 2012 they romped home with top points from both the regional juries and the televoting.

For me, their winning song, 'Waterline', did not have the basic appeal of 'Lipstick', and gave less scope for the twins to display their peculiar strengths as performers. Jedward became the first-ever act to represent Ireland two years in a row, and they attracted media attention again when they arrived in Baku, the capital of Azerbaijan. However, press interest seemed more subdued than in 2011. Perhaps journalists were more engrossed in the scale of that year's contest – which was the most expensive ever staged – or perhaps Jedward's presence had simply become old news. The twins may have picked up some of the coolness in the air, because they announced that – 'win or lose' – this would definitely be their last involvement in the Eurovision.

When they performed in the semi-finals, it was clear that some attempt had been made to increase the visual impact of their performance, and to distinguish it from the previous year. For the semi-final, they wore what appeared to be jewelled space suits, and their act now included a water feature – so that, by the end of the song, the Grimes brothers were both soaking wet. However, perhaps the most obvious difference for most of those watching on TV was that the twins' hair was no longer bouffant, but flat.

Whether it was a wise decision to abandon their trademark 'Viagra' hair style is debatable. At any rate, it was soon resumed after the Eurovision was over. It was true that the title of their song was 'Waterline', but the inclusion of a working fountain on set also seemed much too literal-minded to me. Ireland was the last of the ten songs that had qualified in the semi-final to be announced – to the palpable relief of both Jedward and the RTÉ delegation.

The Grimes brothers had changed their costumes for the Grand Final. The space-age theme was still there, but the sequins had been lost. They delivered their usual high-energy performance, but it did not seem to be as focused as in 2011. The water feature had taken the place of the back projection of the previous year, but it lacked the dramatic impact of the graphics: one was stylish and complemented the feel of the pop song; the other looked like an obvious gimmick, and Jedward's final soaking fell almost as flat as their hair.

In fact, just about everything in the 2012 production seemed to suffer in comparison with 2011. The song, the routine, the backdrop, the costumes – they were both too similar, and yet not as effective as the previous year. When the twins performed in the Grand Final, they scored just forty-six points – roughly half of their 2011 result – and ended up in a disappointing nineteenth place. Inevitably, there was a feeling of anticlimax. While it was understandable that the twins had wanted to compete in the contest again, the wisdom of RTÉ in allowing that to happen so soon after their first appearance was questionable. Given their limited musical talent, the twins remained a novelty act at heart – and the novelty seemed to have worn a little thin as far as the Eurovision was concerned.

Soon after the 2012 contest, Julian Vignoles bowed out of the competition. For the previous ten years, he had been RTÉ's 'Mr Eurovision', and had certainly brought a great deal of personal commitment and enthusiasm to that role. However, in an interview after the Eurovision, he admitted his relief at not having to organise the 2013 contest – since Jedward had failed to win the Eurovision. He said that having to host the event would have been a 'headache', though also a 'privilege'.

Julian seemed acutely aware of all the logistical problems that winning the Eurovision would have created for RTÉ. He believed that the station would probably have had to host the event in an open-air stadium, and this might have required special dispensation from the EBU. He thought that RTÉ might have been forced to rent Croke Park, the GAA headquarters, for up to a fortnight – at great expense – and, since there was a possibility of poor weather, the station could also have faced the prospect of paying to install a temporary roof. Such a roof, he pointed out, would also require planning permission. In any case, he reckoned that there might not have been enough public interest in Ireland to fill the stadium for the semi-finals.

This gloomy prognosis was a far cry from the can-do attitude that had led RTÉ to choose the small village of Millstreet more than twenty years earlier. Given Julian's anxieties, it was perhaps just as well that the chances of the station having to host the contest in any of the previous ten years had been remote. After all, this had not been a decade marked by a great deal of Irish success. In fact, it had been characterised by an unprecedented succession of flops.

In the months that followed their second bid to win Eurovision, Jedward released several new singles, and toured widely in Europe and further afield. However, it was hard to escape the conclusion that this phase of their careers was reaching its end. In 2013, it was announced that Jedward's three-album contract with Universal Music Ireland would not be renewed. Their last album, *Young Love*, had not sold well, and neither had their most recent tour of the UK. The poor result in the Eurovision was also viewed as evidence that their glory days were over. In August 2013, it was reported that the brothers had parted ways with Louis Walsh as their manager, and had enlisted their mother to take over the role.

The twins returned to the Eurovision in 2014 – though only in a modest supporting role. They arrived in Copenhagen on the day of the first semi-final, and I filmed them taking part in a photo shoot with Ireland's Kasey Smith. The brothers were still brimming with energy and able to attract public attention. The next night they appeared briefly on Europe's TV screens. The Danish production featured a humorous running item called the 'Eurovision Book of Records'. This involved allocating mock awards to past Eurovision artists, and they were sprinkled throughout the television coverage of both semi-finals and the Grand Final.

Jedward received two of these awards: one was for having had the highest hair, and the other for wearing the biggest shoulder pads. In a way, this was a back-handed compliment to the twins, but the Grimes brothers seemed happy enough, and they were shown in a quick cutaway shot, waving and smiling at the cameras. For the time being, that marks the end of their involvement in the contest, but, once again, I would not be surprised to see them back in a year or two.

27.
The Only Way is Up

In May 2012, RTÉ confirmed that Ireland would participate in the 2013 Eurovision contest in Malmo, Sweden. In October, RTÉ confirmed that Ireland's song and performer would be chosen by the same mentor system that had been followed in 2011 and 2012. Once again, there were five mentors, and, once again, only one of these could be described as a producer. Two of the others were radio presenters, and two were best known as songwriters.

Three of the mentors had previous connections with the contest. Shay Healy had written the winning song for Ireland thirty-four years earlier. He was described in RTE's press release as having 'contributed' to Latvia's Eurovision song in 2012. '*I was born in the distant 1980s*', the Latvian entry, Anmary, had sung, '*The year that Johnny Logan won*'. Sadly, the inspiration provided by Johnny was not enough, and Latvia failed to qualify for the 2012 final. Niall Mooney had co-written Ireland's Eurovision entry in 2009, which failed to qualify for the final, and again in 2010, which had finished in twenty-third place. The third mentor who had previously been associated with the contest was Stuart O'Connor. He was described by RTÉ in its press release as the producer of both of Jedward's Eurovision performances – which might have surprised Caroline Downey. He was also responsible for the production of a number of Dublin pantos – including *Jedward and the Beanstalk* and *Jedward and the Magic Lamp* – which had both featured Jedward and Linda Martin.

Once again, the five mentors were allowed to select both the song and the act that would perform it, and the winning song was decided on the *The Late Late Show* through a combination of public televoting and regional juries. Two former Eurovision performers also participated in the national contest. Paul Harrington, the 1994 winner, accompanied one of the artists on piano, while Donna McCaul, who had sung for Ireland in 2005, provided backing vocals for another finalist. The Finnish band, Lordi, also performed their winning song from the 2006 contest.

The winning act on this occasion, from both the televoting and regional juries, was Ryan Dolan – another performer from Northern Ireland – who had co-written 'Only Love Survives', the winning song. His performance had featured two backing singers, two dancers who played the *bodhrán*, and another musician who banged away at three large mounted drums – rather like a Japanese *taiko* act. When this ensemble performed in RTÉ's studio, the set had looked rather crowded. However, the arena in Malmo was much bigger and gave more scope for a dramatic presentation of Ryan's song.

The Malmo contest generated a number of controversies. Prior to the final, a Lithuanian production company released a video which suggested that delegates from Azerbaijan were trying to bribe Lithuanians for votes. The EBU determined that the evidence was not convlusive, and that 'every year there are rumours about irregularities in the voting'. After the contest, there were further allegations of vote-rigging against both Azerbaijan and Russia. Since then, the EBU has introduced new rules that will see countries banned from entering for up to three years if they are proved to have engaged in bribery, or vote-rigging.

There were also accusations of plagiarism laid against the German and the Dutch entries, but neither of these were substantiated. A different kind of controversy arose when Finland's performer kissed one of her female backing singers onstage. Krista Siegfrids stated that the purpose of the kiss was to encourage Finland to legalise same-sex marriage. It was reported that the gesture went down badly in some of the more conservative countries who were broadcasting the contest.

Once again, Ireland had to compete in a semi-final in order to secure a place in the main event. It was clear from the semi-final performance that considerable changes had been made in the staging of the Irish song since the national contest. It began, as before, with a flurry of drumming. By this stage, the *bodhrán* had become almost the instrument *de rigeur* for Irish acts at the Eurovision. It seemed that the traditional drum served to signify Ireland's ethnic identity. Perhaps it also represented a small gesture towards *Riverdance*, which had also featured drums – although they were used in a very different context.

The dancers who played the *bodhrán* had changed their appearance since Dublin. They were now stripped to the waist, and displayed tattoos that echoed the designs on the skin of their drums. They wore black leather pants – and so did the third drummer, who was also stripped to the waist. Ryan Dolan was dressed entirely in black leather, but his role was slightly overshadowed by the muscular performance of the three musicians as they beat their drums in a frenetic rhythm. Overall, the visual effect was mildly homoerotic, which might have seemed appropriate – given that 2013 was the twentieth anniversary of the decriminalising of homosexuality in Ireland – but it remained difficult to know exactly what audience this performance was intended to target.

In order to qualify for the Grand Final of the contest, Ryan Dolan first had to figure in the top ten acts in his semi-final. He was able to achieve that goal – although it was later revealed that he had only managed to finish in eighth place. When it came to the Eurovision Final, the limited impact that his song had made with European voters became more apparent: Denmark won the contest with 281 points, while Ryan came last with just five. It was the second time that Ireland had finished last in five years, and the lowest points we had received in a final since 'They Can't Stop the Spring' in 2007.

Many people in Ireland were genuinely surprised at the low points which Ryan received. Michael Kealy, head of the Irish delegation at Eurovision, said they were shocked and disappointed by the poor result, but he found some comfort in the belief that the selection method for Ireland's Eurovision entry had been a success. 'Nobody saw that result coming,' Michael said, 'but we've qualified for the final the last four years in a row, despite a run of some very poor results before that.'

Ryan Dolan took his failure to score well with admirable composure. He admitted that he too was taken aback by the outcome of the final. 'The reviews I have been getting for the song over here have been great,' he told an RTÉ journalist, 'and the crowds were really enjoying the performance, so I do think it is strange we came last.' But Ryan believed that 'the best song won', and that his career would still benefit from the international exposure that he had received. 'I am disappointed,' he admitted, 'but I won't let it bother me too much.'

In fact, Linda Martin seemed to have been much more bothered than Ryan by his failure to win many votes. She had been in the audience for the final in Malmo – where she had won the Eurovision for Ireland back in 1992. The Swedish host – the comedienne Petra Mede – had described Linda during the Grand Final as looking like 'Johnny Logan in drag', a remark that was both insulting and gratuitous. At the time, Linda seemed to shrug off the comment – even claiming not to have heard what was said – but, in the course of the following year, she expressed her apparent disillusion with the contest. She told one journalist that she had walked out of the arena in Malmo after Ryan had finished last and 'watched his mother crying. I thought this is ridiculous, how on earth can we compete?'

Linda believed that the reason for Ireland's run of poor results was the introduction of televoting. 'You get students acting the eejit, and they vote for something stupid,' she claimed. In fact, Ireland had performed well in some contests after the system of televoting was introduced, and Linda had served as the chairperson of the committee that had drawn up the criteria for the Irish selection procedure. Despite her long Eurovision history, Linda insisted that she was no longer wanted to remain involved in the event. 'I was so shocked and downhearted after Ryan finished last, I thought at that point, you know what – I'm just going to leave it,' she said. 'I'm not interested anymore.'

Linda was critical, in particular, of RTÉ's decision to use *The Late Late Show* as the vehicle for the selection of the Irish entry for Eurovision. She believed that the RTÉ studio, in which the national competition was held, was 'misleading' because it was so much smaller than the stage of the actual contest. Linda's fans were no doubt relieved when – just a few days after apparently announcing the end of her connection with the Eurovision – she turned up on the panel of *The Late Late Show* for the national final, where she engaged in a lively on-air row with one of that year's mentors.

The mentor system was back, and, once again, five mentors had been chosen by RTÉ to select the finalists in the national contest. On this occasion, however, none of these had any specific experience as a producer. Instead, they were described by RTÉ's press office as a musician, a singer, a radio presenter, a band manager and a tour manager. One of the songs had been co-written by Don Mescall, who had entered the contest unsuccessfully on several previous occasions. Another of the songs had been written by one of the mentors, and one had been written by one of the performers – Patricia Roe – whose mentor also happened to be her sister. Patricia had first competed – with her sister – in the national contest in 1980.

Jonas Gladnikoff was also back – and had co-written a song with a team that included yet another of the mentors. It seemed that the talent pool from which Ireland's Eurovision entries were drawn remained limited, even after an unprecedented sequence of failures.

The entertainment for the 2014 national contest was provided once again by Johnny Logan – singing a medley of his Eurovision hits – and Paul Harrington and Charlie McGettigan also performed their winning song from

1994. Once again, a panel had been assembled to discuss each entry with the show's host, Ryan Tubridy. This time, it consisted of Louis Walsh, the TV presenters Eoghan McDermott and Maia Dunphy, and Linda Martin.

The composition of this panel was to lead to a dispute on air when Billy McGuinness – one of the mentors and a guitarist with the Irish rock band Aslan – drew attention to the connection between Louis Walsh and one of the performers, Eoghan Quigg. A few years previously, Eoghan had been a finalist on the UK reality talent show, *The X-Factor,* on which Louis was a regular judge. He had also auditioned the previous year for a new boy band that Louis had planned to form, but which had yet to materialise.

In fact, Louis Walsh had connections with other individuals who were involved in the national contest that night. In 2008, Louis – along with Westlife member Kian Egan – had held auditions for a girl band, which became known as Wonderland. The band soon signed a record deal, and released an album and three singles before they were dropped by their recording company. One of the members of Wonderland was Kasey Smith – who performed a song in Ireland's 2014 national final called 'Heartbeat'.

Kasey's mentor that night was Hazel Kaneswaran, who was also one of the credited co-writers of 'Heartbeat'. Hazel was a singer too, and, a few years earlier, she had auditioned for *Popstars – The Rivals –* a reality TV talent show on which Louis was one of the resident judges. Louis had acted as a champion for Hazel, who advanced through the contest and might even have become a member of the winning act, Girls Aloud. However, it transpired that she was ten days older than the maximum age limit specified by the rules of the competition, and she had been disqualified.

Kasey Smith had been a finalist in Ireland's national song contest the previous year – when she has finished third. On this occasion, when the votes were counted, she emerged as the clear winner. She had been supported on stage by Can-Linn – an ensemble of performers that was later described to me by Hazel as 'a concept . . . like *Riverdance*', rather than a fixed troupe. That night, Can-Linn had consisted of two dancers, two backing singers and a fiddle player. As its name might indicate, Can-Linn identified itself with traditional Irish culture, and this gave a kind of Celtic infusion to what was otherwise a standard euro-ballad. The Celtic flavour would increase dramatically in the weeks between the national contest and the Eurovision.

The RTÉ studio had seemed rather too small for the role of the ensemble of performers featured on 'Heartbeat'. However, the song was delivered with a degree of simplicity that seemed to suit Kasey's vocal performance. This would also change in the weeks ahead. Kasey's mentor, Hazel Kaneswaran, was clearly delighted with the win. She believed the song showed why the Irish 'are recognised globally as makers of fine music'. That might seem rather a strange boast since Hazel's co-writers on 'Heartbeat' – Jonas Gladnikoff, Rasmus Palmgren and Patrizia Helander – were not Irish, but Swedish.

The 2014 Eurovision took place in Copenhagen in May. The Danish broadcaster had spent a whopping 112 million kroners on staging the event – and it showed. Thirty-seven countries participated – slightly less than in the previous few years – but the final recorded the largest viewing figures that had ever been recorded for the contest, with almost 200 million tuning in across Europe. Once again, there were two semi-finals in which all countries apart from the 'Big Five' – the UK, Germany, Spain, Italy and France – had to compete to qualify for the Grand Final. Ireland was slated to appear in the second of these.

I was in Copenhagen shooting a documentary film about the Eurovision with Angela Scanlon, and I watched Kasey and Can-Linn as they prepared for the contest. It was difficult not to be impressed by the commitment of all the Irish team. In particular, I was struck by the energy and enthusiasm that Kasey's mentor, Hazel Kaneswaran, brought to the contest.

Hazel is a good singer in her own right, and I often thought over the following days that she would have much preferred to be on stage in Copenhagen, rather than working in the background. She had been a member of the Irish band, Dove, whose cover of Crowded House's 'Don't Dream' had charted in Ireland in the 1990s. After her appearance on *Pop Stars – The Rivals*, Hazel had also popped up briefly on an episode of the comedy-clip show *Harry Hill's TV Burp*. She was selected to act as a judge in the third series of *You're a Star* – when the McCaul siblings won the competition. In more recent years, Hazel had been less involved in Ireland's music scene. She had become a practitioner of Reichi, and a believer in self-healing.

Hazel brought some of this spiritual commitment to her understanding of 'Heartbeat'. '*No story is carved in stone*', Kasey Smith sang. '*Just hold on to my heartbeat.*' For Hazel, these lyrics seemed to hold a profound significance, representing the human journey 'from darkness into light'. She explained that the two step dancers on the Eurovision stage were actually 'Celtic warriors' who symbolised the same eternal struggle between good and evil. 'They're fighting each other', she told us, 'but Kasey is the Goddess, and, at the end, she saves the day.' I had no doubt that Hazel believed sincerely in this interpretation of the song, but I doubted if it would be as clear to viewers of the TV show.

In rehearsals of the Irish entry, I witnessed Hazel bring a sense of passionate intensity to bear. Although she had little prior experience of TV production, she focused on every aspect of the performance – and, at times, I thought that Kasey appeared to wilt under the pressure. If Hazel's sheer will-power could have produced results, then I would have regarded an Irish win as a racing certainty.

There are, however, other factors that help to produce a winning song, and watching the Irish act in rehearsal led me to believe that the performance was in danger of being seriously overproduced – often as great a weakness as underproduction. 'Heartbeat' had undergone many changes since the national final, and I thought that not all of these were to its benefit. The act now began – yet again – with a short burst of *bodhrán* drumming, performed this time by the fiddle player. She was a classical violinist, and told me that she had never played the *bodhrán* before – which hardly mattered, since she only had to mime to a backing track.

In any case, the obvious purpose of this drum was not musical – but rather to suggest the Celtic provenance of the song. That ambition was also evident in the two dancers – who now not only step-danced in the traditional Irish manner, but were both wearing kilts. This emphasis on the 'Irishness' of the song seemed to me to be both unconvincing and unnecessary. After one of the rehearsals, a delegate from another country turned to Marty Whelan, who was commentating for RTE and said, 'We know who you are – you don't have to keep reminding us you are Irish.' I could see his point. None of the seven songs that have won the Eurovision for Ireland involved the sort of ersatz Celticism that seemed to have become a recurrent feature of so many Irish entries in the previous ten years.

That year was the twentieth anniversary of the first performance of *Riverdance*, and, in press interviews, it was repeatedly cited by Hazel Kaneswaran as a point of reference for the Irish song. In reality, such comparisons only served to remind viewers of the significant differences in the quality of the two. At the heart of *Riverdance* was a strikingly original piece of choreography and a wonderful musical score. 'Heartbeat' simply could not compete on either count. Indeed, it seemed to me that the song's overproduction only served to draw attention to its shortfalls. The staging, in particular, threatened to overwhelm the performers. It featured Celtic-inspired shapes – which included Ireland's national colours – set against a gigantic backdrop of churning green seas and crashing lightning bolts. I understood from Hazel that this was meant to symbolise the dark night of the soul – from which the singer emerges into the light. However, it seemed to me to be wildly disproportionate, and to suggest a kind of visual hysteria.

In the national final, Kasey had dressed and performed in a fairly straightforward and unadorned manner. On the Copenhagen stage, she was dressed like the sort of Gothic princess you might encounter in an episode of *Game of Thrones*. Kasey was a young and attractive woman, but the heavy make-up, the encrusted golden dress, and the substantial neckpiece that she wore in the Copenhagen semi-final made her look considerably older – and a good deal more dated.

Kasey appeared somewhat uneasy and uncertain as she tried to match the rapid tracking movements of the cameras. But it wasn't only the huge scale of the rolling backdrop, or the increased role of the dancers that seemed to undermine the centrality of her performance. The official description of the Irish entry as 'Can-Linn – featuring Kasey Smith', implicitly downplayed her role. It seemed that Kasey couldn't even get top billing on her own act.

Ireland was drawn by ballot to compete in the second half of the second semi-final – just after Softengine, a teenage rock band from Finland, and just before Belarus, who were represented by a young singer called Teo. In contrast to the Irish song, both the Finnish and the Belarusian entries were performed simply and without any genuflections towards their ethnic origins. After the last act, all of the performers had to sit in a green room area that was not backstage – as is usual – but which was surrounded by the arena's audience.

As the results began to be announced, there was an early indication that the Irish entry had not polled well. The camera crews, who were covering the reactions of the successful performers, had clearly moved away from the Irish table. It later emerged that the televote had left Ireland in tenth place, which would have ensured that Kasey sang in the Grand Final. However, the juries across Europe only placed Ireland in fourteenth position. When the two votes were combined, it meant that the Irish entry had ended up in twelfth place – and were out of the contest. In a final indignity, Kasey and the rest of Can-Linn had to make their way to the backstage area through dense crowds of spectators who were streaming out of the arena.

I was there when they arrived back at their dressing room. It is easy to be cynical and dismissive of the Eurovision, but the sense of intense disappointment among the Irish performers was moving to witness. I had spent the previous week in their company, and knew the depth of the emotions that had been invested in this competition. As

Kasey and the rest tried to deal with the abrupt termination of their dreams, there were noisy celebrations on either side from the Finnish and Belarusian delegations.

Later, we met up in the same Irish pub in Copenhagen where Ireland's Eurovision entry had been launched a few days before. To say the least, the mood in the Shamrock Bar was now very different. Family members and friends of Kasey and Hazel had travelled to Copenhagen in the hope of seeing the Irish song in the Grand Final. The atmosphere was subdued, and there was uncertainty about who would attend the final now that Kasey wasn't taking part. In the end, neither Kasey nor her immediate family decided to attend.

The winning song that night was 'Rise Like a Phoenix'. It was the Austrian entry, and was performed by Conchita Wurst. Conchita is a drag queen whose original name is Tom Neuwirth. In several respects, Frau Wurst was not a typical drag act. She dressed elegantly, and her manner was diffident and reserved. She did not lip-synch, or use heavy make-up to disguise the shadow of facial hair. In fact, her most distinguishing feature was her black beard – which had led to her nickname of 'the bearded lady'.

Conchita's act was one of extreme simplicity: she was alone on stage – without a backdrop of rolling waves, or the support of acrobats, trapeze artists or half-naked dancers. Instead, she stood directly under a halo of spotlights – almost motionless throughout her song. It was clear, however, that the lyrics had a special resonance for Conchita – *'Peering from the mirror,'* she sang, *'Who can this person be?'* – and she invested her performance of the power ballad with great emotional sincerity. It helped, of course, that she also had a very good voice. I was disappointed to learn that Sir Terry Wogan later described her performance as a mere 'freak show'.

Before she sang, Conchita had stated that her goal in competing was to make 'a statement that you can achieve anything, no matter who you are, or how you look'. Perhaps it was predictable that her performance would arouse anger and indignation in those social conservatives who were watching the contest that night. For them, Conchita's performance only served to promote the rights of gay men, lesbians, bisexuals and transgenders. And, of course, they were partly right. In fact, her success in the Eurovision also highlighted one of the apparent fault lines between Eastern and Western Europe.

Even before she arrived in Copenhagen, petitions had surfaced in Russia and Belarus calling for Conchita to be removed from the televised broadcast. The Russian petition described the Eurovision as 'a hotbed of sodomy, at the initiation of European liberals'. One leading Russian politician described Conchita's performance as an example of the 'blatant propaganda of homosexuality, and spiritual decay' – which, at least, indicated that he had watched her sing with some interest. One of Conchita's fellow performers – the Armenian entry – also labelled her as 'unnatural', and suggested that she should decide 'whether he is a man or a woman'.

In fairness, it must be acknowledged that some liberal commentators in the West also adopted Conchita as a symbol – in their case, of everything that made Western Europe superior to the East. The left-wing British journal, *The New Statesman,* even claimed that every vote for Frau Wurst sent 'a strong message of defiance eastwards'. When it came to the voting, it was true that Conchita averaged higher scores in Western Europe than in those countries that had been part of the Soviet bloc. Nonetheless, she still picked up a substantial number of votes in the East – including Russia – and could not have won the contest without them.

The Austrian President announced that Conchita's victory was 'not just a victory for Austria, but above all, for diversity and tolerance in Europe' – and, perhaps, the result also indicated that viewers of the Eurovision are more open-minded than some of their political leaders. From 1997 to 2007, televoting alone decided the outcome of the contest. If that had still been the case in 2014, Conchita Wurst would have won by a much greater margin. When the juries were introduced back in 2008, the intent was to prevent bloc voting – which allegedly had resulted in Eastern European countries winning too many contests.

However, the breakdown of jury voting shows that juries were even more inclined to vote for blocs than the general public. In other words, the selected juries proved more conservative than the Eurovision's viewers, and this was especially true in Eastern European countries such as Belarus and Armenia, where there was great disparity between the juries' and the viewers' response to the Austrian entry – with the juries giving Conchita significantly less points.

What was indisputable was that the Eurovision contest was still able – almost sixty years after its inception – to stir up passions across the continent, to stimulate social debate, and, perhaps, even to promote the goal of tolerance between European nations that had been part of its original purpose. The rules of the contest have undergone major changes since it was first created, and it has shown a remarkable capacity to adapt not only to new technology, but also to profound and dramatic shifts in the political

283

map of Europe. The number of competing countries has grown, and so has the scale of the Eurovision itself. It now extends over two full weeks – including dress rehearsals and two semi-finals. The Grand Final itself is now three-and-a-half hours long. Despite everything, the contest remains the biggest and most watched live entertainment show in the world.

There is no doubt that further changes are yet to come – both in Ireland and elsewhere. In the aftermath of the 2014 final, the Irish delegation admitted that the method of selection of the Irish entry – which had been followed for the previous four years – was not fit for purpose, and needed to be changed.

When I spoke to Glen Killane, the Managing Director of RTÉ TV, in the run-up to the 2015 national song contest, he made it clear that he would like the station to stage the Grand Final once again. But he also made it clear that he was not aiming for a quick fix solution, and that the goal was not simply to win the contest. 'The first priority', he told me, 'is to develop a clear strategy, and to re-establish our credibility in the eyes of the Irish public. Mistakes have been made in the past, but we can learn from them.' For RTÉ, that means going back to the drawing board, and trying to find a path that could lead Ireland back to its glory days.

That may not be an easy task – but it's not impossible.

Eurovision Chronology

Winners

2014 Austria – Conchita Wurst 'Rise Like A Phoenix.'

2013 Denmark – Emmelie de Forest 'Only Teardrops.'

2012 Sweden – Loreen 'Euphoria.'

2011 Azerbaijan – Ell & Nikki 'Running Scared.'

2010 Germany – Lena 'Satellite.'

2009 Norway – Alexander Rybak 'Fairytale.'

2008 Russia – Dima Bilan 'Believe.'

2007 Serbia – Marija Serifovi 'Molitva.'

Irish Entries

Can Linn feat. Kasey Smith 'Heartbeat' Failed to Qualify.

Ryan Dolan 'Only Love Survives' 26th Place.

Jedward 'Waterline' 19th Place.

Jedward 'Lipstick' 8th Place.

Niamh Kavanagh 'It's For You' 23rd Place.

Sinéad Mulvey and Black Daisy 'Et Cetera' Failed to Qualify.

Dustin the Turkey 'Irelande Douze Pointe' Failed to Qualify.

Dervish 'They Can't Stop The Spring' 24th Place.

2006 Finland – Lordi 'Hard Rock Hallelujah.'

Brian Kennedy 'Every Song Is A Cry for Love' 10th Place.

2005 Greece – Helena Paparizou My Number One.'

Donna and Joe 'Love?' Failed to Qualify.

2004 Ukraine – Ruslana 'Wild Dances.'

Chris Doran 'If My World Stopped Turning' 23rd Place.

2003 Turkey – Sertab Erener Everyway That I Can.'

Mickey Harte 'We've Got The World' 11th Place.

2002 Latvia – Marie N. 'I Wanna.'

Did not participate.

2001 Estonia – Tanel Padar, Dave Benton & 2XL 'Everybody.'

Gary O'Shaughnessy 'Without Your Love' 21st Place.

2000 Denmark – Olsen Brothers 'Fly on the Wings of Love.'

Eamonn Toal 'Millennium of Love' 6th Place

1999 Sweden – Charlotte Nilsson 'Take Me to Your Heaven.'

The Mullans 'When You Need Me' 17th Place.

1998 Israel – Dana International 'Diva.'

Dawn Martin 'Is Always Over Now?' 9th Place.

1997 UK – Katrina & The Waves 'Love Shine a Light.'

Marc Roberts 'Mysterious Woman' 2nd Place.

1996 Ireland – Eimear Quinn 'The Voice'

Winner

1995 Norway – Secret Garden 'Nocturne.'

Eddie Friel 'Dreamin'' 14th Place

1994 Ireland – Paul Harrington & Charlie McGettigan 'Rock 'n' Roll Kids'

Winner

1993 Ireland – Niamh Kavanagh 'In Your Eyes'

Winner

1992 Ireland – Linda Martin 'Why Me'

Winner

286

1991 Sweden – Carola 'Fångad av em Stormvind.'

Kim Jackson 'Could It Be That I'm In Love?' 10th Place.

1990 Italy – Toto Cotungo 'Insieme: 1992.'

Liam Reilly 'Somewhere in Europe' 2nd Place.

1989 Yugoslavia – Riva 'Rock Me.'

Kiev Connolly and the Missing Passengers 'The Real Me' 18th Place.

1988 Switzerland – Celine Dion 'Ne Partez pas sans Moi.'

Jump the Gun 'Take Him Home' 8th Place.

1987 Ireland – Johnny Logan 'Hold Me Now'

Winner

1986 Belgium – Sandra Kim 'J'aime la Vie.'

Luv Bug 'You Can Count On Me' 4th Place.

1985 Norway – Bobbysocks 'La det Swinge.'

Maria Christian 'Wait Until the Weekend Comes' 6th Place.

1984 Sweden – Herrey's 'Diggi-loo Diggi-Ley.'

Linda Martin 'Terminal 3' 2nd Place.

1983 Luxembourg – Corinne Hermès 'Si la Vie est Cadeau.'

Did not participate.

1982 Germany – Nicole 'Ein bischen Frieden.'

The Duskeys 'Here Today Gone Tomorrow' 11th Place.

1981 UK – Bucks Fizz 'Making Your Mind Up.'

Sheeba 'Horoscopes' 5th Place.

1980 Ireland – Johnny Logan 'What's Another Year'

Winner

1979 Israel – Gali Atari and Milk & Honey 'Hallelujah.'

Cathal Dunne 'Happy Man' 5th Place.

1978 Israel – Izhar Cohen & The Alphabeta 'A–Ba–Ni–Bi.'

Colm C. T. Wilkinson 'Born to Sing' 5th Place.

1977 France – Marie Myriam 'L'oiseau et L'infant.'

The Swarbriggs Plus Two 'It's Nice To Be In Love Again' 3rd Place.

1976 UK – Brotherhood of Man 'Save Your Kisses For Me.'

Red Hurley 'When' 10th Place.

1975 Netherlands – Teach-In 'Ding-a-Dong.'

The Swarbriggs 'That's What Friends Are For' 9th Place.

1974 Sweden – Abba 'Waterloo.'

Tina Reynolds 'Cross Your Heart' 7th Place.

1973 Luxembourg – Anna-Marie David 'Tu te Reconnaîtras.'

Maxi 'Do I Dream' 10th Place.

1972 Luxembourg – Vicky Leandros 'Après Toi.'

Sandie Jones 'Ceol an Ghrá' 15th Place.

1971 Monaco – Séverine 'Un Banc, un Arbre, une Rue.'

Angela Farrell 'One Day Love' 11th Place.

1970 Ireland – Dana 'All Kinds of Everything'

Winner

1969 UK – Lulu 'Boom-Bang-a-Bang.'

Muriel Day 'The Wages of Love' 7th Place.

1969 Spain – Salomé 'Vivo Cantando.'

1969 France – Frida Boccara 'Un Jour, en Enfant.'

1969 Netherlands – Lenny Kuhr 'De Troubadour.'

1968 Spain – Massiel 'La, La, La.'

Pat McGeegan 'Chance of a Lifetime' 4th Place.

1967 UK – Sandie Shaw 'Puppet on a String.'

Sean Dunphy 'If I Could Choose' 2nd Place.

1966 Austria – Udo Jürgens 'Merci, Chérie.'

Dickie Rock 'Come Back to Stay' 4th Place.

1965 Luxembourg – France Gall 'Poupée de Cire, Poupée de Son.'

Butch Moore 'Walking the Streets in the Rain' 6th Place.